Through the Brown Mountain Lights

Brown Mountain Lights Book 1

CC Tillery

Spring Creek Press

First Edition
ISBN 0-9894641-5-6
ISBN-13 978-0-9894641-5-4

Published by **Spring Creek Press**

To all of our readers, but most especially our late "Uncle" Donald McAllister who was so inspirational with his continual encouragement and support during the seven years it took to write our *Appalachian Journey* series. We're happy he was around to read the final book in the series and continue to feel his presence cheering us on for this new one. He was deeply loved and will be truly missed.

PROLOGUE

For centuries, the Brown Mountain Lights have been shrouded in mystery. Some people say they're the spirits of Cherokee maidens searching for their lost warriors after a fierce battle between the Cherokee and Catawba hundreds of years before the area was settled. Some claim they're the ghosts of a plantation owner who disappeared while hunting on the mountain and the slaves who went looking for him and never returned. Others believe they're apparitions of a woman and her newborn baby who disappeared in the 1850s and the men who searched for her and vanished. Those of a more practical nature who have never seen the lights claim they're nothing more than figments of people's imaginations while those of a scientific bent say they're some sort of odd phenomenon of nature that occurs occasionally on the mountain. Others not so pragmatic declare they're extraterrestrial beings visiting Earth from other planets.

But they're all wrong. You see, I know the truth behind the Brown Mountain Lights.

I came through them.

CHAPTER ONE

August 1969 → August 1859

The Times They Are a-Changin'

If I had known that a moment's encounter with one of the Brown Mountain Lights on a warm August night in 1969 would forever change my life, sending it barreling in an unforeseen and mystifying direction, would I have reached out to touch it? Perhaps … then, again, perhaps not.

On that fateful night, the clouds played a wily game of hide and seek with the full moon, revealing its brightness one minute then obscuring it completely the next. A slight breeze ruffled the leaves as the night songs of crickets, katydids and frogs from a nearby creek, along with the faint strums of my boyfriend Ben's guitar, wove eerily through the mist surrounding me. The musty smell of damp moss mingling with the sweetness of wildflowers and the sharp tang of smoke from our campfire drifted through the warm, moist air. I could almost taste the hot dogs we'd roasted over the fire for dinner.

I stood on a well-worn path on Brown Mountain, with ferns and wildflowers edging the left side and a high rock cliff on the right, spellbound as a bright light approached through the haze, moving diagonally through the forest, seemingly undeterred by the massive trees in its path. It appeared to me as if the light passed directly through the immense trunks without pausing, but as it drew closer, I could see that it was actually detouring around the trees, moving so fast that from a distance its course appeared straight and unwavering. Curious, I watched as it bulleted toward me. When it neared, I involuntarily stumbled back a few steps, my right arm hitting the rock wall where it jutted out over the path. I jumped when the light came to a sudden stop, close enough that I could reach out and touch it if I wanted to.

My inner voice hissed a warning but I had always been fascinated by science and at that point considered this more a phenomenon of nature than anything threatening. I studied the light while I waited for it to go around me as it had the trees, thinking it looked to be about the size of a beach ball, bright orange around the outside with a darker, almost black circle at the center that pulsated slightly. When it didn't veer around me but remained stationary, the innermost core palpitating in time to my racing heartbeat, I stepped to the side to let it pass by but it moved with me, reminding me of the first time I'd met Ben on the narrow sidewalk to the medical building on the University of Tennessee campus. We each moved to the side, me to the right, him to the left, as if mirroring each other's steps. After the same thing happened two more times, he grinned at me, held out his hand and said, "Would you care to dance?" I'd smiled back at him and we'd been practically inseparable since then.

In fact, it was Ben who had talked me into ignoring the protestations of my father and coming on this trip to Woodstock. We, along with four other friends, had packed up Ben's VW bus and left Knoxville, Tennessee around noon four days before the music festival was scheduled to begin on August 15th on a 600-acre dairy farm in Bethel, New York. We hadn't intended to stop on Brown Mountain but the van broke down outside the little town of Morganton, North Carolina. While waiting for it to be fixed, we'd decided to hike up the mountain and camp there, hoping to see the legendary Brown Mountain Lights.

And now we had … or at least I had. I hadn't been gone more than thirty minutes and wondered if the others back at camp could see the lights. Or was it just me? Later, I would spend a great deal of time speculating whether or not a person had to be alone in order for the lights to do what they did to me. Sort of like the tree falling in the forest when no one is around to hear it.

My eyes stayed on the light as I moved to the side again, wanting to see if it would follow. When it did, I froze, thinking it seemed to be playing with me. Testing, I feinted to the right before changing direction and going to the left, stepping clear of the rock wall. The light, as if knowing my mind, moved in sync with me. A sense of unease began to creep over me when I realized I could no longer hear the normal night sounds of the forest, the musical chorus of the insects mingling with the bellowing bass of the frogs or the wind whispering softly through the leaves. Before the light approached me, Ben's guitar had been barely audible but now my ears couldn't detect anything at all. I should have turned around and run back to the campsite where my friends were all sitting around a warm fire, sharing a joint to ease them into sleeping on the hard ground for the night, but my body seemed frozen in place as I stared into that pulsating center, vaguely wondering if it was in some way hypnotizing me.

As my anxiety grew, I began to regret my impulsive decision to take a walk to get away from the smell of marijuana smoke. I didn't do drugs of any kind, thanks to my strict father and a mother who killed herself using sleeping pills her doctor had been more than willing to overprescribe. Although I had at one time hated her for that and called her a coward, as I grew older, I found myself wondering why she chose that path and if I would be prone to make the same decision.

I blinked hard, trying to break the light's spell, my inner voice whispering maybe one of our friends laced our food or drinks with an illegal substance. Could this be what being stoned or tripping out felt like? I'd never experienced it before but surely not. My mind was too clear and alert, and I hadn't felt any differently before I encountered the light.

The dark center circle of the light pulsed harder than

before. I tried to look away from it by closing my eyes and turning my head, but once open, my eyes returned to the light of their own volition. As if drawn, my hand reached out to touch the brightness at the edge, receiving a light electrical shock when it did. I jerked my hand back and looked at the tip of my index finger, thinking I would see evidence of the contact, but there was nothing. As I checked, I stepped back several paces on the path and watched as the light did the same, appearing to want to get as close to me as possible.

I moved back again, putting out my hand to stop the light from following. This time, I touched the dark center. Instead of the shock I expected, the light enveloped my hand. I didn't feel anything, only a strange numbness as if I had slept with my hand tucked under me and woken to find it frozen, dead to feeling. I tried to pull it back but was met with a powerful resistance, clinging to my hand and dragging me closer, as if it intended to absorb my entire body into its dark center.

I'm not sure how long I stood there, panicked and bent forward at the waist, futilely trying to pull away from this unknown source of power, even more futilely trying to scream for help, but it was as if the light absorbed all sound and nothing but silence issued from my mouth. It could have been seconds or minutes or hours but was probably no longer than a moment or two. The only thing I was aware of during that time was the wind picking up and gusting, blowing my long hair around my face and the skirt of my dress around my legs. And all the while, I tried to free my hand from the powerful grasp of the pulsing center of the light but the pull grew ever stronger, enveloping my arm up to the elbow, making me think of a fly with one leg caught in a spider's web. The rest of my body went numb, almost as if that strange light had the ability to paralyze a person. In only seconds, I couldn't move my legs at all, not even to step back or try to save myself. In desperation, I made the mistake of reaching out with my other hand to try and push the light away, only to have that hand caught and drawn in, too.

Again, I opened my mouth to scream but nothing came

out. The light continued to pulse, quicker now, outracing my furious heart, pounding hard in my chest. My breathing erratic, I strained against the light, to no avail.

I had, at most, a few seconds to panic and then, with a loud whoosh—the only sound I heard—it sucked me in completely.

Into a void so dark I wondered if the light had given me a shock strong enough to kill me. I clamped my teeth together as a jolt tore through my body and left me feeling as if it had ripped me apart from the inside. I tried to scream from the agony but my teeth remained clenched and my mouth wouldn't open. I frantically wondered if this was what death felt like.

There was another loud whoosh as the light released me and I found myself falling, my stomach tumbling in that panicked topsy-turvy feeling you get when you take an unexpected dip on a roller-coaster.

I braced for the impact only to find myself deposited softly on the damp ground, my fingers curled into the pine needles and moss of the forest floor. I lay there for a moment, becoming aware of a steady wind blowing as the feeling returned to my body with a tingling sensation. Opening my eyes, the first thing I glimpsed was the full moon floating high above the rock cliff that seemed to rise a hundred feet or more in the air behind my head. The light had apparently not moved me very far, if at all.

I raised my head and stared at my feet resting at the base of a large clump of what appeared to be tall spears of flowers. A bubble of panic popped in my stomach. I didn't remember those being there before the light. Turning my head to the right, I saw a haphazard pile of stones.

Reaching out, I grasped the top stone, thinking to use it to pull myself up to a sitting position. Instead, I set off a rockslide and the pile collapsed, revealing the empty eye sockets of a skull.

This time when I opened my mouth, a shrill, high-pitched scream emerged, echoing and bouncing off the cliff behind me, becoming louder when I saw the smaller skull nestled in the rocks beside the first one.

Out of breath, I slammed my mouth shut as I sat up and scooted forward, as far away from the gruesome sight beside me as I could get, thinking the light must have moved me after all. The trees in front of me, instead of the aged oaks and pines from before the light took me, while still tall, could not be much more than saplings, nothing like the large, multi-branched, heavily-leafed trees I had noticed earlier. Where there had been a smooth dirt trail before, now there were leafy ferns and ground cover showing no signs of being trampled by human feet.

I fought panic as the wind gusted through the trees, showering me with drops of water as if it had rained recently. The rustling of the leaves brought back memories of the mechanic at the garage warning us to stick to the well-trodden trails due to a large influx of poisonous snakes on the mountain. I looked around wildly but spied no path nearby.

And noticed the light was nowhere to be seen.

Taking a deep, steadying breath, I slowly pulled myself to my feet, holding onto a nearby tree for support, gingerly avoiding stepping closer to the skulls. My heart still pounded but all feeling had returned to my body. Noting I was still dressed in the long maxi-dress I started the day in, my right hand automatically went to the pocket on that side of my dress, feeling for the items I habitually carried there, my driver's license, a small pot of lip gloss, a half-empty pack of Virginia Slims cigarettes with a bright yellow Bic disposable lighter tucked into the cellophane surrounding the pack. The pack of Teaberry gum remained in my left pocket. Nor had I lost the Seiko watch my father had given me when I graduated high school. Holding my left wrist up to my ear, I listened to the slow, steady tick that told me it was still running.

I could no longer hear Ben singing along to his guitar and wondered how long I had been out or if the light had somehow moved me beyond hearing distance of our campsite. Ironic though it may be to me now and perhaps even more so prophetic, when I left the campsite, he had been playing Bob Dylan's *The Times They Are a-changin'*, which I hoped to see Dylan himself perform at Woodstock. I hoped their silence only meant they had all gone to bed for the night or Ben was taking a break from playing to toke on the shared joint and talk to our friends.

Shaking my head, I turned in what I thought was the direction I'd walked in earlier, only to be greeted with confusion. Everything seemed different. I looked in the other direction, growing even more bewildered. There was nothing familiar about this place. Squinting my eyes, I searched for signs of a campfire in the distance and saw nothing but darkness all around me.

Surely the light hadn't moved me so far that I couldn't see or hear any indication of my friends.

I shivered, rubbing my hands along my bare arms. With the wind picking up and the drops from the trees dampening my dress and hair, the night seemed much colder. I needed to find shelter until I could figure out what to do. Or at least find some dry wood so I could light a fire and hope Ben and my friends would come looking for me. Surely they'd noticed I'd been gone longer than the twenty or thirty minutes I'd told them I would be. Or were they all so stoned they didn't even remember I'd told them I was going for a short walk?

I chose a direction, took one step, then hesitated again, debating. I could hear water babbling faintly somewhere nearby. We had camped with a creek to the right of us. Maybe if I could find where the sound was coming from, it would lead me back to my friends. Turning in a slow circle, I tried to pinpoint the direction.

I heard a rustling to my right and whirled around, coming face to face with a young woman wearing a long dress that had clearly seen better days. Her eyes widened, her mouth forming an O of surprise.

"What in tarnation?" she said, as if to herself.

"Oh, hey," I said with relief, pleased to see someone and even more glad that she didn't appear to be dangerous. I forced myself to smile but it was a weak one at best. "I think I'm lost. Can you help me get back to our campsite?"

She jumped at the sound of my voice, backing up a step. "You come from the lights. I seen it myself from back over yonder." She turned to point behind her then swiveled back to me. "At first, I thought maybe you was a haint or somethin but you're a real, live person." She put her hand over her mouth, her eyes darting around. "Oh, Lordy, I hope you didn't bring him back with you."

"Him? I don't know who you're—"

She craned her head, looking behind me then to each side of me as if searching for someone. "Did you see him in your travels? An old feller, so tall ..." she held her hand slightly above her head "... walks with a stoop, has a mean look in his eyes?"

"No, I didn't see anyone. I touched the light and woke up, I guess, here. Have you by any chance seen a group of people camping out? My boyfriend's with them—"

Her brow furrowed. "Boyfriend? What's that?"

I studied her, wondering why she didn't know the word. Was she one of those Appalachians I'd heard about, inbred so many times they were mentally afflicted?

She cocked her head as if hearing movement behind her. "Sarie," she called out, "I reckon you best come on over here."

Sarie? I'd never heard that name before but didn't have time to think what it could be short for before I heard a muffled response accompanied by rustling sounds as someone drew near. A woman stepped out of the trees and I knew at once these two were related in some way, cousins maybe though they looked enough alike to be sisters. This one appeared to be a few years older but she had the same blond hair and eye shape with lips tilting slightly upward at the corners. She also wore a long dress with an apron tied around her waist. When she saw me, she hesitated, her eyes narrowing.

"She come from the lights," the younger one said, her voice hissing.

The one called Sarie drew closer, studying me with wary interest. "Don't look like she comes from around here, that's fer sure."

"No, I'm from Knoxville. I'm afraid I'm lost. I was traveling with some friends and our van broke down. We're waiting for

9

it to be fixed in Morganton. They're camping around here somewhere."

"Van? What's a van?" the younger one said.

"Our car."

She shook her head. "Car? I ain't never heared the word afore." She gazed at me for a moment, as if she'd never seen anything like me. "You sure do talk strange."

I looked back to Sarie. "Are you all from around here?"

Sarie narrowed her eyes, tilting her head to her left. "We got us a cabin a ways over yonder." She stared at me as if waiting for something then finally said, "My name's Sarie Collins." She nodded toward the other woman. "This here's my sister Abbie." She cocked an eyebrow at me in an expectant manner.

It took me a moment before I finally understood what she wanted. "Oh, um, nice to meet y'all. My name's Lizzie, Lizzie Baker."

She didn't acknowledge this, turning to her sister and saying, "You seen Maggie, Abbie?"

Abbie shook her head. "She was followin the lights awhile ago, hopin like ever'body else they'll lead us to Belinda and that poor baby of hers. They gotta be around here somewheres. That no-good husband of hers is too lazy to take em too far afore he'd bury em. *If* he'd even bother to bury em. Probably just covered em over with some leaves or somethin."

"We best go find Maggie, the wind's pickin up and it's gettin cold." Sarie looked at me, seemed to be considering whether to trust me or not. Finally, she nodded and said, "You can come along if you like, look for your friends as we go."

"Uh, yes, sure, that's probably the best thing to do."

Abbie drew near her sister and said in a low voice, "What if she brought Pa back with her, Sarie? What if he's here?"

Sarie put her hand on her sister's forearm. "Are you sure you seen her come from the lights or did you just see a light and then her?"

Abbie thought about this for a moment. "All I know, I was

lookin at that big clump of Joe Pye weed over yonder. See it? Then the light come out of thin air. I closed my eyes 'cause it was so bright, and when I opened em again, there she was sprawled on the ground right beside them rocks there at the base of the cliff."

Sarie frowned, glancing at the ground where Abbie pointed. She caught her breath suddenly, reaching out to grasp Abbie's arm. I knew what she'd seen but couldn't bring myself to turn and look at those gruesome things again.

"Oh, my merciful heavens, is that what I think it is?" Sarie asked.

Abbie turned to look. "What?"

"Look, look there at the base of the cliff, in the rocks."

Abbie glanced down and whimpered like a whipped puppy; clutching her sister's hand. "D'you ... d'you think it's them?" she whispered.

Sarie nodded then turned her attention to me.

I could see the suspicion in her eyes and quickly spoke up in my defense. "They were there when I woke up, I swear. Look at them, they're nothing but skulls. It's obvious they've been there for a while." I glanced at the skulls, then away. "Do you have any idea who they might be?"

"I ain't sure but they might be a woman named Belinda and her newborn baby," Abbie said. "She disappeared a while ago, Belinda did, right after she had the baby. People all over this mountain been lookin for her ever since. Most ever'body thinks she was killed and we all been searchin for her for years but so far we ain't had any luck."

Sarie reached around behind her back and untied her apron.

"What are you doin?" Abbie asked.

"I'm gonna wrap em up in my apron. We'll take em back home with us and give em to Mr. Sanders tomorrow when he comes to collect the hyssop for his wife's rheumatiz. He can take em down to Constable Jackson next time he goes into town."

"Sarie ..."

"Don't worry, Abbie. If the constable comes to question us again, we have her ..." she nodded in my direction "... to tell him they were here before we got here."

"You mean we're takin her back with us? But what if she brung Pa back and he's lookin for her now?"

"Well, I don't see there's nothin else to do except take her with us. And I don't reckon we'll see Pa anytime soon, but if he shows up, we'll handle it."

Abbie leaned toward her sister and whispered, "I don't want him to come back, Sarie."

Sarie rubbed her arm in a consoling way. "I know, Abbie, I feel the same way but I can't think of any way we can stop him if he has a mind to." She shook her head. "I wish you and Maggie would stop worryin about it. If he comes back, he comes back and there ain't nothin we can do about it till he does. 'Sides, look how long he's been gone and he ain't showed up yet so I don't reckon he will."

Abbie leaned close to her sister and lowered her voice. "I pray to God ever'day he don't never come back. Do you think that's a sin, Sarie?"

"I don't know, but if it is, I'll burn in Hell alongside you." Sarie walked over and bent down, picking up the larger of the skulls. Holding it in front of her, she studied it then spread her apron on the ground and placed the skull on top. She gingerly positioned the smaller one beside it before wrapping the apron around both of them, tying the sashes around the skulls to secure them. Holding the bundle gently in her hands, she turned to look at me as she stood. "Whereabouts did you say you're from?"

"Knoxville, Tennessee."

"That's a mighty far piece to come. Do you know where you are?"

"On Brown Mountain in North Carolina."

"That's right." She regarded me for a long moment. "Must've taken you days to get here. Did ya walk all that way or you got a horse and wagon?"

Alarm bells clanged in my head and I put my right hand in my pocket, worrying the items had disappeared. I ran my fingers over them once again to calm myself. Driver's license, lip gloss, cigarettes, lighter. All there where they were supposed to be. I put my left hand in the other pocket, touching the pack of gum. Yep, still there. I drew my hand out and looked at my watch for a moment then glanced up to see Sarie watching me suspiciously. I quickly hid my hand behind my back and unfastened the watch, cupping my palm around it. When she glanced at her sister, I dropped the watch in my pocket with the gum. I didn't know why but it suddenly flashed into my mind that I should find a place to hide all of them. A safe place, close to where I could get to them if I ever found my way out of this mess.

Sarie brought me out of my thoughts when she spoke with irritation. "Well, which one is it? Did you walk or ride in a wagon? How long you been on the road and where's the rest of your things?" She gestured toward my dress. "You can't go around in your nightgown and slippers, it ain't decent."

Confused, I looked down at my dress. It was long enough, reaching to my ankles, with a ruched bodice, but the material was a bit thin and I didn't own a slip so I didn't have one on. I hadn't worn a bra for years—I'd figuratively burned that uncomfortable item of apparel when I started college. I'd always hated them, and since my breasts were on the small side, I figured I'd go along with the majority of feminists at that time. The dress covered me sufficiently, I thought, but apparently Sarie didn't agree. My "slippers" as she'd called them were a worn pair of ballet flats I wore a lot because they were comfortable.

As for her other question about how I'd gotten here, I hesitated. Walk? Wagon? It had taken us only three hours or so to drive over from Knoxville thanks to the relatively new Interstate 40, but I had a feeling I shouldn't tell them that, not yet anyway.

So, I knew I was still on Brown Mountain, but the more important question, the one I couldn't bring myself to ask was, *When was I?*

CHAPTER TWO

Shelter From the Storm

That one all-important question circled in my mind, an endless unanswerable loop going around and around. Along with it was the panicked instinct that I shouldn't ask, not yet anyway.

When a bolt of lightning flashed across the night sky, I jumped and let out a little squeak. Sarie flinched as she looked up at the sky, mumbling something under her breath. It sounded to me like she was counting but I couldn't be sure.

A boom of thunder drowned out her whispers. She looked at Abbie and spoke louder. "That's gettin close. We'd best get back to home or we're gonna get soaked." Then she turned to me. "You comin with us or not?"

I shivered as I stared at the apron-wrapped skulls in her hand.

Sarie huffed out a breath. "Ain't no call to be a-feared. They ain't gonna hurt you or nothin. We ain't gonna hurt you neither so there's no need to be so skittish."

I shook my head. "No, no, it's not that. I know they can't hurt me. They're dead after all. I guess a goose just walked over my grave or something."

I tried a smile but she only pinned me with a baleful stare as she asked again, "Well, are you comin with us or not? We can't stand here all night waitin on you to decide what you want to do."

I had a feeling she didn't like me—or trust me—but what else could I do? I was alone and had only their word that I was still on Brown Mountain so there was no way I could get back to my friends other than to wander off into the dark, stormy night alone. Added to that, I still had absolutely no idea *when* I was.

"Sure, I guess I will." I looked down at my dress, plucking at the damp material of the skirt as if that explained my decision. "I'm wet and I'm cold. So what else can I do?" I added with a shrug.

"All right. We ain't got much but we can give you a dry nightgown and a place to sleep for the night. Tomorrow, you can look for your people if'n you don't find them as we go along tonight." Sarie looked up at the sky. "Storms should blow out of here by mornin."

She held out her hand to Abbie. Abbie took it and, in turn, held hers out to me. Still hesitant, I looked back behind me, hoping Ben or one of my friends would be there. No such luck.

Patience didn't appear to be Sarie's strong point as she snapped, "Are you comin or not?"

I wanted more than anything to find Ben but it was so dark on the mountain and nothing looked familiar. I didn't know what else to do but go with them and try to find my friends in the morning. I gave her a reluctant nod. "Yes, yes, I'm coming."

"Our cabin's not too far from here, but since you don't know the way, it'd probably be best if I keep a grip on your hand," Abbie said.

Sarie glared at me. "Don't let her go, Abbie, I don't want to have to go lookin for her, too."

Abbie squeezed my hand. "I won't." She smiled at me. "Don't let go, Lizzie."

I nodded as I clasped Abbie's hand tight in mine.

Sarie led us into the night, saying over her shoulder, "It's too dark to look anymore tonight and that storm's not gonna hold off much longer. Our cabin ain't much to speak of but it's warm and dry. We'll find you a dress to wear tomorrow while you look for your people. When you find them, you can put on one of your own and give us back the dress. Abbie should be able to wear it if she grows a little more."

I nodded. "Okay, thanks. I really do appreciate the help."

"*Okay*?" Abbie said. "What in tarnation does that mean? Y'all sure do talk strange over there in Knoxville. It's like you're from a different country or somethin."

"Oh, uh, it means yes or all right. I don't know where it comes from, it's just something my, uh, grandmother says. She's part Cherokee so I guess ..."

"We're part Cherokee, too, and I ain't never heared that word afore."

Though Sarie smiled when she looked at her younger sister, the pleasant expression on her face changed to a glower when she turned to me. I sensed she didn't believe me.

"Maybe the Cherokee in Tennessee talk different from the ones over here," Abbie said.

"I guess they do," I said.

Within a few yards, we were enclosed in a thick copse of trees that blocked out the little light we'd had in the open. It also obstructed my view of the cliff where I'd ... landed was the only thing I could think to call it. It was as good a word as any, I supposed.

We walked single file through the trees and the darkness with Sarie in the lead, Abbie in the middle and me bringing up the rear. Abbie and Sarie, it seemed, could see in the utter blackness that surrounded us but I couldn't. After tripping on exposed roots three times, I clung to Abbie's hand, thankful for her guidance. She kept me from falling flat on my face every time.

In a few minutes, we moved out of the thick cover of the trees and onto what appeared to be a well-traveled path. I looked up at the sky, barely managing to contain a squeal when lightning flashed, followed by booming thunder, though I did jump. Sarie glanced back and I saw she was again muttering to herself.

When she nodded and said, "Three, it's gettin closer," I

realized she had been counting to judge how far away the storm was from us.

"We got to hurry," she said to Abbie as she started walking faster. "It ain't gonna hold off for more'n a few more minutes. I want to get back to the cabin afore we get wetter than we already are. We'll look for Maggie as we go, but I'm a-bettin she's already home."

When she tucked the apron-wrapped skulls more securely under her arm, I caught the faint scraping sound when they rubbed together and shuddered, drawing Sarie's attention to me.

I inclined my head toward the bundle. "Did you ... did you know her and her baby?"

Sarie just shook her head but Abbie answered my question. "I reckon we knew her, all right. Her name is Belinda. Was Belinda. Don't know as the baby had a name. Probably did. Belinda would have had a name picked out, but far as I know, she never had a chance to tell anybody what it was."

"Was the baby stillborn?"

"Don't rightly know. The common belief on the mountain is that her man killed her d'rectly after the baby was born."

"Her man? You mean her husband? Why would he do that? Had they been married long?"

"You're a nosy one, ain't you?" Sarie said, irritation evident in her voice.

Abbie, not bothered by her sister's demeanor toward me, answered. "No, they wasn't together long at all. She was a-carryin when she and Jim decided to move in together, so it couldn't've been more'n a few months."

"So they weren't married? They were just shacking up together?"

Sarie turned her head at the unfamiliar phrase but remained silent.

Abbie answered, her voice shaking as we stepped over and around tree limbs lying across the path. "Shackin up? I ain't never heared that afore. Still, it's fittin, I reckon, as that run-down cabin of Jim's weren't hardly more than a shack and they both lived there."

"You mean they just lived together and her parents let her?"

"Yep, people here on the mountain don't usually go through a real marriage ceremony in a church. They move in together and live their lives without ever goin before a minister or judge which is exactly what Belinda and Jim did." She shrugged. "Shackin up is as good a way as any to put it. Trouble is, Jim ain't a very good man and even before Belinda had her baby he wanted rid of her. Said he was in love with another woman named Susie and wanted to be with her. I heard tell he treated Belinda real bad, hopin she'd get fed up and leave so he could live with Susie. Way I hear it, he did everythin he could to get shut of Belinda."

"Well, if they weren't really married, why would she stay with him? Why didn't she just leave?"

"I reckon she stayed because of the baby. Maybe she even hoped once it was born, Jim would treat her better."

"How sad. How long has she been missing?"

"Nigh on four or five years, I'd say. People been lookin for her for that long. Like I said, most of the mountain folk think Jim had somethin to do with her disappearin all of a sudden, maybe even killed her and the baby hisself. Lord knows, he's been acting right strange ever since it happened."

"How do you mean?"

Sarie stopped short. She turned and gave me a suspicious look. "If you ain't from around here, how come you're so interested in all this? Don't seem to me like it should concern you one way or t'other."

I shrugged. "I found the skulls. Don't I have a right to know who they belong to and what happened to them?"

"Don't rightly understand why you'd want to, seein as how you won't be stayin once you find your friends."

Abbie put a hand on her sister's arm. "It's all right, Sarie, she's just curious. I reckon I would be too."

Without replying, Sarie turned around and began walking again.

Abbie gave me an apologetic look. "You was askin about Jim actin so strange and all. Shortly after Belinda disappeared, a cousin or an aunt or some relative found her bonnet not too far from Jim's cabin. It had bloodstains on it so they took it to the constable down in Morganton but he said it didn't prove nothin, that maybe she'd gotten tangled up in a bramble bush and that's where the blood come from. When he asked Jim about it, all Jim would say was Belinda put on her bonnet and went out one day and never come back. But ever'body knew he beat her and wanted nothin to do with her. Proved it, if you ask me, when he moved Susie into the cabin right after Belinda disappeared."

"And that was the end of it?"

"No, Constable Jackson gathered some men together and they started searchin the area where the bonnet was found. While they was lookin, a fire broke out and burned the entire area, destroyin anythin they might've found that might have proved Jim killed her." She glanced at me. "A lot of people said Jim started the fire for that very reason and I reckon it makes sense. It was about then that the lights began to appear on a nightly basis on the mountain, too. Remember that, Sarie? I think that means somethin though I don't know what."

Sarie gave her sister a small smile. "I forgot about that. We don't see them so much anymore, do we, Abbie? But there for a while, they appeared every night. Most people believe they're Belinda and her baby tryin to lead the searchers to their bodies." She held up the apron. "These might go a long way to provin Jim actually did murder Belinda."

"How can they do that?" I asked. "You don't even know if they are Belinda and her little baby."

"Maybe not, but I reckon once the constable gets his hands on them, he's gonna pay another visit to Jim and take the skulls with him."

Abbie stopped, dragging us to a stop with her. "Do you think he really will, Sarie?"

Sarie looked at her sister. "You don't think so?"

Abbie shook her head slowly then startled as another bolt of lightning pierced the sky. "No, I don't think he really cares what happened to Belinda and her baby."

Sarie nodded. "All right, then, we won't give him the skulls. Tomorrow, we'll find a way to get em to the sheriff. They've kept this long, I reckon they'll keep one more night."

"Surely you're not going to keep them in your house?" I said. "That would be like sleeping in a graveyard."

Sarie only shrugged as if she didn't care.

Thankfully, Abbie spoke up to reassure me. "Don't you worry none, Lizzie. We'll put em in the barn for tonight while we decide what we ought to do."

"Maybe I'll take em over to Jim myself," Sarie said.

Abbie gasped. "Oh, no, Sarie, you can't do that. He's awful mean and he, he could get it in his mind to hurt you, maybe even do to you what he did to Belinda and her baby."

Sarie glanced at her sister. "You worry too much, Abbie. I can take care of myself."

Abbie stopped suddenly and I almost plowed right into her. "No, Sarie, no, please. You have to promise me you won't go over there by yourself."

"All right, Abbie. What if we all take them? He wouldn't hurt any of us if we were all there together, would he?"

Abbie thought about it for a moment then said, "No, I reckon not but we should be careful. Maybe we could get old Mr. Stevens to go with us. He's old but maybe havin him there with us would keep Jim from doin anything bad."

Sarie nodded. "I'll think about it, Abbie." She squeezed Abbie's hand and brought it up to rub lovingly against her cheek. "I promise you, little sister, we won't go unless we all think we'll be safe."

Abbie nodded. "All right then."

"Wait a minute," I said, as we began to move again. "I really think you should give them to the constable or sheriff and let them handle this whole thing. I mean, what good is it going to do to show Jim you have the skulls of his dead wife and baby? If they even are his wife and baby. It seems to me if he killed them that would pretty much guarantee he would do something to hurt you, or at least try. Why would you do that?"

Sarie shook her head. "You really ain't from around here, are you?"

"No, I told you I'm from Knoxville."

"Well, I reckon they have fancier ways of provin murder over there but here on the mountain it's said that the skull of someone who's been murdered don't never decay, and if you hold it over the head of the murderer, he can't tell a lie about what he done."

I thought at first she was teasing me but her serious expression belied that. "I've never heard that before. Does it work?"

"Never been around anyone who was murdered so I can't really say."

"Just seems too much like you're pushing fate to me," I said. "Like you're just asking—oh, look!"

I raised my hand, pointing off in the distance at the light I saw gleaming brightly through the trees. "There's a light. Can we go after it? Maybe it can take me back to where I was, to my friends."

"That ain't one of the mountain lights, that's our place," Abbie said. "Maggie must already be home."

We got to the small cabin with only a few seconds to spare before the sky opened up, raining so hard, it drowned out all other sound.

I looked around as I followed Sarie and Abbie inside, watching as Abbie greeted two dogs, both black and white with shaggy fur. When they approached me, I drew back, unsure if they would bite a stranger.

Abbie watched, saying, "Hold out your hand, let em get your smell, then they won't bother you lessen you want them to."

I waited for the dogs to sniff my fist before tentatively petting one, then the other.

"That there's Billy and that un's Bob," Abbie said, introducing me to the two dogs who accepted my attention as if their due then returned to the rag rug in front of the fireplace.

The cabin was small and cramped with only two rooms and a loft overhead. Although it smelled of old smoke and wet dog, it appeared to be immaculate. Even the hearth of the big fireplace had been swept clean and it looked to me as if it had been scrubbed as well. There were no lights, only glass lanterns, and just a couple of those placed strategically to shed light in the center of the room where a large, scarred table took up most of the space in front of the rough wooden counters running along the back wall. Nowhere near enough to light the corners—and who knew what lurked in that inky darkness?—but an adequate amount to allow me to see there wasn't a stove or refrigerator or even a sink.

In fact, there didn't appear to be any of the modern conveniences I had come to expect even in the smallest of houses or apartments in Knoxville. Even my tiny apartment off-campus had been equipped with a small refrigerator and a hot plate, electric lights and heat.

Panic tickled the base of my throat and I bit my tongue to keep from blurting out the question I wanted so desperately to know the answer to: What year is this?

I cleared my throat as I stood in the doorway. As one, Sarie, Abbie and the one they called Maggie, standing by the fireplace, turned to look at me. "Uh, you, you have a nice home," I said lamely.

Sarie frowned at me. "I told you it weren't much but its dry and Maggie has the fire goin to chase the damp away."

She turned away to walk over to the fireplace, saying something in a low whisper to Maggie while brushing a hand over her shoulder. Maggie gave me a tight smile before turning back and bending over the fire to remove a kettle hanging from a hook extended over it. She had the look of the other two though her hair was a little darker and her body a bit curvier. In the dim light, I couldn't see her eyes clearly, but as they were the same shape as her sisters', I assumed they were blue as well. Her hair hung down her back to her hips in a neat braid tied off with a strip of rawhide on the end.

Sarie turned back to me with a foreboding look on her face and all I could think was, that one's going to be a hard nut to crack. Unfortunately, I'd have to try. She was obviously the oldest and the one the other two looked to for guidance. If I couldn't win Sarie over, make her trust me and hopefully help me, I didn't think Maggie and Abbie would be on my side either.

"Did you find anything?" Maggie asked Sarie.

Sarie nodded as she held up the skulls. "Have a look at these."

Instead, Maggie turned back to me. "My sister's got the manners of a dead mule so I reckon I best introduce myself afore it finally occurs to her to tell you who I am. I'm Maggie."

Sarie answered before I could, waving a hand in my direction. "Oh, that's Lizzie. She's lost and we're gonna help her find her people tomorrow." She moved over to the large table and set the skulls on it. "But come look at this, Maggie. I think we found Belinda's and the baby's skulls."

Maggie hurried over to the table as Sarie unwrapped her gruesome package.

Clasping her hands at her waist, she studied the skulls. "Lord-a-mercy, Sarie. Where did you find em?"

"We didn't." She gestured to me. "She did. They were buried in a pile of rocks at the bottom of the cliff over yonder toward Mr. Beecham's place. She knocked the pile over and saw em right afore Abbie found her."

"But Jim and Belinda's cabin is in the other direction. How in the world did they get all the way over there?"

"I guess Jim's not as lazy as we thought he was. He must've taken em there to get em away from his place so when they were found people wouldn't think he done anything wrong. He's just stupid enough to hope the constable will think old man Beecham or one of his sons killed Belinda and her baby." She wrapped the skulls back up in the apron. "I'll take em out to the barn, put em in the loft for tonight."

Maggie nodded as she gave Abbie a reassuring smile. "That's probably for the best. Why don't you wait for the rain to stop so you don't get wet? We can have some tea while we wait."

Sarie put the wrapped skulls on the counter against the wall while Maggie walked over to the table to pour steaming water into three cups sitting there, saying, "Abbie, hand me another cup, why don't you?" Picking one up, she held it out to me. "Here, Lizzie, drink this. It'll warm you right up."

Taking a cup, Sarie held it to her nose to enjoy the

scent. "What did you put in this?"

Maggie smiled. "Just some coneflower and velvet dock to fight off the cold I'm sure y'all will get from bein out in this damp weather with some wild mint to add flavor and a dollop of honey to sweeten it."

Abbie took a sip. "Mmm, you do make the best teas, Maggie. Thank you, sister."

I blew on the surface of mine. "I know what coneflower is but what's velvet dock?"

"Bunny's ears." Abbie smiled when I moved the mug away from my face.

"Oh, stop teasin the girl, Abbie," Maggie said, turning her attention to me. Velvet dock's common mullein. You might know it as flannel flower or Indian tobacco."

I smiled at Maggie then raised my cup to Abbie. "Bunny's ears, it is." I took a big gulp of the tea, savoring the tasty liquid as it warmed my throat and stomach. "Oh, that's wonderful."

"Maggie, Lizzie come through the lights," Abbie said. "I was worried she might've brung Pa through with her but she says she ain't never seen him. Do you think he's gonna come back now?"

A look passed between Maggie and Sarie then Maggie looked back at Abbie. "Didn't Sarie tell you not to worry about that no more?"

Sarie reached out and touched Abbie's hand. "Abbie, I promise he won't come back. Don't you trust me?" She smiled when Abbie nodded. "All right, let's let that be the end of that. We won't never see him again. He's gone and he's gonna stay gone."

I had noticed the change in Sarie's demeanor when their pa was mentioned, the way her body tensed, the uneasy look that crossed her face, as if the subject was uncomfortable and one she didn't want to dwell on. I wondered how she could be so positive that he wouldn't return. Did she know something she wasn't willing to share with her sisters? Or had she done something to guarantee that their pa wouldn't come back … ever? Or was she simply trying to soothe their concern that he might one day appear?

Abbie took another sip of her tea before setting down her cup and taking my hand. "Let's go see if we can find you some dry night clothes to wear, Lizzie." She turned to Sarie. "Don't we still have some of Ma's things in the cedar chest?"

Sarie nodded. "I reckon we do." She looked me up and down, apparently sizing me up. "She looks to be about Ma's size." Placing her cup on the table, she waved her hand in a dismissive gesture. "You stay here, Abbie, and finish your tea. Mine needs to cool for a bit anyway. I'll take the girl and find what she needs."

Abbie gripped my hand tighter in hers. I winced as I wondered what the big deal was. Why didn't Sarie want Abbie to help me? Did she not want us to be alone so we could talk?

"Oh, no, Sarie, I'll do it," Abbie said, "I don't mind a bit."

And why was Abbie so insistent that she be the one to help me?

Sarie frowned as she shook her head then smiled sweetly at her sister. "Stay here with Maggie and drink your tea afore it gets cold."

Stepping closer, she grasped my elbow hard enough to make me stumble. Without any choice, I followed her into the other room. As soon as we cleared the doorway, she dropped my hand then turned and yanked a heavy curtain across the opening, effectively shutting us off from the others.

Slamming her fisted hands on her hips, she hissed, "Who are you and where'd you really come from?" Before I could even open my mouth to answer, she snapped, "I don't want to hear no more lies from you. Tell the truth now. I'll know if you don't."

I took a deep breath and said as calmly as I could, "I told you the truth. My name is Annabelle Elizabeth Baker, Lizzie to my friends and family, and I'm from Knoxville, Tennessee."

She narrowed her eyes, nodding. "All right, that I believe. What I really want to know is *why* you're here."

"W-w-why?" I stuttered. "What do you mean, why?" I racked my brain, searching for a plausible reason to give her. "I wanted to see the lights. I've heard so much about them and … um, I wanted to see them," I finished lamely. That was the best I could do under that hard stare. I prayed she would believe me. When her expression eased a bit, I took a deep breath and continued, "Honestly, that's all there is to tell."

"How did you get here?"

"We … drove. Ben drove and—"

"Who's Ben?"

"He's my …" I hesitated, remembering Abbie's reaction when I called Ben my boyfriend. "He's a friend." Inspiration struck and I hurried to add, "More than a friend, actually, he's my husband. We came over the mountains to get married because my father doesn't approve of him and wouldn't let us get married in Knoxville. He's a pretty powerful man over there and put out the word that anyone who married us would pay the price so we decided to elope. We did it in Asheville, got married, I mean." I grabbed her hand. "Please promise me you won't tell my father."

She shook it off, acting as if my touch repelled her. "He's way over yonder in Knoxville and I'm over here in North Carolina. How in the world could I tell him?"

"You could ca—write him a letter."

"I don't know him from Adam's housecat. Why would I do such a thing?" She waved a hand in the air as if the question wasn't important so I stayed quiet. "Did your pa set the law on y'all?"

"No, no, we didn't tell anyone where we were going, especially my father. We just left."

"You best be tellin me the truth of the matter, girl. I don't want Constable Jackson hanging around here, askin questions, tryin to make trouble for us."

Hoping to turn the trend of this conversation, I said, "Why is that? Are you hiding from him for some reason? Did you do something wrong? Or are you protecting one of your sisters?"

She scoffed at that. "I ain't done nothin wrong and I'm not hidin from nobody. Same can be said about my sisters." Her expression softened. "Law, girl, you met Abbie. A sweeter soul can't be found anywhere and Maggie's a lot like her. They're the closest thing to angels you'll meet here on this earth."

"Then why are you so worried about the constable?"

"It ain't none of your business." She hesitated, eying me warily, then seemed to come to a decision. "Well, I reckon I best tell you anyway 'cause he ain't to be trusted and you don't need to be talkin to him. No tellin what you'll say if you do." She contemplated for a moment before continuing. "It ain't that I'm worried exactly. I just don't like him and I don't trust him any farther than I can spit. He don't like me neither and is always comin around here actin suspicious and askin a lot of questions."

"Well, if you haven't done anything wrong and you don't have anything to hide, that shouldn't bother you. Tell him to leave you alone and he probably will."

She huffed out a breath. "I have told him to leave me alone but he keeps comin back, starin at me with those beady eyes of his and askin me the same questions over and over."

"What kind of questions?"

"About my pa and where he got off to, about Belinda and her baby and what happened to them. About anything he can think of that might bring me grief."

"Where is your pa?"

She straightened, that look crossing her face again. When she noticed me watching her, she glanced away, busying herself smoothing the quilt covering the bed. "I don't know and I really don't care. I'm just glad he's gone. He weren't the nicest person to live with."

I had the feeling she was lying to me but didn't want to give her any more reasons to dislike me so didn't question it further "You didn't tell the constable that, did you? 'Cause I think if you did, that would only give him more reason to come around."

"Don't you think I know that? I ain't stupid enough to say somethin like that to him. I only said I didn't know."

"Is there someone you can report him to? Somebody higher up than him?"

"There's the sheriff but he don't like to be bothered with what he calls petty dislikes and squabbles." She glared at me. "I'm tired of answerin all these questions you keep throwin at me. Like I told you, none of this ain't none of your business so just let it be."

Weariness had me lowering myself to the bed, wishing I could just stretch out and close my eyes for a few minutes. Lightning flashed outside, brightening the room to daylight, followed closely by the loudest clap of thunder I'd ever heard. Sarie turned to look at me when I shivered hard enough to shake the bed. Thunderstorms had always frightened me.

"Storm's right on top of us," she said then studied me as I shivered again, not so violently this time. "You cold? Guess we should get you out of that wet night dress first."

I wrapped my arms around my torso as she moved to the cedar chest sitting at the end of the bed. Opening it up, she pawed through the top layer of clothes. I watched as she pulled out a long, white gown made of flannel with little pink flowers dotted everywhere. What looked to be a hundred tiny pink rosebud-shaped buttons ran down the yoke in front with a lace-edged collar around the neck. It was prim but beautiful and all I could think was that I would roast in that darn thing.

"This ought to do it." She held it up, smiling as she looked at it lovingly, lightening her dour looks.

Caught by surprise, my lips curved as I thought she looked so much prettier without the frown.

Her gaze darted to me and the scowl was back. "Get out of that wet thing and put this on afore you catch your death. I'll look for a dress you can wear tomorrow when we go out to look for your man."

"Ok—um, all right."

I clutched the gown to my chest and waited for her to leave but she went back to searching the chest, which left me in another quandary. For some reason I couldn't explain, I didn't want her to see the items I had in my pockets connecting me to the future and felt the need to hide them. But where? I looked frantically around for a good hiding spot that I could get to without her seeing what I was doing.

Sarie pulled out a plain dress made of calico with long sleeves, this with pink and blue flowers dotted all over. "This should do you for tomorrow." She closed the chest and draped the dress over it then turned to me. "Shy, are you? Best get over that if'n you're gonna stay around here. Abbie don't believe in secrets or closed doors and you're gonna be beddin down with her up in the loft while you're here. Maggie can sleep with me down here." She continued to stand there, looking at me expectantly.

I couldn't have her watching while I tried to find a hiding spot. "I, I'm not shy exactly but I do need to use the bathroom. Where exactly is it?"

She stared at me like she thought I was crazy. "You want to take a bath? What for?"

My mind raced. They thought a bathroom was only for taking a bath? How far back in time was I?

"Oh, no, I need to, uh, relieve myself." I shuffled my feet from side to side, doing a little dance that I'd seen young kids do when they really needed to go. I hoped she would get what I was talking about.

She watched me for a moment before the light dawned. "Oh, you mean you want the outhouse. It's out back, a-course, but you don't want to go out there in the dark." She bent down and pulled a metal bucket out from under the bed. "Use this. It's not as pretty as one of them fancy chamber pots the rich folk use but it'll do."

I hesitated.

Her forehead furrowed, the irritated expression I was well-familiar with by now claiming her face. "What's the matter with you? I thought you had to go."

I glanced at the bucket.

She shook her head, acting exasperated over dealing with someone who obviously didn't know which way was up. "It's a sure thing you're a city girl. Ever'body on the mountain knows it's a lot safer usin a bucket at night than goin to the outhouse in the dark. There ain't no chance of meetin up with a stray timber rattler or a copperhead in here."

The mechanic's warning about snakes on the mountain

echoed in my mind again. I hated snakes more than I hated thunderstorms.

"The outhouse is safe durin the day but they's a lot of nasty critters runnin around out there in the dark. Better to use the pot." She waved her hand in a dismissive gesture. "Just shove it back under the bed when you're finished. We'll empty it tomorrow mornin."

"All right." I looked at her and raised my eyebrows. I needed her gone but I couldn't come right out and say it since she was already suspicious of me. "Um, can I ... can I have some privacy, please? I can't go with someone else in the room."

She shook her head as she turned around and went through the curtain, muttering something about "skittish girl" as she did.

I stood still for a moment, fingering the gum in my left pocket as I searched for a good hiding place in the small room. There weren't many options so I finally decided to wrap everything up in my panties and bury them under the things that were in the cedar chest. Hopefully, none of the sisters dug around in there very much.

Moving as fast as I could, I took off my panties and emptied my pockets of every last item, adding my watch to the lot before wrapping it all up. It took precious seconds to get to the bottom of the chest but I managed, constantly darting looks toward that curtain in case one of the sisters stepped through. Then I squatted over the bucket to relieve myself, grateful that was one less lie to add to the heaping pile I'd told that night.

I quickly pushed the bucket back under the bed then pulled off my dress and folded it neatly. I placed it on the chest and shimmied into the flannel nightgown Sarie had laid on the bed. It fit as if it had been made for me, but I'd been right, it was too warm for the summer night, even with the windows unshuttered and open. Oh, how I wished for cool air, but like electricity and phones, there wasn't an air conditioner or even a fan to be seen.

Slipping on my ballet flats, I thanked God I'd worn them for my little walk in the woods instead of my go-go boots. I could only imagine what the sisters would have thought of those. As it was, they had mistaken my footwear for slippers. Shoving up the sleeves of the flannel nightgown for comfort, I slipped through the curtain into the other room to join the sisters.

CHAPTER THREE

I'd Hate to Be You on That Dreadful Day

I slept fitfully that night, lying beside Abbie on a mattress lumpy and hard, pondering my still unanswered question. I knew there were people in the Appalachian Mountains who still lived without electricity or indoor plumbing but suspected I had been transported to a different time, one much earlier than the 20th century. Things here were too primitive. I hadn't seen a car or any hint of artificial light anywhere on the mountain. The rustic cabin was much like one I had visited in Old Fort from the era of the 1800s. The sisters wore long dresses I had seen in pictures depicting the 19th century. Nowhere were there signs of electricity or running water.

Had I been pulled into the light and ended up in a different time and place? If I had somehow traveled in time, how in the world would I get back? Was Ben searching for me? What must he be thinking? Would I ever be able to go back? These questions looped through my mind over and over and it was all I could do not to scream my frustration, fear, powerful longing to return to the year 1969.

I finally drifted off near daybreak and woke to the smell of strong coffee and soft murmurs. I turned over and noticed Abbie had apparently vacated the bed. I sat on the side of the mattress for a moment, praying hard, something I had never done in my life, to a God I wasn't sure existed, to be returned home safely and quickly. Using the hem of my nightgown, I wiped my eyes before climbing carefully down the ladder to join the sisters in the kitchen. I forced a smile at Abbie's cheerful, "Good morning, Lizzie," before stepping through the curtain to retrieve the dress Sarie had laid out for me the night before. Tugging off my nightgown, I pulled the dress over my head, glad to see it fit perfectly. Before going back out through the curtain, I knelt at the chest and fished out my pack of cigarettes and the lighter. After pulling a cigarette and the lighter from the pack, I reburied the bundle beneath the clothes. I got to my feet, checking my dress for pockets. Finding none, I slid the cigarette and the Bic up the sleeve. I needed a smoke badly.

When I pulled aside the curtain, Abbie turned, smiling brightly at me. "My, don't you look pretty, Lizzie. That dress coulda been made for you. Here, have a strong cup of coffee to get you goin. I suspect you didn't sleep right good last night, what with worryin about your friends and all."

I took the proffered cup, nodding my thanks before sipping the bitter, hot liquid. Sarie and Maggie studied me for long moments before returning to their chores. I sat at the table, watching Maggie stir something in a pot hanging on the hook over the fire while Sarie dropped biscuits into a cast-iron skillet. "Is there anything I can do to help?"

Sarie gave me a suspicious look. "With what?"

I shrugged. "Breakfast?"

She shook her head. "Almost done. You look like you didn't rest none. I reckon it's best if you just sit and drink your coffee and stay out of our way. We'll take care of things."

Abbie placed tin plates and old wooden utensils on the table then sat beside me. She leaned close and whispered, "Don't worry, Lizzie, things will work out for you."

I nodded, feeling numb with anxiety.

After everyone was seated and Sarie had dished each of us a bowl of oatmeal, which she called porridge, Abbie led the family in a prayer. While we were eating, she said, "I reckon we ought to take them skulls on up to Jim this mornin and see what he has to say about them."

Maggie hesitated, her spoon near her mouth. "You ain't plannin on turnin em over to Constable Jackson?"

Abbie gave her a look of incredulity. "Maggie, you know good and well Constable Jackson ain't gonna do a thing about them skulls."

Maggie shrugged. "You're probably right. He won't do a blessed thing other than suspect us since we found the skulls." Her eyes darted my way. "Thanks to our visitor."

Abbie sighed. "What's done is done, I reckon. 'Sides, the way he watches us like a hawk, he probably already knows we found em and'll try to find some way to claim what we did's against the law."

"Why would he want to do something like that?" I asked.

Abbie glanced at Sarie. "'Cause Sarie rejected him and he can't forgive her for that so he's takin it out on all of us."

I looked at Sarie, who glared back at me. "This ain't none of your concern, Lizzie."

I shrugged. "You're right, but you can tell him I found the skulls, not you. He can't accuse you of something you didn't do."

Abbie shook her head. "Won't do no good." She looked at each sister in turn. "I got a feelin about this. I know sometimes you don't believe me when I say I know things but I know this. That man killed his wife and baby and he needs to pay for it. Since Constable Jackson probably won't do nothin about it, we need to make sure Jim's punished for it."

"Punished for it?" I asked. "In what way?"

Sarie gave me an irritated look. "It'd be best if you remember you're only a visitor here and ain't got no business with any of this."

"Well, of course. My only concern at the moment is getting back to my boy—friends and returning home."

Sarie nodded. "We'll pay a visit to Jim then try to find your friends. We can ask others on the mountain if they've seen them as we go along. Hopefully they're tryin to find you, too, and I'm sure somebody's crossed paths with em. Before the day's over, you'll be with em and headin home."

"Thank you, Sarie," I said, tears coming to my eyes. "I so

want to go back."

"I reckon you do." Her eyes darted to Abbie and Maggie. "Let's finish eatin and get on our way. It's a few miles to Jim's cabin and we want to get there as quick as we can."

After breakfast, I asked Abbie where the outhouse was.

"Out behind the cabin, Lizzie. You'll see the path to it as you go around back. Be sure to watch for snakes 'cause it's a sunny mornin and they like to sun themselves on the rocks beside the path."

I nodded, resisting the urge to ask her to come with me in case there were any snakes, but I needed desperately to be alone.

When I opened the door, my eyes widened as I watched what looked to be a small wild boar galloping toward me, making small squealing noises. I quickly closed the door.

"What's wrong?" Maggie said, with alarm.

"There's a wild boar out there."

Maggie glanced at Abbie, a smile playing around her lips. "That's Abbie's pet, he won't hurt you."

"They're wild animals," I said. "They have tusks, they're dangerous."

Abbie opened the door, saying, "Curly ain't dangerous a'tall, Lizzie. Come on out and meet him."

She stepped onto the porch, leaving the door open. I closed it most of the way and peeked out, watching Abbie greet the little boar, picking him up and kissing his porcine face. The boar squirmed with delight as Billy and Bob circled around Abbie, vying for her attention.

"Abbie's always bringin home animals she finds that are sick or hurt," Maggie said from behind me.

Sarie sighed. "She's a sweet girl, cares too much for people and animals alike, and I fear that will be her downfall."

I nodded before stepping onto the porch, stopping to pet the two dogs before joining Abbie. "Can I hold him, Abbie?"

She smiled as she handed him over. "Careful of those tusks, they can cut you, but he won't do it on purpose."

I held the small boar, his fur bristly against my skin, smiling when he rubbed the side of his head against my arm.

When he began to squirm, I put him down and watched him dart into the house, Abbie and the dogs following behind.

As I picked my way up the path to the privy, I kept my eyes on the ground, watching for any slithering form that might come my way. I wiped away tears prickling at my eyes, wondering why I was here, in a time and place so primitive and unfriendly. I can't live like this, I thought, as I opened the door and stepped inside the small building, reeling back at the odor that greeted me from the covered hole that had been dug in the ground. I sat on the wooden seat built over the hole, casting my eyes around in the dim light for signs of spiders or other insects. Finished, I looked around for toilet paper then realized if I actually had gone back in time, chances were it hadn't been invented yet. I spied corn husks neatly stacked in a basket nearby and deduced that must be what they used. Oh, God, why did this happen to me, I wondered, as tears filled my eyes and I put my fist in my mouth to hold back a sob. I sat there for several minutes, trying to gain control, and once I felt I could speak without bursting into tears, got up and opened the door.

Before returning to the cabin, I stepped behind the outhouse to smoke. Cigarettes had always calmed me and as I puffed away, waiting for my anxiety to ease, I wondered what I would do when the pack was empty. I knew they probably grew tobacco in this area and more than likely smoked it some way but had cigarettes been invented yet? Hopefully I wouldn't be here long enough to have to find out, I told myself, taking the last puff then burying the butt in the ground and hiding the Bic lighter up my sleeve once more. On the way back down the path, I told myself to buck up and be strong. Things were what they were and all I could do was be patient and try to find a way back.

When I stepped inside the cabin, Sarie eyed my red eyes but didn't comment on them. Instead she said, "I reckon that dress fits you well enough. It'll have to do you till we find your friends. It was our Ma's so you best be careful with it."

I resisted the urge to snap at her. She'd told me enough times that the dress had belonged to their ma. Why did she feel the need to remind me again? Swallowing my anger, I only said, "Thanks, Sarie."

After Sarie collected the skulls, we went on our way, Abbie in the lead. As we walked along, I studied the terrain around me, searching for anything that might look familiar, praying hard I'd look up and see Ben's anxious face.

To my dismay, all I saw were trees, ferns and wildflowers, all shrouded in a low-lying mist swirling near the ground. It was a little creepy but it was also beautiful the way the mist hugged the tree trunks and plants. Even as I wondered if the delicate haze hung around all day, it began to shred apart as the sun came out from behind a cloud, beaming in thin rays through the gaps in the leaves overhead.

We walked for perhaps an hour, one in which I kept vigilance for snakes, the mechanic's words echoing in my mind yet again, but luckily we didn't cross paths with any. I finally couldn't stop myself from saying, "If you don't want to turn the skulls over to the constable, why not the sheriff, and what's the difference between the two anyway?"

Sarie eyed me for a long moment before saying, "The sheriff's over the whole county, Constable Jackson's only over our district." She snorted. "He's only supposed to serve papers and such but he's got it in his head he has power to do everythin the sheriff does. Sheriff seems to like their arrangement well enough long as it don't interfere with his duties." She shook her head. "Not much we can do about it. They's a system in place and ever'thing on the mountain has to go through Constable Jackson afore the sheriff gets involved."

"Even murder?"

She shrugged. "Best to follow the rules where the constable's concerned. He don't like it if we go around him. We found that out the hard way." She didn't elucidate and I wondered if there was more to the reason he disliked the sisters other than being rebuked by Sarie. "'And knowin the constable, he's liable to think we had somethin to do with her death seein as how we have the skulls."

"But that makes no sense. They've been missing for a

long time and obviously dead for a good long while, since they're nothing but bones."

"That ain't how Constable Jackson will see it."

"We'll make him see it if he doesn't," I said stubbornly.

She stopped and studied me for a moment. "I reckon our way of justice on the mountain might not be the way it is over there in Knoxville."

I shook my head. "I'm not sure what you mean."

"Tell her about what happened to Frankie Silver, Sarie," Abbie said. "Maybe then she'll understand."

"Who's Frankie Silver?" I asked.

"If you listen, I'll tell you." Sarie turned around and began walking, speaking over her shoulder. "We're related to Frankie through our pa's side, though I don't rightly know how, and this is what's been passed down through the family. Lord knows, Pa told the story at least once a month like he was proud of it. It took place afore any of us was born but it's a fair account of the way justice works around here to this day.

"The story goes that Frankie killed her husband Charles in the winter of 1831. After he was dead, I reckon she panicked and cut him up with an axe. To keep anybody from findin out what she'd done, she tried to burn the parts. When that didn't work, she tried hidin parts of his body by buryin some of them under the floor of their cabin near Toe Creek and the rest outside around the cabin.

"I ain't fer sure how the sheriff found out what she done but he did and arrested her for it. Frankie was put on trial in March of the next year for the murder of her husband. The jury, made up entirely of men, a-course, judged her to be guilty and sentenced her to be hanged to death at the next term of the North Carolina Superior Court. Her lawyer asked for an appeal and got it but the State Supreme Court judged her to be guilty."

She paused to step around a fallen log then waited for us to do likewise. "Frankie was hanged on Damon's Hill in Morganton on July 12, 1833." She turned and eyed me. "You ever heared of Daniel Boone?"

"Of course. The frontiersman. We studied him in history."

"Ain't sure what you mean by that but his nephew John Boone was sheriff of Burke County then and it was either him or one of his deputies who hung her. It's said people come from everywhere to see it and they sure wasn't disappointed. I've heard tell that Frankie wrote some verses or a song or something but it later come out they was written by a Methodist minister, I forget his name. Anyway, they printed them verses on strips of paper and passed em out to the people who came to watch her hang. Most said they was as good as a confession but I don't know about that 'cause I never read em.

"They was some people who said the killin was justified, that Charlie had mistreated Frankie all throughout their marriage and she killed him while tryin to defend herself in a beatin, but I reckon we won't ever know the truth of the matter 'cause Frankie weren't allowed to testify during the trial. In fact, she weren't allowed to utter a single word. And then they killed her and silenced her forever.

"Mr. Woodfin, her lawyer, now, that's a different matter. He went around tellin ever'body she was innocent till the day he died, sayin if she'd been able to testify, the jury never would have found her guilty. He even wrote a petition sayin she didn't have no choice in the matter, that Charlie would've killed her if she hadn't killed him first. Said he come home drunk and started beatin her with a stick, and when she struck back, she killed him in what he called self-defense. Lawyer Woodfin went all over these mountains, gatherin lots of signatures, but the governor refused to interfere. And the clerk of the court at the time also claimed she was innocent but that didn't do Frankie no good neither. They still hanged her."

I stopped. "Wait a minute. They hanged Frankie without letting her testify in her own defense? That's not a fair trial."

"Maybe not, but at the time all this happened, most of North Carolina still abided by the English justice system which don't allow an accused person to testify in court."

"But that isn't right. It's in the constitution ... or I think it is anyway. I don't know exactly what it says but when we find Ben I'll ask him. He's studying to be a lawyer, he'll know."

39

Sarie held up her hand, palm out. "Well, it so happens I agree with you but it's the way things went. Besides, it's all in the past anyway. You getting all het up about it ain't gonna change what happened to Frankie Silver. It's done and ain't nobody can change it, not even your lawyer husband."

Abbie beamed at me. "You're married? I didn't know that. I thought he was just your ... boyfriend. Isn't that what you called him?" She turned and looked at her sister, reaching out to take her hand. "Oh, Sarie, we got to help her find her husband."

Sarie held up her hand again. "Shh, Abbie. We'll do that soon as we can, I promise, but right now she needs to hear what I'm sayin. And she needs to take heed of it else we're gonna find ourselves in a heap-load of trouble."

"Trouble, what trouble? How is she gonna bring us trouble?"

"It'll come is all I'm saying if'n she don't listen to what I tell her and keep her mouth shut around the constable."

Abbie looked directly at Sarie. "Lizzie ain't gonna bring no trouble here. Not that I can see. We got to help her, don't you see? It's the right and only thing to do."

Sarie patted Abbie's hand. "Didn't I promise? We'll help her if we can, don't you worry none. Hush now and let me get this out. It's gettin late and we've still got a ways to go."

Abbie nodded.

Sarie smiled at her sister then turned back to me. "This ain't about what's right or what's fair, Lizzie. This is about showin you what passes for justice here in the mountains."

I nodded. I'd heard of mountain justice but still couldn't grasp how the constable would think me or the sisters guilty of murdering someone just because we found her bones.

Abbie stopped suddenly.

"What's wrong?" Sarie asked.

"Somebody's comin," she said in a quiet voice.

Sarie shook her head with frustration. "With our luck, it'll be Constable Jackson."

"It ain't him." Abbie waited then held her hand up. "Zeke, Thomas, over here."

"Why are you callin them over?" Maggie asked.

"I don't reckon we're strong enough to hold Jim down while we hold the skulls over his head. We need help 'cause I shore don't figure he'll be too het on just sittin there," Abbie said, her tone matter-of-fact.

Neither sister responded to this.

Within moments, two mountain men appeared on the path ahead, ambling their way to us. When I gasped, Sarie turned to me. "What?"

"Nothing," I said, glancing away. One of the men looked exactly like the mechanic who had worked on the van, the one who warned us about snakes on the mountain. The only difference was this man's hair was sandy blond while the mechanic's had been more of a chestnut color. Their brown eyes and face shape were the same, as was their tall, lanky build. I looked at the other man, who was older and bore a slight resemblance to the younger one.

I shivered as I studied them, wrapping my arms around myself. This unexpected meeting, as well as the dampness of the forest, actually had me grateful for the long sleeves on my borrowed dress.

When the men reached us, they took off their hats, nodding their greeting. "What's goin on?" the older man said.

"We need your help," Abbie said.

He smiled. "Well, we're right happy to help in any way we can."

"We shore do thank you," Abbie said and explained to them about the skulls and the sisters' intentions.

"My granny always said the same thing about skulls," the older man, who Abbie had called Thomas, said. "Why, I reckon if she was here today, she'd insist I go on with y'all and help get the truth out of that bastid. Ever'body on this mountain knows he killed that sweet Belinda and her baby. I'll help you, all right, and so will Zeke here."

Zeke nodded his agreement.

As we set off again, I couldn't help but sneak glances at Zeke, wondering what his last name was. The mechanic had to be a descendent of his. They looked almost identical. He caught me looking at him once and smiled. "Howdy, ma'am."

"Hello," I said, glancing away.

"This here's our cousin Lizzie from over Knoxville way," Sarie said.

Both men nodded at me.

"Nice to meet you," I said, ducking my head and staring at the ground.

Within the hour, we stepped into a small clearing in the middle of which sat a small cabin made out of wooden planks with a front porch that dipped and swayed and looked ready to cave in. The roof had holes in it and I wondered what they did when it rained or snowed. The chimney canted to one side and looked about ready to topple over but apparently still worked, a thin stream of smoke puffing out and dissipating in the air.

As we approached, the door creaked opened and a man stepped onto the porch, watching us. He was short and stocky, with greasy black hair and a beard that rested against his chest. "You ain't got no business here, so go on, git," he said, making a shooing motion.

"We've found somethin you might want to see, Jim," Sarie said, walking closer, holding the skulls in her apron which she had folded so that they weren't visible.

"Cain't think of nothin you got I'd want to see." He hawked up phlegm and spat it into the yard.

A woman stepped onto the porch behind him. She stared at us but remained silent. She looked considerably younger than the man, with strawberry-blond hair and a heavy build. This must be the woman he had moved in shortly after Belinda disappeared. I tried to remember her name. Was it Susie?

Thomas stepped up beside Sarie. "I reckon we got business to discuss, Jim, and it best be done inside."

He studied the men, who were considerably bigger than him, before finally saying, "Well, come on in, then, but best make it quick. I got chores that need doin." He stepped aside, gesturing toward the door.

As we went onto the porch, Sarie said, "Ain't no need for Susie to come inside. I reckon she best stay out here till we're done."

Susie straightened up, looking as if she were about to protest, but Maggie stepped in front of her. "I'll stay outside with Susie. Lizzie can, too."

I wanted to see what happened when they held the skulls over Jim's head but couldn't think of a valid reason to request I be allowed to watch. As it turned out, even though they closed the door, it opened right back up so I was able to witness the whole thing.

Thomas pulled a rickety chair from the table, which looked to be uneven, and told Jim to sit in it. "I don't see no need to sit," Jim said, a stubborn cast to his face.

Zeke reached forward and pushed him down into the seat. Jim made an effort to rise but Zeke pushed him down again, keeping his hands on his right shoulder to hold him in place. Thomas stepped to the other side of him and put his hands on his left shoulder like Zeke had done.

Jim looked at Sarie and I thought I could detect fear settling into his features. "Show me what you got then get out of my house."

She unfolded the apron and lifted the skulls up, one in each hand.

Susie, who had moved to stand beside me, peered inside. She gasped and put her hand to her mouth. "Oh, my sweet Jesus, what is that?"

Jim startled, as if someone had goosed him, then sat back in the seat, trying to get as far away from the skulls as he could.

Sarie stepped close to Jim. "I reckon you've heard the tale, Jim, that when you hold a skull over the murderer, he can't lie about it. So we've come here with Belinda's and her baby's skulls, to ask you if you killed em."

Jim's eyes were wide, his mouth open. He tried valiantly to get out of that chair but Zeke and Thomas held him in place. "Don't put them skulls over me," Jim cried, his voice panicked. "I don't want em near me." He moved his head from side to side as Sarie held them aloft so that he wouldn't be directly under them. Zeke put one large hand on the back of his neck to hold his head still.

"All you got to do is tell us you didn't kill your wife and her baby, Jim," Abbie said, her voice calm and soft. She glanced at Sarie, who held the skulls above his head. I stared at the baby's, thinking how very tiny and fragile it looked. "Say it," Abbie said.

Jim had gone pale and began to tremble all over. He worked his mouth but couldn't seem to say anything.

"Say it," Abbie repeated.

Drool began to slide down Jim's chin and he shook his head from side to side. His body shook so violently, it was all Zeke and Thomas could do to hold him in the chair. This went on for several minutes while Abbie and Sarie placidly watched. I felt movement beside me and turned to see Susie fleeing into the yard, where she stood with her hands to her mouth, looking away into the woods.

Sarie finally said, "I reckon we got our answer even though he didn't say it." She put the skulls back in her apron and folded it over. I was relieved to see the tiny skull disappear and hoped I never saw it again.

When Zeke and Thomas let go of Jim, he fell to the floor, curling into a fetal position, continuing to shake and drool.

"Is he having a fit of some sort?" I asked Maggie.

"Fit of guilt, I'd say," she said.

"I reckon we best ought to turn these over to the constable now," Sarie told Zeke and Thomas.

They nodded their agreement and all came out onto the porch.

"Should we oughtta stay with him till Constable Jackson comes?" Thomas asked.

Abbie shook her head. "He ain't goin nowhere." She glanced back at Jim, still on the floor. "I reckon we ought to give somethin to Susie to help that poor soul."

I looked at her. I had never heard Abbie speak in that tone of voice, cold and unfeeling, even though the words belied the tone.

Sarie nodded. I watched as she stepped off the porch and approached Susie, pulling something out of her apron pocket. Curious, I drew closer to listen.

"Susie," Sarie said, taking her hand and placing a small folded packet tied with string on her palm. "Jim looks to be in distress. I brung along some tea that will help calm him. Make him some and give it to him right away afore he starts bangin his head on the floor or hurtin hisself in some way."

Susie stared stupidly at the packet in her hand.

Sarie nudged her. "Go on now, make him some. It'll calm him down, bring him back to his senses."

Susie stumbled forward a step then looked back at Sarie. "I shore will, Sarie. I thank you for that." She glanced at the cabin then back to Sarie. "You reckon he did it?" she whispered.

Sarie didn't say anything.

"I didn't have nothin to do with that if'n he did," Susie said. "He told me she run off from him, that they weren't married no more. I wouldn't have moved in with him if he hadn't told me that, Sarie."

"You go on now, tend to your man," Sarie said. "He'll want to be in a good mind when the constable pays him a visit."

After Susie went into the cabin, Maggie and Abbie joined Sarie. They exchanged meaningful glances and I wondered what exactly was going on here. Zeke and Thomas stepped off the porch, shaking their heads.

"Well, he didn't say it but I'd say from his actions he shore did it," Zeke said.

Thomas nodded. "If'n you want, Sarie, I can take them skulls over to the constable. Zeke and me was headed into town when you hailed us."

I didn't miss Sarie's look of relief. "That would be mighty fine, Zeke. Save us a trip into town when we've got other things to see to."

"Why I'm happy to do it," he said.

I turned away when he reached for the skulls. I couldn't bear to look at them anymore.

After they said their goodbyes, we made our way back toward home. We hadn't gone far when I realized we hadn't asked them if they'd seen Ben or any strangers around. When I mentioned this to Sarie, she assured me if they had seen anyone about they didn't know, they would have mentioned it to us, simply to see if we were aware strangers were on the mountain.

Sarie led us to the place where Abbie had seen me come through the lights and we searched until dark for any evidence that anyone had been there. There was no abandoned campfire, no downtrodden foliage or path that had been recently used. Nothing looked familiar, and I wondered if the light had moved me to another place on the mountain. The thought of spending another night without finding Ben and my friends filled me with dread. I clutched at my stomach, sick at the thought that I might never return home.

Abbie, seeing this, put her hands over mine. "It'll be fine, Lizzie, I feel it. You just got to have patience."

I nodded but felt no consolation from her words.

CHAPTER FOUR

You Ain't Goin' Nowhere

The next day, Sarie and Maggie left early to check on several slaves at a nearby plantation who had come down with chicken pox. Abbie elected to stay behind with me, telling Maggie and Sarie she would take me with her to see Pokni.

"Who's Pokni?" I asked, taking the large basket she handed me and hurrying to catch up with her.

"An old Choctaw woman who lives on the mountain, supplies us with herbs from time to time. She don't usually like white folk, but she took to us, I reckon 'cause we're healers like her." She hesitated, eyeing me, before saying, "She can help you."

"How?"

She gave me a mysterious smile. "You'll see."

I wondered what she meant as I followed her down an overgrown path, deeper into the forest. I tried not to panic at the thought of snakes but could not take my eyes away from the ground, where I feared one lay in wait, ready to strike at any moment. I had by this time come to the conclusion I had a phobia about snakes.

Abbie, though, seemed unconcerned, as she walked ahead of me, talking over her shoulder. "Pokni is Chocktaw for granny. She tells me the Chocktaw are the original people, they was here before the white man, even the Cherokee."

"Where did they go?"

"You heard of the Indian Removal Act? Well, the Cherokee wasn't the only Indians Jackson removed. He took the Chocktaw, Creek, Chickasaw and Seminole, too. Some hid out, some went south, but most were herded west." She made a disgusted sound. "Like they weren't nothin but a bunch of buffalo or cattle."

As we walked along, I tried to remember what I knew about the American Indians, discomfited that the only tribe I had any knowledge of, and that was very little, was the Cherokee. And only because I was part Cherokee.

Abbie interrupted my musing when she spoke. "My sisters think I'm slow in the head. They say it's 'cause my pa beat me when I was a young'un, but to tell you the truth, I don't remember it. Sarie said I was passed out cold for two days, and when I woke up, I had to learn to talk all over again. They think my mind plods along way behind theirs. But that don't mean I'm stupid or slow or they're smarter than me. When he hit me, hit my head, why I reckon he opened up a whole new world for me. That's why I could forgive him though Sarie never would. But since then? The earth speaks to me. I can tell you when it's goin to rain or snow, even when the wind decides to shift its course and blow a whole 'nother way. I can sense what animals are thinkin in their minds. That's why I don't believe in killin em, they feel pain just like we do and have their own purpose on this earth, nothin to do with man. I see things others don't and that's another reason they think I'm touched in the head." She glanced at me before continuing. "I reckon I've seen a haint or two but I'm not bothered by them. They remain here for their own reason and it ain't for me to interfere. And the lights. Sarie don't say it but I know she thinks I'm crazy when I say they're a door to another time, another place. But I know different. And you proved me right, Lizzie."

That stopped me. She walked on a few paces then seemed to sense I wasn't behind her any longer and glanced over her shoulder at me.

I stared at her, waiting.

She nodded as she returned to stand beside me. "I know you're from another time, Lizzie, and that you want to go back. I can tell by the way you act, the look on your face, like a wild animal caught in a trap."

I grabbed her hand, put my face close to hers. "You truly believe that, Abbie, that I'm from another time and place?" I asked, my voice going high.

"A-course I do. I seen you step out of them lights, plain as day. You heard me tell Sarie that. I kept tellin Sarie the lights would lead us to Belinda and her baby, and they did, and you right along with them."

"And you'll help me? Go back, I mean."

"If that's what you want, as long as you don't help him get back here."

"Him?"

"Pa. He's meaner than a striped-eyed snake and I don't bear him any ill will but Sarie does." She looked away. "Ever since Pa beat me that time, I got what my granny called the sight. I know things are gonna happen afore they do, but when it comes to those I love? It's like I go blind in my mind. So I can't see when he's comin back or if he ever will. But I got a feelin somethin bad's happened to him or is gonna if he comes back. I'm a-scared Sarie might kill him if she gets the chance, she hates him that much."

I squeezed her hand. "I promise, Abbie. I'll steer clear of him if I run across him." I fell into step beside her as she began walking.

"I reckon it's gonna take some time. We have to make sure you go back through the same light you stepped out of else you might end up somewheres else." She glanced at me. "Where did you come from anyway?"

"From right here on the mountain, like I said."

"Well, then, I reckon it's better to ask *when* you come from 'cause I knew right off you wasn't from our time."

"1969."

Her eyes widened. "Over a hundred years hence?"

Over a hundred years? I swallowed audibly before I

asked the question that had plagued me since I'd arrived here. "What year is it now, Abbie?"

"Why, it's 1859."

I shook my head, unable to believe this. "Yes, over a hundred years, a hundred ten."

She regarded me for a long moment. "What's it like then? Is it as hateful as it is now?"

"Hateful?"

"All this uproar over slavery, which I don't abide by one whit, all this meanness in the world."

I thought of the Vietnam War and the way protesters had been treated by our government. Of how the vets from that war were spit on when they returned to America. Of the way women and black people had to battle so hard for equal rights. Of the assassinations of John F. Kennedy, Martin Luther King, Jr. and Bobby Kennedy, all in the span of five years. All the brutal inhumanity in the world. "No, there's still a lot of meanness there, Abbie, but it is a different world than this."

"How so?"

"Oh, in thousands of ways. I guess the most important way would be that we have electricity."

She squinted her eyes at me. "Electricity? What in tarnation's that?"

"You know how everything you do here centers around having to have a fire and wood to heat the cabin and cook meals? Well, in the future, we don't have to depend on fire, we have electricity."

"Electricity." She repeated this, as if savoring the word.

"Yes. If it's cold outside, we're warm inside. If it's hot outside, we're cool inside. All because of electricity. And we have indoor bathrooms, with flushing toilets and running water."

"What's a toilet?"

"You know, a commode." Seeing her confusion, I went on. "The seat over the hole in the outhouse we squat over? In the future, you sit down on this commode, toilet, with water in it. When you're finished relieving yourself, you push a lever which flushes the water and your, um ..."

"Shit?"

"Yes. Or pee goes right down the toilet and out of sight. No odor, no mess. Then you go to a sink and turn on either hot or cold water and wash your hands. No need to step outside to do any of that, it's all right there in the bathroom inside your house, all nice and warm or cool, depending on the weather outside."

She shook her head. "Lawsy mercy, wouldn't that be nice when it's cold and rainy outside?"

"Oh, it is. You can also take a bath inside the house, in the bathroom, in a roomy bathtub with warm water, or hot if you want. Or a shower. Oh, Abbie, I miss showers."

"What's a shower?"

"You stand in a stall and turn on the faucet and water just, well, sprays over you, like standing outside in a warm rain shower. You can wash your hair, wash your body, using soap that smells good and is mild and gentle on your skin. Most people shower or bathe every day in the future."

"I bet everybody smells right nice, huh?"

"Those that bathe do."

She wrinkled her nose. "Most of them on this mountain don't take a bath but maybe once a month, if that. Why, some of these mountaineers don't do it but once a year and that's only if'n they get the urge to. Gets to where you can't get used to the stink when you're around a lot of em at one time. I can't abide that. Sarie says I got a sensitive nose, she says you get used it after a bit, but I can't. I always carry a hankie with me wrapped around crushed flowers to hold to my nose. It helps some but not all the time."

I nodded. "I read somewhere that that's how bridal bouquets came to be, to cover the stench of unbathed bodies."

"Shore makes sense to me."

I resisted the urge to sniff under my arms. I hadn't bathed since I'd come through the lights and was beginning to feel grungy. My hair, which tended to be oily, felt greasy and clumpy. "Speaking of which, I need to clean up when we get back. Where do you all bathe, Abbie?"

"Oh, in the crick when it's warm like today. They's a nice

deep place just for that. I'll show you when we get back. During the winter, we got us a big tub we fill up. Takes a long time heatin the water but it's worth it to me."

I silently said a prayer I would be gone long before winter set in.

Abbie brushed a limb aside and waited for me to step up beside her. "Tell me more about your time, Lizzie."

I closed my eyes for a moment, thinking back. "You walk into a dark room and with the flick of a switch, it's light, like being outside in the sun."

She made a small contented sound beside me.

"You need to talk to someone, even if they're miles away or on the other side of the country or world for that matter, you pick up a phone and dial a number and you're speaking to them."

"Oh, Lizzie, I can't imagine it," she said. "If'n I can find some paper, can you draw some of them things for me?"

"Sure, I'll be happy to. Oh, and there's no traveling by horse or feet if you don't want to, we have cars and trucks for the ground and airplanes for the sky."

"Sky? You mean you can fly like a bird?"

"In a machine with wings, called an airplane, that flies like a bird."

She glanced up at the sky, as if searching for one. "I shore would like to see that," she said, with wonder.

I smiled to myself, remembering my first trip on an airplane. Back when my mom was alive and all was right with my world.

"We're here," Abbie said, stepping into a small clearing edged by a shallow creek, in the middle of which stood a roundhouse covered in bark.

I stopped and stared, wondering how long it had been there. An elderly woman sat outside near a fire, her hands rolling something on a rock. Although she wore a long dress much like the sisters, her features clearly were those of an American Indian. She looked up when we neared and smiled at Abbie. I noticed most of her teeth were missing and those that remained were dark and stained. Her long, white hair trailed down her back in a single braid but her dark eyes were alert and seemed that of a much younger woman. As she kneaded what looked to be clay, I watched her fingers, which were gnarled and bent, and wondered if she suffered from rheumatism or arthritis. This didn't seem to bother her, though, as she deftly worked the clay.

"Hey, Pokni. Is this your pottery makin day?" Abbie asked as she bent down to kiss her cheek then sat beside her.

The old woman smiled before darting her eyes to me, giving Abbie a questioning look.

"This here's Lizzie, she come through the lights."

Pokni nodded as if this made perfect sense to her as she gestured for me to sit.

"Nice to meet you, Pokni" I said, sitting next to Abbie.

She didn't acknowledge this as she worked the clay into a long coil then placed it around a flat base.

Abbie turned to me. "Pokni makes the prettiest pottery, Lizzie. Trades it down in Morganton if she needs to barter for somethin or other."

I was fascinated by the old woman's hands as she worked the clay and the pot began to take form. When her dress shifted, I noticed a tattoo of a coiled black snake on her shoulder that climbed the side of her neck.

I leaned forward to study it. "That's beautiful. I've never seen one like it."

Pokni turned her attention to me, and when she spoke, I was surprised at how articulate she was, television having given me the mindset of 19th century American Indians who grunted or only said one-syllable words. "My husband was a war captain, although during his time there were no major wars to fight." She shrugged. "An occasional skirmish with other tribes but they weren't serious, not like the big one. But in the before, the backs of respected war captains were tattooed with two blacksnakes, one on each shoulder blade. The respected war captain would also have those things he held special tattooed to mark them as his." She smiled a secret smile. "And he held me most special of all, so as a gift to him, I had myself tattooed." She looked away, lost in thought. Abbie and I remained quiet, giving her whatever memory was running through her mind. Eventually she looked back at us, her eyes sad and filled with pain.

"Is he here?" I asked, intrigued by her.

She glanced away, toward the forest edging her homeplace. "He is buried here and so will I be, when I decide to join him."

"Do you have any people nearby?" I asked.

She shook her head. "My people were south of here in a place called Alabama. The Chocktaw were the first to walk when the Great Removal began, back in 1831. My war captain would not go and chose war instead but the others who did not walk fled and refused to fight. It took many a night to convince him this was a war we could not win but he finally listened. So we came here, to the mountains to hide, and here we stayed." She continued to talk as she worked the clay into long lengths then coiled it around into the shape she wanted. "He was a good man and I loved him like no other. When he died, it felt as if a fire inside me had gone out and left nothing but ash and dust. When I see him again, the fire will ignite and burn fierce, like it once did." She darted a glance at me. "Until then, I wait."

What would it be like, I wondered, to love someone the way she seemed to have loved him.

We watched in silence until she finished the pot. She set it aside and looked at Abbie expectantly.

"We come for some burdock root, Pokni. Some slaves has come down with the chicken pox and we figured we'd try it since it works so well on poison ivy."

She tilted her head toward her roundhouse. "Inside with my other herbs. I also have wild mint oil, which will help."

Abbie touched Pokni's hand then got to her feet and went inside the small roundhouse. While she was gone, the old woman studied me, her eyes intent. "When did you come from?"

I blinked, not expecting this. I leaned closer to her and lowered my voice, although there was no one to hear us. "You know about the lights?"

"During my time on this mountain, I have seen them many times and have come across one or two others who

54

stepped through the lights."

I moved closer to her. "Did they go back? Were they able to go back, Pokni?"

"One did, or I think so. He disappeared one day so I assumed. The other decided to stay."

"Why in God's name would someone stay in this place?" I asked, unable to contain the spite in my voice.

Her eyebrows pitched. "Your time is better?"

"Of course. We have so many more amenities there."

She nodded. "So said the one who left. He told me of a world I couldn't even imagine."

"Yes, exactly. Did he tell you what year he came from?"

"2053."

I gasped. I wanted to ask her what his world was like in that time but Abbie came out of the roundhouse, saying she found what she needed.

Pokni glanced at her. She reached out, took my hand. "If you go back, you must go back through the same light you came here through."

I nodded, smiling at Abbie who joined us. "Abbie told me that."

"But you must also remember to think of the time you want to travel to or you may find yourself in another time, like this one, or different from your time."

"I'll remember."

Pokni squeezed my hand. "When you see the light, before you step through, consider your life here and your life there. Choose wisely, daughter, or you will regret it the rest of your days on this earth."

I smiled as I squeezed back. "I promise." I had no intention of doing that, I knew exactly when I wanted to be and it wasn't during this time. "Thank you, Pokni. I hope to see you soon."

"You will." She smiled as Abbie kissed her cheek and we left to return to the cabin.

I held Abbie's hand. "Did you hear what she said, Abbie? She's known two others who've come through the lights."

"She told me that afore, Lizzie. Said one went back but one stayed."

"What happened to the one who stayed, do you know?"

Abbie's eyes darkened. "Pokni told me she came afore I was even born. The way Pokni talked, she weren't like you, Lizzie. She says she went half-mad and talked about the time she come from to anybody who'd listen. Most thought she was crazy or a witch. Pokni asked her why she decided to stay and she told her she couldn't go back to her time." She shrugged. "Maybe the law was after her or she'd done somethin she felt bad about and felt it best to stay away. Wasn't long afore she met up with some feller from Asheville and went off with him and that's the last anybody heard of her."

"Did she say what time she was from?"

"Close to your time, I think it was 1940, if I remember right."

For the first time since I'd stepped through the lights, I felt hope and excitement. One had gone back. If he could, I could. But you don't know if he went back to the right time, my inner voice reminded me.

Abbie's voice drew me out of my musings. "I been thinking about your predicament. I reckon you ought to tell me what happened when you come through the lights and maybe we can figger from there how to get you back where you belong." She crossed over to a fallen log and sat down, staring at me expectantly.

I sat down beside her and took her hand, tears coursing down my cheeks, so grateful to have someone to talk to about this. Just as I opened my mouth to tell her, I heard movement behind me and glanced around. A tall, muscular man stood there, watching the two of us, his lips set in a firm line. Thick, black hair framed an angular face with dark eyes and brows above a long, straight nose. I would have found him handsome but for the look in his eyes, cold and dead and cruel. I imagined a smile rarely touched those wide lips of his. He held the reins of a tall, black horse, its flanks foamy with sweat. When the horse bent his head to the ground to graze, he yanked on the reins so that the horse couldn't reach the grass, the bit of the halter biting cruelly into its mouth. You hateful bastard, I thought, what does it hurt you to let the animal eat?

He glanced at me before speaking to Abbie. "I been to the cabin to talk to Sarie about them skulls Zeke and Thomas brought me, but she wasn't there, so I reckon you'll do for now."

"What do you need to know, Mr. Jackson?" Abbie asked.

When she said Jackson, I knew immediately this must be the constable.

"Where you found em, for one."

I listened as Abbie described the place they located the skulls and how they were positioned, noting she didn't implicate me in any way in the discovery. I found it odd the constable didn't question her very much about the finding of the skulls other than to ask the time and who was present, and wondered about that. When they finished, he said, "Tell Sarie I need her to show me exactly where y'all found them skulls and that I'll be by later to get her and Maggie's statements about em." His gaze shifted to me. "As for you, I reckon it's time we had us a little talk."

Abbie squeezed my hand as she rose to her feet, pulling me up with her. "About what, Mr. Jackson? She ain't done nothin wrong that I can see."

"About who she is, for one, and where she came from, and my suspicion that she's somehow tied to those skeletons of Belinda and her baby. Seems awful strange she shows up the same night y'all say you found the skulls."

"This here's Lizzie," Abbie said, gesturing toward me. "She's our cousin from over Knoxville way, just this week come for a visit. She didn't have nothin to do with Belinda and her baby, why, she wasn't even here when they disappeared."

He studied me for a long moment, his eyes traveling up and down my body, and it was all I could do to remain quiet. He finally turned his attention back to Abbie. "Your pa never told me you had relatives in Tennessee."

"She's from our ma's side. He never liked em, didn't want to have nothin to do with em but he ain't here no more so ..." Her voice trailed off.

His eyes narrowed. "That's right, he ain't and I reckon I'll find out what happened to him in due time." He held up his hand when Abbie moved. "Don't go telling me the lights took him, Abbie. That's just your feeble mind trying to rationalize what happened to him. I suspect sooner or later somebody's gonna run across his body on the mountain. I just hope it's soon enough that I can figure out how he really died, whether it was by knife or gun." He lifted his eyebrows. "Or poison."

I looked at Abbie, standing there with her fists clenched and tears in her eyes. I put my arm around her waist as I met his gaze, wondering what in the world he had against these sisters other than being rejected by Sarie. That didn't constitute good enough reason to harass them, in my opinion. "I don't think you need to talk to her like that. There's no reason to tell her you think something sinister has happened to her father if you don't have proof."

He sneered at me. "I reckon you believe what she says about the lights."

He carried a superior attitude, honed, I'm sure, by his official status and I doubted he had any compassion or empathy for anyone. I had known men like him in my time, men who used intimidation to cower others, and wanted so badly to tell him that would not work with me but sensed if I did so, this would only pull me into his area of focus and I did not want that. But I would not lie and hurt Abbie in the process. "I do."

He studied me for a long moment. "Is that right? Well, I reckon I got some questions for you, seeing as how you showed up all of a sudden, so mysterious and all. We can talk here or we can head on into town and talk there. It's your choice."

"Then we'll talk here. What is it you want to know other than the fact that I'm a relative from Knoxville here to visit my sweet cousins who have promised to show me their healing methods? The fact that I happened to be present the night the skulls of the woman and her baby were found is happenstance only, Constable, and I don't understand why you find my presence here so suspicious. Certainly I'm not the only visitor Brown Mountain has ever had." I met his eyes, telling myself not to challenge him, but God help me, I hated this man for no reason other than the way he talked to Abbie.

He glanced at Abbie then back to me. "I'm thinking it might be a good idea to get in touch with the sheriff over there in Knoxville, just to make sure you're who you say you are."

I smiled at him. "You caught me. Actually, I came through the lights, from the year 1969. If you can go forward in time and check with the sheriff of Knoxville then, I'm sure he'll be able to ascertain I am an actual person from that area and that time."

He glared at me. "You don't want to go messing with me, missy."

"I'm just curious why you're messing with me, Constable. If you have verified the skulls are of Belinda and her baby and they'd been murdered, why in the world would you think I have something to do with their deaths? I only just arrived as I'm sure you know since I understand you find it necessary to check on the sisters quite frequently, and I've been told Belinda and her baby have been missing for quite awhile. So I have no idea why you would want to question me about something that happened years ago. I have nothing I can give you on that matter."

He studied me for a long moment. I stared right back, determined not to let him bully me. He finally stuffed his hat on his head. "I reckon we'll see about that. For the time being, I'll make my inquiries elsewhere but I ain't through with you, girlie, not by a long shot." He climbed on his horse and nodded at me. "I'll be sure to keep an eye on you."

"Eye me all you want, there's nothing of importance you'll find, I'm sure."

"We'll see about that." He looked at Abbie. "Don't forget to tell Sarie what I told you." He clicked to the horse, jerked on the reins and rode away.

Idiot, I said to myself. Why couldn't I just keep my mouth shut? If he checked with the sheriff of Knoxville, there would be no record of me and that would only arouse his suspicions further.

Abbie turned to me, a smile flitting around her lips. "I liked to died when you told him you come through the lights, Lizzie. I was half-afraid he'd believe you."

I shook my head. "Men like that only use a small portion of their brain for thinking, Abbie. I doubt he'd ever even consider the possibility of something other than what he perceives to be normal. Even if he saw the lights, saw me step right out of them, he'd find some way to rationalize it."

"You reckon he'll contact that sheriff over in Knoxville?"

I shrugged. "Even if he does, what can he arrest me for? I haven't done anything." But I suspected that man would find a reason to arrest me if he wanted.

"You need to be wary of him, Lizzie, and tread light. He's a dangerous man. He's already got his sights on Sarie 'cause she rejected him, so just be careful."

I nodded. "I will, Abbie, I promise."

When we returned to their cabin, I asked Abbie to show me the place in the creek where they bathed.

"I reckon you'll want some soap," she said.

"Yes and shampoo."

Her forehead wrinkled. "What's that?"

"What you wash your hair with."

"Ain't never heard of it. We just use soap."

If they didn't have shampoo, I wondered at the soap. "What kind is it?"

"Lye."

I remembered reading how harsh lye soap was. "Do you know what it's made from?"

"Ashes and animal fat. We trade for it in Morganton seein as how I don't believe in killin animals for their meat or fat."

"Well, if that's what you have, I guess I'll use that," I said.

After Abbie collected the soap and a rough towel which looked more like burlap cloth to me, I followed her to the nearby creek, stepping into the woods along a trail that led to a large rock overlooking a wide area of the stream which Abbie explained was deep enough to stand in. She stood back and watched me expectantly.

I peered over the rock into the clear water below. "Are

there snakes?"

"I reckon so. They don't usually bother us, so you should be fine."

I nodded as I turned back to her. "Thanks, Abbie. I think I can handle it from here."

When she didn't leave, I said, "Are you going to bathe as well?"

"Nope, did that last night afore supper."

We stared at one another. I finally sighed. "If you don't mind, I'm a bit shy. I'd rather bathe in privacy."

She turned her back on me. "You can have all the privacy you want but I ain't leavin. We always have somebody with us to warn if there's a bear or anybody else around."

I winced. I'd been so busy watching out for snakes I hadn't even thought about bears or any other wildlife, for that matter. "Oh, well, that makes sense," I said with resignation, beginning to remove my clothes while stealing glances around me for a lurking wild animal or human.

The rock rested on a larger one leading into the water. I gasped when I first entered the creek, goosebumps rising all over my body. "It's cold."

Abbie laughed. "Don't get no warmer than that, Lizzie, it's a mountain spring and they's all cold. You'll get used to it though."

As I lathered up with the lye soap, trying to ignore its harsh odor, I began to contemplate how to make a more sensitive, nicer smelling soap. Hadn't the American Indians used something I'd read about once, a root or something that turned sudsy? And body lotion, surely there was an herb that could be used for that. I scrubbed my underarms, trying to recall what I knew of deodorants. I decided I'd ask Pokni next time I saw her what herbs were good for personal hygiene.

Finished, I climbed onto the rock and quickly toweled off, feeling refreshed, my body buffed from the rough soap. Although I felt exposed on the rock, which was warm and flat, I had to resist the impulse to just lie down and let the sun beam down on me. Abbie didn't turn around until I spoke. "You know where I can lay my hands on a razor?"

She turned to me with a frown. "What in tarnation you want with a razor, Lizzie?"

I pulled up the gown and ran my hands over my stubbly legs. "In my time, women shave our legs and under our arms. Well, there's a movement lately not to do that but I do simply because it feels so much cleaner and fresher. I'd like to shave if you have a razor I can borrow."

"Pa had one but I ain't seen it in forever." She cocked her head, contemplating. "Makes your skin smooth, huh?"

"As silk."

She gave me a secretive smile. "I'll see if I can find it. Might be I'll do that myself if it feels so good." She winked. "But don't tell Sarie, she'll think us heathens if she finds out."

I smiled at her, then startled a bit realizing this was the first time I'd probably smiled for real since I got here.

Walking back to the cabin, Abbie resumed our conversation before Constable Jackson interrupted us, asking me to tell her once more what happened when I came through the light.

I described seeing it moving through the trees, my curiosity at first when it moved with me, then fear when it enveloped my hand and began to pull me into its grasp. She studied the ground as we walked, listening intently. Just before we stepped into sight of the cabin, she stopped, placing her hand on my forearm to keep me with her. "You got to keep in your mind the color of that light, Lizzie, 'cause that's the one you need to go through to get back to your time."

I nodded.

"We'll go out at night, after Sarie and Maggie have gone to bed, start lookin for it. The lights are always more active in the fall so it might take till then for us to find it."

Despair coursed through me and I couldn't stop myself from saying, "That long? Abbie, I don't know if I can stay here that long. That's weeks away."

"You ain't got no choice so you better make the best of it." Seeing my face, she reached out and touched my hand. "We'll look until we find the light, Lizzie. I promise you that."

I hugged her hard, tears streaming down my face. "Abbie, thank God you believe me and will help me. I don't know what I'd do without you."

She hugged me back then stepped away and began walking once more. "Just don't tell Sarie. She don't believe in them lights and she won't like us out at night searchin for em."

CHAPTER FIVE

The Devil's Been Busy

As the days passed, I found myself spending more and more time with Abbie. I liked not only her sweet nature but her simpleness which I knew was not due to brain damage but merely her acceptance of the world around her. We spent much time in the woods foraging for herbs and one bright sunny morning a week or so after my arrival were in search of St. John's wort. It was a beautiful summer day, the skies a prettier blue than I remembered ever seeing during my time, with large white fluffy clouds drifting across.

As we walked along, Abbie told me about Lori, a young woman on the mountain who became so depressed after losing her baby, Sarie feared she would kill herself. The sisters wanted to give her the herb, which Abbie told me helped ease depression. She pointed ahead. "Look there, Lizzie, you see them pretty yellow flowers with tiny black dots at the tips of the petals? That's St. John's wort. It's best to harvest em when in full bloom but we'll have to dry the flowers afore we can use em, a-course." She knelt down by the plant, setting her basket beside her.

I studied the herb with its erect stem and oblong, yellow-green leaves, admiring the pretty flowers. "What else is it used for, Abbie?"

"Oh, it can help heal wounds and treat swelling. Good for

just before your monthlies when you feel like tearin the world apart, but Sarie likes it most of all for treatin them folks trapped in their own black world."

A rustling sound behind us drew our attention. I looked around, expecting to spy Constable Jackson standing there, looking harsh and mean, and was surprised to see a black woman hurrying toward us, leading a small black horse by the reins. She was tall and very slim, with warm, chocolate-colored skin, wearing a bright red bandana around her dark hair. Her beautiful face was contorted with agony, her eyes wide and frightened.

Abbie rose to her feet, saying, "Tillie, what's happened?"

When Tillie noticed me, she hesitated, her gaze darting from me to Abbie.

"It's all right, Tillie, she's my cousin Lizzie from over Knoxville way."

Tillie gave me a slight nod then turned her attention to Abbie. "I went to the cabin but ain't nobody there. I need you to come quick, Miss Abbie. It's Samuel. He run away but the master's overseer tracked him down and brought him back and whipped him near to death. He's bleedin all over his back and in so much pain he keeps passin out. Oh, please, Miss Abbie, you got to come help him."

"I'll go to the cabin and get my medical bag then we'll be on." Abbie immediately began walking toward the cabin, Tillie and I falling in on either side of her, the horse trailing behind.

Tillie wrung her hands together. "Can you stop the blood, Miss Abbie? I's afraid he's going to lose so much of it he can't come back to us."

Abbie, walking so fast she was almost running, nodded. "A-course, Tillie, if he needs blood stopping, I'll do it. You go on now, get him inside out of this heat and put him on his stomach. We'll be along soon as we get what we need. Don't you worry none, we'll take good care of him."

With a nod, Tillie mounted the horse and rode away. We returned to the cabin, where Abbie handed her basket to me and took down an old, tattered saddlebag hanging from a peg beside the door. As she began placing bottles in the saddlebag, I looked for Sarie and Maggie but didn't see them anywhere.

"Where are your sisters?" I asked Abbie.

She glanced up at me. "Probably off helpin others, Lizzie. I reckon we ought to leave them a note, tell em where we'll be."

"I can come?"

"Better you do. I might need your help."

I glanced around the cabin but saw no evidence of paper or writing utensils. Did they have pencils or pens back then, I wondered to myself. I knew in colonial times, they used the tip of a feather dipped in ink for writing. But what about the mid 19th century in the mountains?

Abbie looked up and, as if sensing my confusion, said, "Get a piece of old charcoal out of the fire there and write on the wall, right next to the door. That's where we always leave our messages."

I glanced at the wall, noticed a spot much darker than the wood surrounding it. "Where are we going?" I asked as I fished charcoal from the hearth, glad there hadn't been a recent fire in the fireplace.

"The Hampton plantation."

I wrote a brief note to Sarie and Maggie, cursing to myself when the piece kept breaking on me. Finished, I looked up and saw Abbie heading out the door, her saddlebag thrown across her shoulder. I threw the remaining charcoal in the fireplace and rushed to follow, wiping the charcoal dust off on my apron.

Abbie ran to the small corral behind the barn and called to a large horse grazing inside. I had noticed him before but hadn't gotten close to him, being a bit afraid of an animal this big. He was a beauty, with dark brown hair and a blond mane and tail and dark, soulful eyes. Abbie handed the saddlebag to me as she put a halter around the horse's muzzle and laid the reins along his back. Using a stump, she hoisted herself onto the back of the horse then held out her hand. When I started to hand her the bag, she said, "Take my hand and get on behind me."

I stepped back. "I've never ridden a horse before, Abbie,

especially one bareback. Can't we walk there?"

"We need to get there as fast as we can, Lizzie, and if'n we walk, it'll take some time. Besides, riding ole Buck here's about as dangerous as sittin in a rockin chair. He's a gentle old soul, he won't buck you off. Hurry up now, Lizzie, we need to get there quick afore it's too late."

I stood on the stump, placed my hand in hers and let her tug me onto the horse. "I'll hold the bag," I told her as she picked up the reins and clicked her tongue to get Buck moving.

As we set off at a fast trot, I clutched Abbie around the waist with one arm, fearful of falling off. But that fear proved to be unfounded because the horse had a gentle sway to him, much like rocking in a rocking chair as Abbie had described, and I soon relaxed. Although the sisters' cabin was closer to the bottom of the mountain than the top, it took longer than I expected as we meandered down a trail where the going was rough enough in places to slow us to a walk But once we reached the flatlands at the bottom of the mountain, the land smoothed out, and at Abbie's cluck, Buck began to gallop, causing me to clutch her around the waist once more. I squinted my eyes and ducked my head against the dust from the road swirling around us as we made our way to the plantation. When Abbie clucked to the horse again and he began to slow, I looked up, noting a white, two-story house with a large portico set back from the road, with plowed fields off to the right and back, a row of rugged cabins nearby. Abbie bypassed the house and went straight to the cabins.

Tillie stepped out of one, relief clearly on her face as she held Buck's halter so we could slide off. "I'll take care of Buck, see he gets some water," she told us.

Abbie didn't respond as she hurried into the cabin Tillie had stepped out of. I followed her in and had to take a moment for my eyes to adjust to the dimness inside. The room smelled of sweat and blood and moldy hay. I watched Abbie approach a wooden table, on which a large black man lay on his stomach, his shirt off and back exposed. He was perfectly still and didn't make any sound so I assumed he must be unconscious. When I drew closer, my stomach clenched and I was glad he wasn't awake, thinking the pain would be unbearable. Even in the dim light, his back looked like it had been shredded and I wondered if there was any attached skin at all as I forced myself to peer closer, but there was so much blood it was hard to tell. It had pooled on his back and spilled off onto the table, dripping onto the floor. Flies buzzed around, settling on his back, then rising into the air. Although it was already stifling hot in the cabin, we needed to find a way to stop the influx of flies.

I waved them away as I glanced up at Tillie. "Could we close the door to keep the flies out and do you have a candle or lantern so we can see his back better?"

She went to the door and closed it, then crossed over to the wooden mantle over the fireplace where she fetched a candle, dipped it into glowing fire embers in the fireplace and brought it to the table.

Abbie glanced at me, whispering, "Sarie normally uses goldenseal to stop the bleedin but too much can be poisonous. Samuel's whole back's bleedin, I can't tell if he left him any skin at all. Oh, Lizzie, I wish Sarie was here. She'd know what to do."

"Tillie asked if you could stop the blood. What did she mean by that?"

Abbie shook her head, saying, "I ain't never done it in this kind of situation. His back's tore up pretty bad and there's an awful lot of it but I don't see none pumping."

I wondered if she had heard my question then forced myself to concentrate on the matter at hand. "Maybe what we're seeing isn't fresh blood. If we cleaned his back, we could get a better idea of what needs to be done."

She reached out to touch his back and I grabbed her hand. "You need to wash your hands first, Abbie. You've got germs on your hands, they can get into his blood and cause an infection."

She gave me a questioning look. "What in tarnation's germs?"

I shook my head. "Never mind. Let's wash our hands then find some clean rags to wipe off his back." Tillie stepped closer and I said, "Have you got warm water, soap, some clean rags? We need to wash his back, get all this blood off."

Nodding, Tillie returned to the fireplace, where a large black pot hung over the glowing ashes. She placed a log on the embers then stoked them until flames shot up around the log and it began to burn.

I noticed movement in a corner of the room and looked that way. Two small children hovered together, watching us. I wondered if they were the children of the man on the table. If so, they didn't need to see this. Well, no child should. I stepped over to them, knelt in front of them. "I wonder if I could ask you two to go to the other cabins and get me as many clean rags as you can. Could you do that for me, please?"

"Yes'm," the little boy said as he clutched the little girl's hand and they rose as one. I couldn't help but notice their clothes were nothing but rags, their faces and hands and feet dirty. I watched him lead the little girl out of the cabin, their gaits stiff and forced. They must have been terrified seeing something so horrific. I hoped they hadn't witnessed the whipping which brought it about.

Abbie poured water into a chipped bowl and washed her hands with a small piece of lye soap. Finished, she took the bowl to the door and emptied it into the yard, brought it back and refilled it from the black pot. I followed suit, then we both stood over Samuel, who hadn't regained consciousness. Tillie joined us, the newly filled bowl in her hand, holding out rags in the other, and we set to work, dipping the rags into the water, washing as tenderly as we could the flayed skin on his back.

I straightened for a moment, stretching and blotting sweat off my forehead with my apron. With the door closed, the fire had quickly turned the room into a furnace. "I pray he doesn't wake up, Abbie. I don't think he'd be able to stand the pain."

"Then we best work quick." After a long moment, she said, "'Sang."

I looked at her.

"Sarie's used that before to stop the bleedin."

"What's sang?"

"Mashed ginseng root. Look in the saddlebag, see if you can find some."

I knew what the plant ginseng looked like but wasn't sure about the mashed roots so simply searched for what might be roots that had been crushed together. I held up a canning jar and said, "Abbie?"

She glanced around and nodded. I took the jar over to the table, and after we patted his back dry, we both began to apply the ginseng root concoction on the areas that were still bleeding.

"He'll be scarred for the rest of his life," I said.

She shook her head. "Sometimes I wonder why God don't take things into His hands and destroy this world. How can He look down on somethin like this and be proud of what He's made?" She stopped and glanced around at Tillie, who had gone to the door to empty the blood-filled bowl. She turned back to me, her voice dropping to a whisper. "Tell me it gets better in the future, Lizzie, tell me this all ain't for naught."

Oh, how I wanted to, but I came from a violent time, filled with hostility and hate, inequality and unrest. "I wish I could, Abbie, I really do." I could not stand the look on her face so returned my attention to Samuel's back. One large gash still oozed blood, and as I dabbed that away, I noted it was so deep I could see the muscle beneath. "This needs to be stitched."

Abbie leaned over to have a look. "I ain't never stitched anyone before. I've watched Sarie but …"

"I have." She looked at me, her eyes filled with curiosity. "I can do it." I leaned close and whispered. "What do you use?"

"Needle and thread. It's in the bag." She watched me as I returned to the saddlebag and found what I needed, appalled that they used a sewing needle and thread made of cotton. I returned to the table. "What do you use as an antiseptic?"

She shook her head. "I ain't got no idea what that

means."

"Something to sterilize the needle and thread."

"Sterilize?"

How did anyone remain alive during this time, I wondered, if they didn't take sanitary measures to treat someone injured or ill? "Alcohol?"

Abbie shook her head.

"Liquor? Moonshine? Have you got any of that?"

Abbie looked at Tillie. "The master don't allow it but I reckon I can find some hidden away somewhere." She looked agitated then said, "Please, Miss, don't tell him we has it or somebody's liable to get the whip or worse."

"Of course I won't, Tillie. I promise."

With a nod, she turned on her heel and left the cabin.

I glanced at Abbie and noticed her regard. "I was in medical school before I … that doesn't matter. I went to medical school, learned how to treat injuries, illnesses, for a little while."

She looked shocked. "You mean you was learning to be a doctor?"

"Yes."

A look of wonder crossed her face. "It can't all be bad when you come from, Lizzie, if women can be doctors."

"No, it's not all bad, not at all." A feeling of homesickness overcame me, so powerful it brought tears to my eyes. Oh, Ben, I thought, are you looking for me? Abbie reached out and touched my hand. Our eyes met. "I wish I could go back there, Abbie. I don't belong here."

"We'll find a way," she whispered just as Tillie came through the door.

Both watched as I poured the moonshine over the needle and thread then soaked a rag with it and patted the skin around the gash. Samuel moaned but I continued on, ignoring him. Tillie knelt close to his head, murmuring comforting words to him. As I sewed his back, much like I would a garment, I began to design in my mind a needle for stitches while I tried to put his skin back together. He began to stir and I hesitated.

"Keep going," Tillie said. "He won't stop you."

"Almost through," I told him. "It won't be much longer now."

Samuel had fully regained consciousness by the time I finished. Although I could tell he tried hard not to show his pain, he couldn't keep moans from escaping his lips. His body was covered in sweat and at times he trembled as if trying to hold the pain in. I put my hand on his shoulder, close to his neck. "Try not to move, Samuel. We need those cuts to heal, and if you move around, you're liable to keep opening them." I placed the salve over his stitches and covered it with a clean cloth.

Abbie had returned to the saddlebag and was searching through it. "If I can find some feverfew, we can brew up some tea to help keep him calm and treat any fever he might get."

"Do you have anything we can give him for the pain?"

"The feverfew ought to help him a bit."

The door opened, flooding light into the room, and Abbie and I both sighed with relief when Sarie and Maggie stepped inside. I noticed each carried their own saddlebag much like Abbie's.

"We found your note," Sarie said, crossing over to Samuel.

"How'd you get here so fast?" Abbie asked, continuing her search.

Sarie picked up the candle and leaned over Samuel, studying his back. "We run across Thomas on the trail. He loaned us his horse so we could get here quick." She looked up at Abbie. "What'd you use?"

"'Sang. I was afraid goldenseal might be too much. I thought I had feverfew to help keep him calm but there ain't none in my bag. You got any?"

"Maggie?" Sarie asked.

"I do. I'll make a tea for him."

As she set to work, Sarie ran her finger over the gashes.

"You probably shouldn't do that until you wash your hands," I said.

She gave me a hard look.

"Your hands are probably dusty from traveling, will have

germs all over them. They can get into his blood system and cause infection."

"She told me the same thing," Abbie said. "It's somethin to think about."

Sarie studied me for a long moment then returned her attention to his back. "Did you stitch him up, Abbie?"

"No, I shore didn't. Lizzie did that."

Sarie straightened up. She glanced at Maggie, then looked at me, one eyebrow raised. "You did a right fine job, Lizzie. I reckon there's more of a mystery to you than I thought."

"Could have done a better job if I'd had the right kind of needle," I quipped before I could stop myself. At her questioning gaze, I said, "In Knoxville, they use different type needles for stitching. They're hooked so they curve into the skin and out, which makes it easier."

Maggie handed Tillie a tin cup filled with a steaming liquid and we watched as Tillie knelt beside the man, encouraging him to drink. It took several minutes but she was able to get him to finish the tea. He lay his head back down with a groan and seemed to visibly relax.

Sarie moved aside when Maggie approached the table with small balls of what looked to be silken thread.

"What is that?" I asked.

"Spiderwebs," Maggie said.

We all watched as Maggie placed a small ball into a long gash where the skin had pulled apart and carefully unrolled it, being sure to entirely cover the cut and overlap the skin on either side. She continued to do this until all the gashes that were too shallow for stitching but still leaking blood had been tended to. The man's breathing eased and he seemed to be sleeping.

I leaned over him, fascinated by this. "What do the cobwebs do?"

Maggie smiled at me. "They help the flesh pull together and keep the bleedin down."

"Amazing."

"Also helps the wounds to scab faster although he'll itch somethin terrible," Sarie said.

"Oh, man, that is so cool. Sort of like nature's Band-Aid."

The sisters gave me questioning looks.

I ignored that as I asked Maggie, "Do you collect them and how do you do that?"

"We get them from Pokni," she answered. "Takes too long to collect enough to use, especially on ..." She trailed off as her eyes returned to Samuel's back.

Sarie began to unpack her medical bag. "All right, we need more cloths to cover his back, Tillie, to keep the flies away. I'll leave some medicine with you to treat his back but he needs to stay still as much as he can while those gashes heal. The feverfew will help with that."

While Sarie and Maggie explained to Tillie what she would need to do to treat the wounds, Abbie and I stepped outside. I breathed deep, trying to cleanse the acrid stench of blood and sweat from my nostrils. "Does this happen a lot, Abbie?" I asked as we walked away from the cabin.

"Happens too much," she said. "Don't see the need to damage a person simply 'cause they want to live free like the rest of us. It just ain't right, Lizzie."

I squeezed her hand. "That does get better in the future, Abbie. In a couple of years, there's going to be a war between the states over the issue of slavery, and when it ends, slavery will be abolished and illegal. It's going to be a bloody war with families fighting against one another and thousands will die. But it's only the beginning for the blacks. The time I come from? Black people are marching to have the same rights as whites do, and it's dangerous for them but they persevere and I hope one day will be treated as equally as whites."

She stopped walking and stared at me. "I can feel the war comin, Lizzie, have for some time now, and though I hate the thought of men fightin each other and dyin, I'm right glad it will bring about their freedom. No man or animal should have to do another man's biddin unless they're willin to." She glanced up at the sound of approaching footsteps.

A man strode toward us, carrying a whip with leather thongs, each tied at the end. He was short in stature, with a wiry build, and walked with a bowlegged gait. His sandy-colored hair was receding and his whiskers were streaked with silver. When he reached us, he stopped in front of Abbie. "You and your sisters tend to him?"

She straightened, giving him a defiant look. "Weren't no need to whip him like that, Eustus. You liked to killed him."

"He knew he was chancin a whippin when he run. Mr. Hampton don't put up with his slaves takin off like that."

I glanced at the whip, dried blood caking the leather. "I can't imagine anyone using a weapon like that on another living being. I'd say it takes someone who gets perverse pleasure out of the deed to do what you did to that man."

He looked at me, his eyes hard and flat. "Don't rightly know what perverse means, but the way you said it, I won't take it as a compliment. It ain't none of your business anyway, missy. I only did what needed to be done."

"I wonder what Mr. Hampton will say when he learns one of his valued slaves won't be able to move for a good while. You did so much damage, Samuel will be scarred for life, won't be able to work until his back heals, which is going to take some time seeing as how you didn't leave an inch of skin untouched."

His eyes flickered and I hoped that meant he was concerned about what his boss would say over this whipping. But what kind of man was this Mr. Hampton if he let a cruel sadist like this tend to his workers?

Abbie grabbed my hand. "We best get back inside, Lizzie."

"Shouldn't we talk to Mr. Hampton, explain to him how badly damaged Samuel is, what needs to be done for him?"

"Sarie will talk to him. Let's go see if they need help." She jerked on my hand and I reluctantly followed her.

At the door, I turned and looked at the overseer. The ominous look he gave me was not lost on me.

Inside, Abbie let go of my hand. "You best watch what you say around Eustus, Lizzie. He's a mean man with a temper to match. He won't hesitate one second to use that whip on you."

"What? Me, a woman, someone he doesn't know, someone he has no right to touch?"

She glanced at her sisters, who were watching us. "This ain't like where you come from. Women ain't looked upon the same way here."

I clenched my fists. "I wish I'd taken that damn whip away from him and used it on him."

All three sisters gasped.

Sarie stepped closer and said, her voice calm and low, "And you'd be dead if you had. Listen to what Abbie tells you, she knows the way of it. There will be other ways to deal with that man."

I looked into her eyes, could see a promise there. But of what?

Abbie nodded. "Time will come he'll need our help. Life on this mountain's rough. He'll get hurt, maybe cut himself, fall off his horse. We'll tend to him then, Lizzie, but you got to let it be for now."

I looked back at Sarie, then Maggie, who gave me a slight smile. I forced myself to relax, my mind to let go of the anger I felt. "I'll hold you to that," I said.

CHAPTER SIX

Disease of Conceit

Each day for the next week, I accompanied Sarie to the Hampton plantation to check and treat Samuel's wounds. He was a fast healer and began to recover fairly quickly although Sarie cautioned him to act more hurt than he felt when the overseer was around. When I gave her a questioning look, she said, "He'll put Samuel back in the fields if he thinks he can work but we can't let that happen. Samuel's liable to open up them wounds on his back and he needs to heal. He'll be scarred enough as it is. Bendin over a field will only make it worse."

Although a large, strong man, I found Samuel to have a gentle soul and voice. I knew we hurt him when we treated the wounds but he never complained and always had a smile for us. He seemed to accept what had happened to him without placing blame on anyone. "I reckon it's my fault for gettin caught," is all he would say when I asked him if the whipping angered him. I wondered if he had become lackadaisical or simply felt defeated over his predicament and chose to accept the life of a slave, which I found unacceptable.

Each time I visited, I became more and more dismayed by the way the slaves were treated. At times, it was all I could do not to march up to the main house and have words with the owner. The cabins occupied by the slaves were old and roughly built with dirt floors, unscreened windows, and large gaps showing between the planks. I hated to think how cold they must be in the winter without insulation between the planks to keep the cold air or snow from seeping in. Samuel slept under a tattered blanket on a pile of hay in the corner and he only had a fireplace for cooking. The only furniture in the room was the rickety table and a couple of chairs. Sarie told me they worked six days a week and were only allowed Sundays off because that was the day of prayer. Many worked from sunup to sundown with a short lunch break. Their clothes were tattered and dirty and most went barefoot although Samuel assured me they were given shoes to wear during the winter. All endured the wrath of the overseer who marched around with that damned whip, snapping it here and there in intimidation. Each time I saw him, I wanted to snatch that whip away and use it on him but forced myself to ignore him.

We only saw Tillie on Sundays, when we would find her visiting Samuel. I learned from Sarie that she and Samuel wanted to be married but the overseer wouldn't allow it. I knew why when I saw him approach Tillie and touch her in a way he had no business doing. "Is he screwing her?" I asked Sarie.

She frowned. "I ain't fer sure what that means."

I hesitated, uncertain how to explain it to her. "Lying with her, like a husband and wife?"

She shook her head. "Can't stop him if he wants to," was all she said.

The rage that came over me was so powerful, I had to sit down, holding my arms around my waist, clenching my fists so I wouldn't use them on him. In my protected life before I came through the lights, I had never felt such hate for a person as I felt for that man. I hoped with all my might that he would get hurt so the sisters could treat him. I would encourage them to give him whatever they had given Jim, who could no longer speak and now lived alone and alienated and was thought by some to be insane.

About a week after the whipping, Sarie had been called away to treat a sick child so Abbie and I rode down the mountain to see Samuel.

"Abbie, how many slaves are there in this county?" I asked.

She thought a moment. "I ain't never tallied em up, Lizzie, but I'd say closer to a thousand than not."

"Who owns the most slaves, do you know?"

"I reckon that'd be old man Waightstill Avery and his son Isaac. I know they own well over a hundred."

I tried to think back to history classes I'd taken in high school and college. I knew the Southern States began seceding in January, 1861, shortly after Abraham Lincoln was elected president. I remembered there was much conflict before then over slavery. Had it reached this mountain by now? Surely there were other people like Abbie who didn't believe in it.

Abbie interrupted my musing, saying, "It's bad enough these men own slaves but even worse we got a plantation owner trainin em and shippin em off again."

"Who's that?"

"Man named William Walton, Jr. brings in slaves from a place called Africa. He has a slave trader name of Z. D. Lancaster, who brings the slaves here from Charleston, where they teach em English and how to farm then sell em to plantation owners."

"Sounds like a human trafficker to me."

"What's that?"

"Someone who buys and sells humans, much like they would animals or produce."

"I reckon that'd fit."

When we arrived, we found a man close to my age sitting on a stump outside Samuel's cabin, speaking to him in a low voice. He immediately rose to his feet when he spied us. Samuel stood up as we dismounted, his mouth forming a large smile, showing strong, white teeth. "Good mornin to you, Miss Abbie, Miss Lizzie," he said.

Abbie grabbed the saddlebag, saying, "Mornin to you, Samuel, Mr. Josh."

I smiled at Samuel as I joined her, a bit unsettled by the scrutiny I received from the man who openly stared at me. Abbie ignored him as she asked Samuel how he was feeling.

The man named Josh smiled at Abbie before tilting his head at me in greeting, saying, "Ma'am," in a soft, Southern drawl. He was tall, over six feet by my calculation, with a lean physique and wide shoulders. His sandy-blond hair framed a strong, masculine face with dark-green eyes and a straight nose above well-shaped lips.

I nodded before following after Abbie and Samuel, who had stepped inside the cabin. When Josh followed us, I turned and said, "Maybe you should wait outside."

"Oh, it's all right, Miss Lizzie," Samuel said, "Mr. Josh is welcome to stay if'n he wants."

As we treated Samuel's wounds, which were now scabbed and healing well, he and the man talked as if they were old friends. I wondered what his role on the plantation was and if he could have done something to stop the overseer from the brutal whipping he'd delivered to Samuel. Finally, unable to contain my curiosity, I said, "Who exactly are you?"

Everyone grew quiet, looking at me as if I'd said something offensive. Abbie nudged me, and when I looked at her, she shook her head.

"I apologize if I sound rude, but no one has officially introduced us." I stuck out my hand. "I'm Lizzie Baker and you are?"

The man stared at my hand as if I held a snake in it. He finally placed his hand in mine and gave me one quick shake then withdrew it. His eyes danced with amusement when he looked at me. "I'm Josh Hampton. Nice to meet you."

Anger flared in my brain. "Hampton? You're the owner of this plantation?"

He shook his head. "The owner's son."

I drew myself up. "And you let that blasted overseer whip Samuel raw?" I said, my voice rising.

"That's enough, Lizzie," Abbie hissed at me.

Josh stared at me for a long moment but I held that gaze, hoping to see some sort of remorse or shame. He drew closer and dropped his voice. "Believe me, if I'd been here, I couldn't have stopped it but I would have made sure it wasn't as bad as it turned out to be."

"You're the owner's son, you could have totally stopped it," I protested.

"My father gives all control to Eustus." He looked away, then back. "But once he's gone and I have this plantation, we won't have one slave working here, not one, and that damn Eustus will be gone." He turned and strode away, his back rigid with anger.

I looked at Abbie, then Samuel. "I'm sorry, Samuel, I hope I didn't make things worse for you."

"No, ma'am, not with Mr. Josh. Why, I reckon he's been my friend since we was little young'uns runnin around here. He meant what he said, he'd have stopped Mr. Eustus if he'd been here. It ain't his fault what happened. He tried to help me."

"In what way?"

He glanced at the door but only shook his head and refused to say more.

When we left, I saw no sign of Josh but spied Eustus in a distant field berating a field worker, threatening him with the whip. My fists clenched, and without thinking about it, I turned in that direction.

Abbie hauled me back, saying, "You got to leave it be, Lizzie. This ain't none of our business."

"How can you say that?" I said, pulling my arm out of her grasp. "He doesn't have the right to do that. You saw the damage he did to Samuel. His back will be scarred for life."

"This ain't your world," she said, her eyes staring into mine. "It ain't your time and there ain't nothin you can do so just let it be." She grabbed my elbow and steered me toward the path that would take us up the mountain and home. "You'll only make things worse for Samuel and put a target on your back. Eustus ain't the type of man to take kindly to somebody, especially a stranger ..." she eyed me "... a woman stranger telling him he ain't got the right to whip a slave. Like I told you, he wouldn't think twice about takin that whip to you."

I shook my head with despair and reluctantly let her lead me home. Once my anger passed, I had to admit to myself she was right. This was not my time nor place and I did not need to call any further attention to myself. Tears filled my eyes and I wondered if I would ever find a way out of this mess. I remembered what Pokni had said about the other time travelers she had met. Maybe she could tell me more, I thought, as I said to Abbie, "I'm going to go visit Pokni. I'd like to talk to her."

Abbie studied me for a long moment before averting her eyes. "I reckon if you've a mind to visit Pokni, you should. I can't go with you, though, I got chores to see to when I get home."

"That's fine, Abbie, I remember the way."

When it came time to part paths, I reached out and squeezed her hand. "I'm sorry I got so angry. I understand what you're telling me. It's just hard to see that and not be able to do anything about it."

Abbie nodded.

"Abbie, I know you see things. Will there come a time when I find my way back? Have you seen that?"

"You'll get your chance, Lizzie, that's all I can tell you. As for you goin back, that lies with you."

I tried to smile but failed miserably. "Well, at least it's something," I said before waving and continuing on my way to Pokni's.

I found her laying herbs to dry on large rocks around her property. She smiled when she saw me. "I see you are still here."

"Afraid so." I watched her, wondering what the different herbs were for. Abbie had called her a healer and I was curious how that came to be. "Were you your tribe's medicine man, or woman, Pokni?"

She shook her head. "My father was and he taught me many things." She gestured toward her fire. "Come, sit with me while I boil the leaves and bark of witch hazel."

"What do you use that for?"

"To make a poultice for infected cuts or sores."

After we were settled, I said, "How did your father come

to be medicine man? Did your chief appoint him or was he simply a natural healer?"

A small smile flitted along her lips. "He was chosen by Bohpoli."

"Who is that?"

"Bohpoli lives deep in the forest. He's very small, only so high." She raised her hand up at a height I gauged to be two feet tall. "He has been known to throw sticks or stones at those passing by but they never see him because he ducks out of sight. If you hear a loud banging on the pine trees, that is him, as well, and he is warning you that you are too close to his cave."

"Really?"

She nodded. "Bohpoli lives in a cave concealed by large rocks so you would pass by without knowing he was there."

"If he's so secretive, how did your father meet him?"

"Bohpoli will strike up a friendship with children, which is easy to do since they consider him a child as well because he is so short. After awhile, he will take the child to visit inside his cave. There, he introduces the child to three elderly spirits with white hair. The first spirit will offer the child a knife, the second one poisonous herbs and the third medicinal herbs. If the child accepts the knife, he will grow up to be a violent mad man and will kill his fellow Choctaws. If he accepts the poisonous herbs, he will become an evil medicine man, and if he chooses the medicinal herbs, he will become a wise and good medicine man. My father chose the medicinal herbs and was instructed by Bohpoli and the spirits."

"Did he ever tell you about meeting Bohpoli?"

"Yes, and only because he was a man. They are not allowed to speak of him when they are children. Only when they are grown can those who meet Bohpoli tell about their experience."

I considered that as I watched her stir the pot. "Pokni, when I come from, we have a softer soap than lye as well as shampoo." I plucked at my dry hair. "It's for washing the hair and smells good and makes it soft. Do the Choctaw use herbs for washing the body and hair, and also for making the skin soft? We call that lotion."

"The Choctaw have herbs for everything, child." She pulled the braid from her back and placed it over one shoulder. "See how my hair shines? I have, what was the word you used?"

"Shampoo."

"Yes, I make shampoo ..." she said this word as if tasting it "... from the yucca. I will give you roots to boil which will form a lather which you may use to wash your hair, or you can simply crush the plant and use that."

Excitement traveled through me. "And soap? What do you do for soap?"

"Ashes and pig fat, then add wild mint for scent, which also is good for itching if your skin is dry. I will give you soap I have made."

"And lotion?" I held out my hands, which were raw and red. "To soften the skin?"

"Mash rose hips and you will have a fine lotion." She smiled. "I like that word, lotion."

I lifted my arm and pointed to my armpit. "We have what is called deodorant in my time, which helps to control sweat and the smell."

She nodded. "Sage oil. When my warrior was alive, I used it because I wanted to smell nice for him. Since he's gone, I see no need. There is no one to smell me but me." She gave me a sad smile.

I reached out and touched her hand. "And when you meet him again?"

"Look to the sky, child, for the two brightest stars. That will be us riding the sky together."

I smiled at that image. By then shadows began to seep over the mountain and I knew if I didn't start for home, it would be dark before I got there. After Pokni collected the soap, shampoo and lotion, I wrapped them in my apron. I told her I would gather herbs for her in payment then bid her goodbye.

I hadn't traveled far when Constable Jackson stepped into my path. I stumbled back with a squeak, losing my grip on the apron, spilling my precious toiletries. I immediately dropped to my knees to gather them up.

He gave me a lewd grin. "What you got tied up in that apron that's got you so riled up over dropping?"

I stood to my full height, wrapping the toiletries in the apron once more. "Herbs from Pokni. Now if you'll excuse me, I'd like to get home before dark." I sidestepped around him but he moved in front of me again.

"I sent a telegram off to the sheriff of Knoxville," he said in a casual tone.

I met his eyes. "And?"

"Ain't heard back yet but reckon I will soon."

I shrugged as if it made no difference to me. "Don't know as he'll know who I am since I don't socialize with him and I've never been arrested so he'll have no record of me."

"Maybe he will, maybe he won't." He cocked his head and studied me. "I find you a bit of a mystery, Miss Lizzie. Ain't never heard the sisters or their pa talk about you or your family back there in Knoxville and then out of the blue you show up on the very night they found them skulls."

"Actually, I found the skulls, Mr. Jackson. The sisters didn't have anything to do with that."

His eyes narrowed. "You take up for them all you want but I know they had something to do with that, just like their pa. Seems awful strange he disappeared all of a sudden after he made an arrangement with me about Sarie. Seeing as he ain't here, I can't hold him to that." He gave me a curt nod. "But when I find him, dead or not, I'll make her carry through with our agreement, you see if I don't."

"Oh, get over it," I said before I could stop myself.

He glared at me. "Don't intend to, now or never. I'll find out what you and them sisters are up to and it won't be long afore the lot of you'll be sitting in my jail cell."

"For what?" I asked. "I understand the sheriff concluded it couldn't be determined if those skulls were Belinda's and her baby's nor what caused their deaths. Seems to me if anyone should interest you in that regard, it would be Jim, but you chose to harass Sarie and her sisters instead. From what I hear, you didn't even question Jim during your investigation."

He regarded me for a moment. "That's another thing I find mysterious, the way Jim changed after you and them sisters paid him a visit. Weren't no way I could talk to the man 'cause he ain't said a word since." He narrowed his eyes at me. "Susie told me about that tea Sarie gave her for Jim. Makes me wonder if y'all put something in that tea so he couldn't talk after he drunk it."

I shrugged. "I imagine the real reason was seeing the skulls of those he killed. Must have traumatized him something awful."

"I reckon we'll see about that." He stepped closer to me, causing me to move back, almost tripping myself in the process. "Eustus told me what you said to him over whippin that slave. Seems to me you need to learn your place on this mountain, girl. You see, Eustus, he has power over them slaves, and if he decides to whip one, that's his decision and no one can stop him. Just like I have power over this mountain. I can do anything I want to you and them sisters and nobody can stop me. You best remember that."

I couldn't stop myself from saying, "Power? That would lie with the sheriff, wouldn't it? Aren't you more a glorified process server?"

He loomed over me, his face growing hard, his fists clenched. "You keep talking to me like that and you'll find out how powerful I am."

I stepped back, out of his reach. "I have to get home."

He glared at me for a moment longer before finally stepping aside so that I could get by him.

I made a wide berth around him and rushed down the path. When I glanced back, he stood there staring after me and it was all I could do not to bolt when he called out, "You remember what I said, girl."

CHAPTER SEVEN

It's All Right, Ma (I'm Only Bleeding)

Sarie insisted I earn my keep, so most days, I accompanied one or more of the sisters as they made their rounds on the mountain, checking on patients who were sick or healing, or being called upon to administer aid. Other days were spent performing chores around their small homeplace, from washing clothes outside in a large kettle over a fire to chopping kindling and firewood to planting and weeding their garden or doing whatever was needed to maintain their primitive cabin and lifestyle. I developed calluses on my fingers and suspected I was losing weight, as the two dresses Sarie had found for me to wear now hung loose on my frame. I alternated the dresses, wearing one while the other was washed then draped over a bush to dry, mourning the comfortable wardrobe I had in my time, hip-hugger jeans and gauzy tops, long maxi dresses, jeans shorts and halters or cropped tops. At times, it seemed we went from daybreak to dusk with no time for rest and I constantly found myself longing for my former comfortable life, with long lunches and afternoon naps and more than enough time to sit and talk with friends, read, watch a movie, or any of a dozen ways I found to relax. I worked hard at tamping down my eagerness to return to my time, my hatred for the primitive way we were forced to live, my only hope being the nights when Abbie and I snuck away to search for the lights.

From time to time, I would spy Josh Hampton going about whatever business occupied him, or if we were in town, walking along the sidewalk. We attended church irregularly, but when we did, he was always present with whom I assumed were his parents and siblings. It did not escape my notice that he seemed popular among young, single women who eagerly sought him out. I had to admit he was a handsome man, but when he greeted me or smiled at me, my response to him was cool bordering on rude. Although Samuel claimed Josh was his friend and helped him, I could not fathom how he could do anything for anyone in such dire straits, especially if he were overruled by a sadistic overseer. Did he not have any sort of influence with his own father, I wondered, if he so blatantly disagreed with slavery.

It seemed we were called to the Hampton plantation quite often, treating illnesses or wounds suffered by the slaves working in the fields. One morning, Tillie found Abbie and me foraging for mushrooms in the woods. She told us she'd been to the cabin but couldn't find Sarie or Maggie to come tend to a child with chicken pox, which seemed to be making its way all over the mountain. Abbie told Tillie we'd be right along and we immediately returned to the cabin for Abbie's saddlebag.

Abbie explained to me once we were on our way to the plantation that a good tonic for chicken pox would be catnip tea. "It ain't real tasty but it helps," she said.

"In what way?"

"Helps keep the young'un calm, also brings down a fever." She glanced at me. "We give it at times for bad headaches. Old Ellie Stephens, lives up near the top of the mountain, she gets these headaches somethin fierce, makes her go near blind they're so bad. Can't stand light, can't stand noise, gets sick to her stomach."

"Sounds like migraines."

She looked at me. "What's that?"

"In my time, that's what we call the type of headache she has. Migraine."

She thought for a moment. "Seems like such a calm word for something so awful."

I nodded. "My mom had them. She would be in so much pain sometimes we'd have to take her to the hospital."

"What'd they do for her?"

"Gave her a shot that seemed to help. Made her sleepy anyway."

"That's what the catnip tea does for Ellie. But she's got six kids livin in a one-room cabin. Ain't no way she can get any sleep without somethin to help with that much noise around her."

As we walked along, I tried to imagine what it would be like sharing a small cabin with so many other people. All this did was remind me of my own apartment back home, which was spacious in comparison to the homes of these mountain people except those belonging to plantation owners. Which brought me back to Josh Hampton and the mysterious way Samuel claimed he helped him. Was it possible he had helped him escape? I wondered if the Underground Railroad was active this early and, if so, if it was here on Brown Mountain.

Abbie leaned into me for a moment and lowered her voice. "I know you're homesick somethin terrible and I reckon you're so anxious to go back you can't stand it at times. But until we see that light you said took you, there ain't nothin I can think of we can do to get you back to your time, Lizzie."

"I know but—"

"If you step into the wrong light, you might end up in another time and place," she reminded me.

I nodded.

She sighed. "Although, might be, anyplace you end up would be better than here."

"I'm sure there are far worse places."

She didn't answer and we trod on in silence until we reached the plantation. We found the cabin with the little boy with chickenpox, but before we stepped through the door, I placed my hand on her arm to stop her. "Have you had chickenpox before?"

"When I was a little 'un."

"Good, then you can't get it again."

"What about you, Lizzie? Have you had it?"

"Yes, I'm good."

We fixed catnip tea for the little boy who was so miserable, he lay moaning on a blanket on top of a bed roughly made of hay. I held his head in my lap while Abbie coaxed him to drink the tea. His body was covered with red blisters and I knew the itch must be unbearable. "What do you give him for the itch?" I asked Abbie.

"A mixture of porridge and water's good," she said, going to the fireplace to make more tea for the mother to give to the boy. "I got some porridge in my saddlebag there if you want to mix it up and put it on him."

As I mixed the solution, I said, "What about the burdock root? Did that work?"

Abbie shook her head. "Works right well for poison ivy and Sarie said it worked well enough for chicken pox but no better than the porridge. Since I ain't got the burdock root, we'll have to use the porridge."

I returned to the boy and began to apply the mixture to his body. The tea seemed to help calm him while the porridge soothed him and he fell asleep. I felt his forehead. "He feels a bit cooler."

"That's good."

While Abbie instructed his mother on how to fix the tea and oatmeal solution, I stroked the boy's forehead, humming softly to him, hoping what we had done would keep him from scratching the blisters, which could become infected and could scar him. He seemed so innocent, so fragile, and I worried about his health in this small, grimy cabin with its dirt floor and warped, handmade furniture. The odor of ash and sweat and cooked food hung in the air, and I imagined it was near impossible to keep anything clean in such conditions. I wanted to tell him that in a few more years, things would be different for him and other slaves, that they would be free and not forced to live in such deplorable conditions.

The door flew open and Samuel stood in the doorway, looking huge and dangerous. Sweat covered his face and blood soaked his clothes.

"Miss Abbie, young Joseph was choppin some kindlin and the axe slipped and cut into his leg. We can't get the blood to stop. Can you come quick?"

Abbie snatched up her saddlebag and rushed to the door. "Take me to him, Samuel, but you got to hurry."

I eased the boy's head back to the floor and after squeezing the young mother's hand and telling her her boy would be fine in a few days ran after them.

We flew down the path in front of the cabins and ran toward the back of the plantation house where several men were gathered around a large stump, talking in low voices. As one, they turned when they heard us, looks of relief falling across their faces. I searched the yard, looking for the injured boy, and spied him lying under a shade tree, blood pooling around his leg. As we neared, I heard several say, "It's the Bloodstopper." I vaguely wondered what they meant as I followed Abbie and Samuel to the young man's body. The coppery scent of blood hung in the air and I immediately began to breathe through my mouth, finding the smell nauseating. Someone had tied a rope around his upper leg to stem the flow of blood but it didn't seem to be helping. He's dead, I thought to myself, watching the blood pump from the wound, noting his pale countenance. Flies were everywhere, lighting on his leg and flying away only to return. I brushed my hand in the air, trying to chase them away, to no avail.

Abbie knelt beside him, tore open the saddlebag and frantically searched inside. She finally pulled out a well-worn Bible and flipped it open to a marked page. She eyed the sky as she rose to her feet then walked away, reading from the Bible. I pressed close to her, trying to hear the words, realizing that she was repeating the same phrase, "'And when I passed by thee, and saw thee polluted in thine own blood, I said unto thee when thou wast in thy blood, live; yea, I said unto thee when thou wast in thy blood, live.'"

After she said this three times, she turned around and went back to the young man. I heard gasps and looked down at his leg, shocked to see that the blood no longer poured from his body. Had he died? Had he lost all his blood or had his heart ceased pumping?

Abbie put her head to his chest then smiled. "He's alive."

A woman shouted, "Oh, praise the Lord, and thank Him for the Bloodstopper." She raised her hands to the skies. This was followed by shouts of "Hallelujah" and "Amen" with much laughter and joyousness.

I knelt beside Abbie and put my fingers to his carotid artery. I could feel the heartbeat, slow and regular. I watched as he inhaled and exhaled then looked at Abbie, stunned. "He should be dead," I whispered.

"Another minute and he would've been," she said in a matter-of-fact tone. She put the Bible back in her saddlebag and pulled out a jar of yellowish-green powder.

"What's that?" I asked.

"A mixture of dried stems, leaves and flowers of the yarrow plant. It'll keep the leg from bleedin again."

She reached into her bag for clean rags to bind the wound. I helped her treat the gash then wrap the rags around the boy's thigh and secure them. I kept watching his chest rise and fall, waiting for it to still, but he continued to breathe regularly and appeared to be simply asleep.

Finished, Abbie rose to her feet, accepting thanks and well wishes with only a simple nod as she walked away.

I put my fingers on his wrist, feeling for a pulse, relieved that it continued to be steady although a bit weak, which was to be expected after that much blood loss. Assuring myself that he was not in danger of dying, I followed after Abbie, wondering what in the world had just happened.

I caught up with her on the road leading off the plantation. Abbie gave me a vague smile.

"They called you the Bloodstopper."

She nodded. "I reckon that's as good a name for it as anything."

"Is that what you do, Abbie, stop blood?"

"I reckon so."

"By repeating a phrase from the Bible?"

"Three times while walking East."

I thought for a moment. "Can anyone do that?"

She shook her head. "It's a gift, least that's how I look at it. My granddad, he come from the Ozarks, had it but he called it a power. There's a secret to it he told me just afore he passed on. He said I can share that secret with three others, three men. That's the way it works. A man shares it with three women, a woman shares it with three men."

"So you can't share it with me?"

"If'n I did, I'd lose the power."

"What if you shared it with four men?

"I'd lose the power."

"Abbie, that was like a miracle. I've never seen anything like it."

She didn't answer.

"How often have you done this?"

"Oh, more times than I can count, I reckon. People cut theyselves all the time choppin wood, or women birthin lose too much blood. Seems somebody's always in danger of bleedin to death on this mountain."

I stared at her, wondering if there were Bloodstoppers in my time. If so, I had never heard of them. I contemplated what had happened as we walked the rest of the way home in silence. Just before we stepped out of the forest, I said, "Abbie, I think the miracle is you."

She gave me a beatific smile.

"That explains how you became a healer, Abbie. What about Sarie and Maggie? Who taught them?"

"Our granny was a healer, too. Why, I reckon since Sarie and Maggie were little more than babies, they followed her all over the mountain, collectin herbs and learnin how to treat the sick and injured. They both took a likin to it, Sarie using the herbs and Maggie midwifin. I helped both of them till my granddad told me the secret. Blood stoppin's what I do best." By then we had reached the cabin. Before opening the door, Abbie hesitated, looking toward the forest surrounding us. "We left our herb baskets in the woods."

"I'll get them," I said. "I've been wanting to visit Pokni anyway."

"You sure? I can go along with you if you want."

I shook my head. "I'm fine. I'd kind of like to be alone anyway."

Abbie nodded her understanding as she closed the door.

I set out, eager to visit the old Choctaw woman. I had become quite enchanted with Pokni and loved accompanying her as she would gather herbs, listening with rapt attention as she told me their medicinal benefits, hoping to learn as much from her as I could. At first, although polite, she had been a bit distant toward me but with each visit seemed to become more curious, querying me about my time and the differences the future held.

When I arrived, I found her rolling tobacco in dried corn husks. I smiled as I sat beside her, giving her a brief kiss on the cheek. This was another reason I looked forward to our visits, Pokni being more than willing to share her handmade cigarettes with me. I had long since depleted the pack I brought with me and had traded Pokni my yellow Bic, which she seemed fascinated by, for cigarettes, an arrangement that worked well for the both of us. After I used the Bic to light the cigarette she handed me, I drew the first puff in, savoring it for a moment, loving the sweet hint of honey from the beeswax she used to seal the maize mingling with the acrid tang of the tobacco.

As we smoked, I told her about Abbie stopping the boy's blood, noting Pokni's acceptance of what to me was a true miracle.

"I think God has blessed our Abbie," I said.

Pokni made a snorting sound. "Not your god, perhaps my people's."

"The Choctaw have their own god?" I asked rather naively.

"Yes, he is called Nanishta."

I smiled. "I wonder if he's like ours."

She gave me a sidelong glance. "We are the first people, Lizzie, here long before the white man. Our god is the true god."

I blew smoke in the air, relishing the taste of real tobacco without all the toxins added during my time. "How so?"

"He created the world."

"So did my god."

She shook her head. "Nanishta created the sun and moon, the underground world of the grasshopper goddess Eskeilay and the surface world of the Earth. Next he created animal and plant life forms, then water for the water fowl and fishes. He then combined Earth and water to form the swamplands and undergrowth for the frogs and alligators and put the goddess Abohli in command. Following that, he created the brothers Choctaw and Chickasaw."

I found it interesting the white man believed in a hell overruled by a horned red devil with a forked tail and trident while the Choctaw's underworld was ruled by a grasshopper. And that my god created a man and woman while Pokni's god created two men. For the most part, though, the similarities of how the world was created between the two gods were astounding.

"The brothers Choctaw and Chickasaw," she continued, "were the only human beings in the underground world. After 70 years, they asked Nanishta for mates so that they might multiply like other life forms. Nanishta used the same yellow clay he used in making other life forms to sculpt the first human females and gave each a heart more like his own than the hearts he had given to Choctaw and Chickasaw. He warned them that since women had his more tender heart, men should treat them gently and with respect." She stopped to take a few puffs from her cigarette. As I watched her, I thought that lesson hadn't been handed down to men during this time or mine, as women still weren't treated with the respect I felt they deserved.

She studied the tip of her cigarette for a moment before continuing. "The females were little girls, as Choctaw and Chickasaw had been little boys when they were created, so Nanishta sang an aging song to hasten their development so that they would quickly reach womanhood and could be wives.

"Choctaw and Chickasaw were ageless but their wives were not, so when they died the brothers took new wives, and this continued on for generations although their children, unlike the brothers, had limited life spans like the first wives. Eventually, the human population crowded the underground world so much that Nanishta ordered their exodus through the Earth womb at Nanih Waiya."

"Is that here?" I interrupted.

She shook her head. "We are here for a reason, which I will tell you soon." She smoked for a bit then continued. "The day came when Nanishta decided that the people led by Choctaw and Chickasaw should become separate but kindred nations, so he caused the Misha Shipokni ..." she glanced at me "... which means river older than time, to overflow its banks in the great autumn flood. This drove a wedge between the Choctaw and the Chickasaw and forced the Choctaw people to evacuate to a higher ground far away."

I smiled. "Here in the mountains?"

A faint smile touched her lips. "We shall see." She put her hand on my forearm. "Nanishta warned the Choctaw and Chickasaw to not marry people of other races but they did not listen. But there will come a time, daughter, when they will wish they had. Nanishta will prevent summer from coming and allow most of the trees to disappear and days to become shorter. The hair of all children will turn white as if from old age. The land will be unfarmable which will lead to widespread famine. At that time, Nanishta will come back down to Earth for what is called the Third Removal. He will gather all the Choctaw and Chickasaw who have not abandoned their heritage and will lead them toward the mountains where game animals will have already been evacuated to."

I smiled. "Here."

"Yes, child, here. This is why my warrior captain wanted to come here and would not leave. He waits for Nanishta."

"Of course," I said.

"Along the way, the Choctaw and Chickasaw will begin crying, like so many did during the Great Removal, and

Nanishta will transform those falling tears into a flood that will kill all the other people of the world. The Choctaw and Chickasaw will be safe in the mountains while everyone else will die trying to reach higher ground. When the flood waters subside, the Choctaw and Chickasaw will return to repopulate the earth while nature heals itself to the point that the land will be lush and green as it was centuries before."

I pondered her words as we finished our cigarettes, thinking of the similarities and dissimilarities between her god and mine. We remained quiet after that, smoking another cigarette together, but before I left, I kissed her cheek. "I like Nanishta's philosophy that women should be treated with respect. I'm afraid the white man, especially during this time, but even still in my time, has not learned that lesson."

She nodded. "Women are regarded with great respect among our people. It is Nanishta's way."

"As it should be." I smiled at her. "I'm glad you were the first, Pokni, and maybe it would be a better world if you were the last."

"It is prophesized," she said, with gravity.

I nodded. "Groovy."

She smiled at me. This was another reason I liked Pokni so much. I could speak my language around her without getting confused looks or being asked for an explanation. She seemed to understand what I meant and it was a relief to be able to say what I wanted without having to think about it first.

I leaned into her for a moment. "Perhaps I will witness it."

She kissed my cheek before I rose to my feet. "Perhaps."

CHAPTER EIGHT

A Hard Rain's a-Gonna Fall

I breathed a sigh of relief as Maggie and I stepped into the relative coolness of the house after a hot, sweaty hour collecting eggs from the none-too-friendly chickens. Maggie snickered as I swiped an arm across my dripping forehead. For some reason the heat didn't seem to bother her as much as it did me and she'd teased me endlessly about sweating so much as we went about our chore.

It took only a glance at her older sister's expression to quell the laughter.

"What's wrong? Has there been an accident? Is somebody hurt?" Maggie said as she shoved the basket of eggs into my hands and rushed over to the table where Sarie and Abbie were packing Sarie's saddlebag with dried herbs and wildflowers.

"Nobody's hurt. Where's the damn Joe Pye weed?" Sarie muttered as she searched through the bottles on the herb shelf.

Hearing Sarie curse had my mouth falling open.

"There, there it is." She grabbed a jar and stuffed it into the bag.

Maggie gripped her arm hard enough to have Sarie hissing out another swear word.

"Sarie, quit cussing at me and tell me what's wrong."

"It's nothin, Maggie. I got to go to the Hampton plantation to see to one of the slaves." Sarie pried Maggie's fingers free then held onto her hand as she looked her sister in the eye. "I promise, it ain't nothin for you or Abbie to worry about."

Abbie grabbed Maggie's other hand. "She won't let us go, Maggie."

"Why?" Maggie demanded. "Why do you have to go and why can't we come with you? Whatever it is, we can help."

Sensing an ally, Abbie squared her shoulders and glared at her older sister. "That's what I told her but she won't listen. She said I'm not to go anywhere near the Hampton plantation till she tells me I can."

"Not this time," Sarie snapped.

Appealing to Maggie again, Abbie practically whined, "She won't tell me what's goin on. Mr. Hampton sent one of the slaves over here to get us but Sarie says we're not to go with her."

Sarie huffed out a breath. "You don't need to go with me, Abbie, or you neither, Maggie. I can handle this one on my own."

"But why?" Maggie insisted.

Closing the saddlebag, Sarie jabbed a finger in my direction. "I'll take her with me. Could be she can help but I don't want neither one of you going anywhere near the Hampton place till I tell you different. You got plenty of chores to keep you busy. 'Sides, we need somebody here in case anybody else on the mountain needs doctorin."

I set the basket of eggs on the table. "What is it, Sarie? What's going on?" When I didn't get an answer other than a belligerent look that sent my stomach sinking down to my knees, I said, "All right. Let me wash the chicken stink off my hands and we'll go."

I hurried over to the washtub Abbie had been using to wash the breakfast dishes, dipped my hands in the warm, soapy water while giving Abbie what I hoped was a reassuring nod.

Turning back to Sarie as I dried my hands on my apron, I pointed to the saddlebag. "Do you have everything you need in there?"

She frowned as she nodded. "I sure hope so."

I patted Abbie on the shoulder, smiling at her and Maggie, mouthing "Don't worry," before following Sarie out the door.

I had to run to catch up with her and held my silence until we moved into the dim, cool air of the barn. Dust motes floated through the air as she snagged a bridle off a hook then clucked to Buck. I said, "Okay, Sarie, tell me what's going on. What is it you don't want your sisters to know about?"

She slipped the bridle over the horse's ears, adjusted the fit before opening the stall door. "Come on, Buck," she muttered as she flipped the reins over the horse's neck and led him out of the stall. "Good boy." When she finally turned her attention back to me, she frowned. "All right. I ain't sayin I believe you or nothin, but you told Abbie the lights brought you here from the future."

"Yes, that's right."

"And that you were trainin to be a doctor?"

"Yes, I'd been through pre-med and two years of medical school. Still have a long ways to go but when I get back—if I ever do ..."

"Well, I reckon we're about to find out if you're tellin the truth or not." She stared at me for a moment then took a deep breath, lowering her voice to a whisper. "What do you know about small pox?"

My right hand automatically went to the small scar high up on my left arm where I'd been vaccinated when I was a child. Unlike some people, the mark left by the vaccination was barely noticeable on me and I rarely, if ever, thought about it but just the words "small pox" were enough to send my stomach tumbling again.

"Small pox? I've never seen it in person, if that's what you're asking. But I had one class that touched on it. In fact, I wrote a paper about the disease and the history of the vaccination."

She arched her brows. "Vacci—I ain't fer sure what you're sayin."

"A way to keep people from ever getting it. Small pox

isn't something we think about much in my time. It's almost a thing of the past since most people are vaccinated against it at a young age. In fact, it's a disease that's close to being wiped off the face of the earth. It's rare for anyone to come down with it. It happens but mostly in small, impoverished countries overseas."

"Well, it's still pretty common around here and ever once in awhile it flares up." She buried her face in Buck's mane and sighed. "She'll know. As soon as she gets over her hissy fit, she's gonna do whatever it is she does in her mind and she'll know."

"You mean Abbie?"

She sighed again. "Yes, I mean Abbie."

I started to question her about Abbie's ability, but when she raised her head, I could see she was struggling with tears, so I only said, "Yes, she will know."

Sarie shook her head before swinging up onto the horse's bare back. "Nothing to be done," she muttered. "Hand me the saddlebag." When I did as she asked, she positioned it in front of her then held out her hand to help me mount behind her. "Like I said, we have outbreaks ever now and again. Not as severe as they once was, but bad enough to kill some of em what get it."

I grabbed her hand and swung up behind her. "It's a horrible disease, I know that. If I remember my studies correctly, it's fatal in about thirty percent of patients. And those who do survive are scarred for life."

She nodded then clucked to the horse and we were off. As we rode, she said in a loud voice, "Not much we can do except do our best to keep the sick 'uns as comfortable as possible while they go through it ... and pray to heaven they do get through it."

My heart softened toward this oldest sister who never seemed to have any use for me and, after weeks of living with them, still distrusted me. Right now, she was only trying to protect her sisters. I had to admire that. "Have you ever treated it, Sarie?"

She was quiet for a moment. "Once, with my granny, when she was alive. She showed me what to do but wouldn't let me near the sick ones. I was close enough I reckon I could have caught it but never did so maybe I can't get it." She glanced at me over her shoulder. "What else can you tell me about it?"

"It's highly contagious. Is that why you didn't want Maggie and Abbie to know, because you're afraid they'll catch it? But what about you? Your granny was smart for not letting you near the infected ones but you're still just as susceptible as they are."

"Maybe I am but I ain't willin to risk their lives. I don't want them to know anything about this. Especially Abbie. You know she can't stand to see any animal hurtin. She's the same with people. And she has a special sort of, oh, I don't know, protectiveness when it comes to them slaves. Knowin her, she'd be over there in two shakes of a mule's tail if she found out."

"All right, I won't say anything to them when we get back, but if you're right and Abbie senses it, she's going to tell Maggie. Then they'll probably show up at the plantation."

"I know, Lizzie, but there ain't nothin we can do about it now."

"No, there isn't. I assume you know all the symptoms of small pox, the incubation period, and all that?"

"I reckon I know it takes one to two weeks after being exposed afore any sign of it can be seen and one or two days more after that afore the rash sets in. Red spots come up, mostly on the face, feet, and hands before spreadin to the whole body and gettin larger, then they start to look like blisters that itch somethin terrible until they scab over, dry up, and fall off. *If* the person is lucky enough to live till they fall off."

"Yes, and those who survive, while terribly scarred, are immune from ever getting the disease again." I gripped her arm. "You can't go anywhere near someone who has it, Sarie. You're almost sure to get it if you do."

She shook off my hand. "I'm the closest thing to a doctor on this mountain. There ain't nothin to do but take my chances, girl."

"Take your chances?" I admired her for doing what she

could to protect her sisters but was outraged that she would put herself at risk. "You can't, Sarie. What would Maggie and Abbie do without you?"

"They'd get by, I s'pose. 'Sides what else can I do? Those slaves have it bad enough as it is and I shore don't want nobody to suffer any more than they have to. Mr. Hampton will do what he can to save his property, you can bet on that."

"That's horrible."

She shrugged. "That's pretty much all they are to him, his property since he paid for em. I reckon it's safe to say he'll do whatever he can to protect what's his."

Outrage poured through me at her words. I wanted to rant and rave at the atrocity of one person owning another, thinking about them as property, but I forced myself to put it aside. Sarie had heard my views before. Right now, I needed to do what I could to keep her safe.

I clutched her arm again. "Stop and let me down, Sarie. I'll go by myself. I'll do what I can to help them but you should go back to your sisters."

She pulled on the reins to stop the horse before swiveling around to look at me. I guess she saw that I meant it because she shook her head. "No, I can't let you do that, Lizzie."

I slid down off the horse. "Why not?" I demanded. "I've been vaccinated. There's no chance I can get it but you can."

She shook her head again, holding out her hand to me. "Get back up here, or I swear, I'll go on and leave you standin here like the fool you are." She clucked her tongue to the horse.

I grabbed the halter and held on. "Whoa," I shouted, bracing my feet to hold Buck still. I took a deep breath. I wasn't above begging at that point. "Please, Sarie. Please, let me go alone. Think about Abbie and Maggie. They'd be lost without you. You can't do this to them."

She looked down at me. "The Hamptons don't know you, 'ceptin Mr. Josh. More important, the slaves don't know you well enough to trust you. They're gonna be scared enough as it is and I doubt they'd want you to treat em. You might even do more harm than good if you go out there alone. Knowin Mr. Hampton, he'll get out his shotgun and put a load of buckshot in your tail to chase you off his property."

"But if you introduced me to him and told him—"

She shook her head again.

I started to protest but something was circling in my brain, something I'd heard or learned at school, so I kept my mouth shut and concentrated on holding the horse. Sarie said something about the slaves and Mr. Hampton but I tuned it out.

Letting go of the halter, I held up my hand to hush her. "Just stop yammering at me for a minute and let me think, Sarie." I paced away from the horse, trying to remember what it was.

It surprised me Sarie didn't just ride away but she waited me out as if she knew I was trying to figure out something important. When I finally turned back to her and the horse, she simply held out her hand. "Come on if you're comin. I ain't got time to sit out here like a bump on a log and wait for you to get over your snit."

Still thinking, I took her hand and got back on the horse. We were nearing the Hampton plantation when it suddenly came to me, thanks to seeing a herd of cows grazing serenely in the pasture that ran along the front of the property and one side of the drive to the house.

"Cow pox. We need a sick cow."

Sarie turned to frown at me.

I pointed at the field. "Where there are cows there might be cow pox."

Sarie shook her head with a frustrated look.

"Do you know what cow pox is?" I asked her.

"Cow pox? What in the Sam Hill does that have to do with anything? We're dealin with small pox and as far as I know they're two different things."

"Different, yes, but cow pox is similar to small pox only much less deadly for humans. Not sure what it does to the poor cows but we can't worry about them right now."

Her voice shook as Buck cantered over the rough path.

"Will you please tell me why the devil you're so happy about some cows and the possibility they might or might not have cow pox?"

"In the late 1700s, a doctor in England, um, Edward Jenner, or was it Joiner? Never mind, this doctor used cow pox as a treatment or, really, as a vaccination, a way to inoculate people against small pox."

She blew out a breath but I could see she was listening so I went on. "I remember learning about this while I was researching my paper on the history of small pox and its vaccination. Dr. Jenner noticed that milkmaids rarely contracted small pox when there were outbreaks and wondered why. After studying on it some, he concluded that it had something to do with the fact that the milkmaids had contracted cow pox from the cows and that made them immune to small pox."

Sarie snorted rather indelicately but I ignored her. "Dr. Jenner went on to successfully inoculate people against small pox using some of the secretions or the infectious material from cows that had cow pox. Oh! And wasn't there something about another doctor here in the United States … no, no, wait, not a doctor, it was Thomas Jefferson. You've heard of him, haven't you?"

"You talkin about President Thomas Jefferson?"

"Yes, well, I can't remember if he was president at the time but he fully supported the cow pox vaccination. He even handled a lawsuit for it or something, but I think that was before he became president. He believed in the cow pox vaccination, encouraged people to have it and was vaccinated himself in his early twenties. In fact, he planned on sending his wife to Philadelphia for the vaccine but she never made the trip and died several years later before she got the vaccination. I don't know if her death was caused by small pox or not but that doesn't really matter. Jefferson also had his children, other members of his family and all his slaves vaccinated."

"How is it you come to know so much about President Jefferson?"

"Well, I kind of went through a biography phase when I

was in the sixth grade. I can't remember what triggered it but I spent the whole summer with my nose buried in a biography book about somebody or other. I read every one our small library had available and even had the librarians watching out for more." I sighed, remembering how the books had taken me away from my miserable life. "In sixth grade I was tall, taller than all the boys in my class, and lanky with it, and really, really shy around people. In fact, I avoided people at all costs and didn't have any friends. It was a hard time for me so I immersed myself in books and, like I said, lots of them were biographies of famous people."

When Sarie made a frustrated sound, not so subtly reminding me to get to it, I changed course. "Anyway, back to the vaccination. There was … oh, I can't remember what it was right now, but another kind of vaccine using another kind of pox that was common in the states during Jefferson's time." I snapped my fingers as I tried to bring it clear in my head. "If I remember right, it was carried by cats and rodents that lived in the woods. They called it … kine pox, yes that's it, kine pox. Or maybe that was just what they called the cow pox since kine was commonly used to mean more than one cow. I can't remember but I do remember the part about cats and woodland rodents having some form of pox that wasn't nearly as fatal as small pox."

"How in the Sam Hill does knowing all that help us?" she said with exasperation.

I pointed at the cows lazily grazing in the sun. "Well, if any of those cows have cow pox, we can use it to inoculate all the slaves and you, too, since you're being stubborn about exposing yourself." I threw my arms around her and hugged tight. "We can fix this, Sarie, I know we can."

She squirmed and shrugged until I dropped my arms. "I'm sorry, I got a little excited there for a minute. But it could work, Sarie, I really think it could. And if it does, we can also vaccinate Abbie and Maggie so they don't get it either." I wiggled behind her in a sort of sitting down victory dance.

She merely turned and aimed a hard stare at me until I settled down. But I continued to smile at her. "We can fix this, Sarie, at least I think we can. You just have to trust me."

I patted her shoulder, trying to reassure her, to convince her I knew what I was talking about. "Please, Sarie, we have to try."

She brushed my hand away with more force than necessary. "All right, say we decide to do this, do you remember enough about it so that we can do it without puttin my sisters or the slaves at risk?"

That stopped my grin, but after thinking about it for a few minutes, I nodded. "I'm pretty sure I do. No, no, strike that, I'm sure I do. I wrote a theme paper on the development of various vaccinations when I was in med school. It was fascinating stuff." I shrugged. "I told you I was a bit of a nerd."

She turned and frowned at me. "Nerd? What are you rambling on about?"

"It doesn't matter. All we need to do is find an animal that's infected and scrape some of the lesions to get the secretions. Then we smear it on an open cut or scratch on the patient. We may have to cut them but it's just a small cut, nothing more than a scratch, really, and shouldn't hurt too much, or, or, wait, no they didn't cut us, they punctured us with a two-pronged needle when they vaccinated us. So, no need to scratch but we will need to find a sharp needle."

"What about a sewing needle? Would that work?"

I smiled. Apparently I'd convinced her we could do this. "Most likely. I think we need to put our heads together and see what we come up with."

"All right, we'll do that. But first, we need to see what's goin on here at the Hampton place. Maybe we're jumpin the gun and it's not small pox at all. Maybe it's only chicken pox. We been treatin a lot of that lately."

"But you don't think so, do you?"

"No, Big Thom—the slave Mr. Hampton sent to get me, he's one of the stable boys—described it, and from what he said, I'm right sure it's small pox. I reckon there's no harm in hopin, though."

"All right, then, let's see what we've got and then we can go home and plan what to do. But, Sarie, you need to take precautions while we're there. Do you have a handkerchief or a scarf or something?"

In answer, she pulled an embroidered handkerchief out of her sleeve and waved it in the air. I recognized it as Abbie's work, the tiny, precise stitching that only she could achieve. "This is all I got."

"I don't suppose you have a pair of gloves tucked in there, do you?"

She shook her head. "What would I need gloves for? In case you haven't noticed, it's high summer and as hot as Hades out here and I ain't exactly some fancied-up lady callin on my neighbor for tea."

"You need protection and gloves will keep you safe, or safer, than you would be without them. I guess the handkerchief will have to do but promise me one thing."

"What now?"

"You won't so much as lay a finger on any of the people who are sick or even the ones we suspect are sick unless and until we find some gloves for you to wear. This is very important, Sarie. Small pox can be spread by physical contact, by touching someone who has it. If we need to examine anyone, I'll do it and you stay as far away as possible."

"All right, I reckon I can do that. What's the handkerchief for?"

"You'll wear it over your face, covering your mouth and nose. The primary way small pox is spread is through germs released in the air by people who have the disease when they cough or sneeze or even just talk to you. All you have to do is breathe the same air. So don't get too close to any of them and keep the handkerchief over your nose and mouth at all times."

As we approached the main house of the Hampton Plantation, I was struck by the total silence, broken only by the occasional lowing from one of the cows in the field, the faint buzz of flies hovering around the piles of manure. The windows of the house were all shuttered despite the heat of the day.

Sarie slowed the horse to a sedate walk and I felt her stiffen as if to brace herself against some unknown and, as yet, unseen danger.

"What is it, Sarie?" I whispered.

"Do you see anybody around?"

"No, no one. Maybe they're all inside having lunch. It is about that time, isn't it?"

"There's always somebody outside. Slaves in the fields or a couple of em out sweepin the porches or even Mrs. Hampton or one of the girls sittin on one of the chairs on the porch there. They're not even comin out to greet us." She shook her head. "I've never known it to be so quiet and still. It's unnatural which probably means it is small pox and Mr. Hampton has ordered everybody to stay inside."

"What should we do?"

As if hearing my question, Josh stepped out of the barn and held up a hand in greeting. My heart took a little leap in my chest then settled when I saw he wasn't smiling. His grim expression spoke volumes.

As we neared the barn, he spoke. "Good morning, Miss Sarie, Miss Lizzie. Thank you for coming."

"You knew we would, Mr. Josh," Sarie said. "Is it small pox for sure?"

"I can't say but we're treating it as if it is. Pa's got my mother, sisters and brothers inside the house and ordered them to stay there. The slaves are back in their cabins. The only ones he allowed to stay inside with the family are Elijah and Selma." He shook his head in disgust. "Gotta have somebody to take care of things. Lord knows, Mama and the girls aren't able to."

"Are they sick?" Sarie asked.

A slight smile touched his lips. "No, no need to worry about them. They're all fine, and if Pa has anything to say about it, they'll stay that way. I wish I could say the same for everybody else."

Sarie tightened the reins when Buck shifted as an old hound dog meandered out of the barn, let out one sharp bark then turned around and went back inside. "Whoa, there, Buck. Hop on down, Lizzie."

I did as she said. Josh, ever the Southern gentleman, hurried over to help me. Then he reached up and took the saddlebag from Sarie before setting it on the ground to help her down, too.

"I'll have Big Thom see to your horse and then I'll take you back to the cabins. This is bad, Miss Sarie. Viola says she's sure it's the pox and there's nothing she can do to help them. I had her separate the sickest, those showing visible signs, and put them in her cabin. The last time I checked, there were only three. Could be she's found some more by now but they should all be in Viola's cabin."

"How did it get started, Mr. Hampton?' I asked. "Does anyone know?"

"Pa picked up five slaves from a slave trader out of Charleston a little over a week ago and brought them home to work in the fields. We think one of them must have been infected, maybe all five."

Sarie scoffed. "Don't surprise me, comin from a no-good slave trader. Some of em don't treat the slaves right at all, keep em in grimy little one-room shacks, ten or more in each one with no way to wash and barely enough food to keep em alive. You can bet if one of em has anything he can pass on to the others in the cabin, it don't take long."

Josh handed Buck's reins to a large black man—Big Thom, I assumed—standing in the barn door. "Brush him down and see that he has water and give him some oats, please, Big Thom." He turned back to Sarie. "They should be shot, or at the very least, made to live like the slaves they bring in. But try to tell that to Pa or, hell, all the plantation owners around here." He seemed to remember he was in the presence of ladies and grimaced. "Sorry, Miss Lizzie, Miss Sarie, didn't mean to cuss. Anyway, they all go to slave traders when they need field hands. At least old man Walton cleans them up, teaches them to speak English and trains them to our way of farming." He waved that away. "Best I can figure, one of the ones Pa picked up must have had small pox but none of them was showing any outward signs of it. Yesterday afternoon, the overseer sent one of them, Ned, to Viola. Said he collapsed out in the field." He looked at me. "Viola takes care of the slaves, Miss Lizzie." He turned his attention back to Sarie. "She took one look and kept him with her while she sent word to Pa that we may have a small pox outbreak. Ned's still in Viola's cabin, along with a few others that aren't showing any outward signs, but they all have fevers. Viola says that's one of the first signs of small pox."

Sarie nodded. "Fever could mean a lot of other things, too, Mr. Josh."

"So Viola says. I've put the four other slaves Pa purchased from the slave trader in a separate cabin and I've placed the men who shared living quarters with them in another. I figure if anybody's likely to get it, it would be them."

I couldn't stand to see the worry on his face and reached out to touch his arm. "Don't worry, Mr. Hampton, we're going to do everything we can. That was a smart thing you did, separating them that way. I'm going to go back and examine everybody at Viola's place first. Then I'll go cabin to cabin and check on everyone else. Depending on what I find, we may have to move some more into Viola's cabin or quarantine another one if Viola's is too small to contain them all."

I touched his arm again when he continued to frown. "Sarie's going to help me and we'll let you know if we need anything more than what we brought with us." I looked at Sarie. "Tie that handkerchief over your nose and mouth before we get any closer. Try not to touch anyone or anything, Sarie, but if you do, put something over your hand first, your skirt or ... wait." I turned back to Josh. "Could you go get us a pair of your mother's gloves for Sarie? Thin, lightweight cotton would be best if she has any. We'll probably need to wash them."

He looked confused as he said, "I reckon so. Do you mind me asking what you want gloves for in this heat?"

I grew momentarily distracted when I glanced at the plantation house, reminding me of houses I'd seen in older, well-to-do sections of Knoxville. A memory of the appalling, ubiquitous cast-iron statues of black stable boys with their perpetually foolish grins, red jackets and white gloves sitting outside some of those houses flashed into my mind. I'd always hated those things.

When he cleared his throat, I turned back to him, forcing that image away. "What? Oh, the gloves will protect Sarie. She's never had the pox and the main way the disease is spread is by air and contact. She shouldn't touch anyone while we're here. That goes for you, too." Waving that away, I continued, "If your mother doesn't have any gloves we can borrow, would Elijah have some or one of the stable boys? Certain servants are often required to wear them, aren't they?"

He nodded. "Elijah wears them when he's serving. Mama insists on it. I'll get a pair and bring them out, but what about you, Miss Lizzie? Aren't you in danger, too?"

I smiled. "No, Mr. Hampton, I'm immune. I had small pox when I was a child, and once you've had it, you can't catch it again. There's no danger for me."

Sarie gave me a sharp look. I raised my eyebrows, mentally asking her if it would be better to lie or tell him the truth. She gave me a small nod of agreement.

Josh apparently didn't see our exchange, as he said, "All right, I'll go see what Elijah has. It won't take me but a minute and then I'll take you back to Viola's cabin."

"Oh, but—" I started but Sarie cut me off.

"I'll take Lizzie to the cabin and then I'll come back here and wait for you to bring the gloves. You shouldn't go around the sick ones, either, Mr. Josh. It's too dangerous if you haven't had the pox and I think I would've heard about it if you had."

"No, I haven't had it but I spent most of the morning out there with them. If I'm going to get it, I'd venture to say I already have."

Sarie raised her eyebrows at me. I shook my head in answer to her unspoken question then addressed Josh. "There's no need taking any chances, Mr. Hampton, and no guarantee that you already have it. In the next couple of weeks you need to watch for fever, headache, and an achy feeling in your muscles. Those are the first symptoms. If you have any of those, you'll need to send for us right away. And tell your family the same thing. Oh, and has anyone reported this to the slave trader? He'll need to check his people to make sure no one else has it."

"Not that I know of but I reckon we should. I'll tell Pa he needs to send someone over right away."

"All right. Thank you."

He shook his head. "No need to thank me. I should be thanking you for being here." He gave me a thin smile. "I'll go get those gloves. If you'll excuse me, please."

I took the saddlebag Sarie held out to me. "Sarie, if you can just point me in the general direction of Viola's cabin, I'll find it. If and only if Josh can get you some gloves then you can come back but only after you have the handkerchief over your nose and make sure your mouth and hands are covered." I reached out to take her hand then remembered her reaction to physical contact from me so dropped it. "Promise me. This is very important. I can handle the ones that we know have already contracted it. You should go to the other cabins and start talking to everyone else, see if anyone is showing physical signs of the illness. If they are, send them on to Viola's cabin."

She nodded. "I'll do as you say but you promise you'll be careful, too. Don't take any chances. Abbie will have my head if anything happens to you."

"I won't. Now tell me where Viola's cabin is."

"I reckon you know the slaves' cabins are all at the end of this path here," she said, pointing to a well-worn trail that disappeared beyond the barn. "Mr. Josh was smart to put the sick ones at Viola's cabin 'cause it's the last one. I reckon it stands several feet beyond all the others. You can't miss it, she's got a big cast-iron cook pot outside her door stuffed full of cattails and reeds. And more'n likely you'll probably hear her singing, too.".

CHAPTER NINE

Don't Think Twice (It's All Right)

Sarie was right, there was no way I could have missed Viola's cabin. The door stood open and her lovely, clear soprano soared over the unnatural quiet and stillness. I stopped for a moment just to listen and allow the splendor of her voice to surround me, to calm me. I didn't recognize the song but appreciated the words which spoke of hope and an undying faith in God. And I admired that someone in her situation could find the heart to believe life would be better if she just trusted in a higher power.

I'd felt the same way at one time in my life, many years ago, before my mom died and my father couldn't be bothered to take me to church on Sunday mornings. I hadn't really missed it, but right at that moment with Viola's voice ringing in my ears, the late summer sun warming my skin and the faint breeze washing over me, I bowed my head and said a silent, tentative prayer, asking for guidance to help me save these poor people.

When the song ended, I raised my head and walked with determination onto the small front porch of the cabin, brushing my hand over the velvety softness of the cat tails as I passed then knocking lightly on the frame.

"Viola? Is it ok—all right to come in?"

A small, wizened black woman who looked to be older

than the God I had just prayed to, hustled over to the door. I saw immediately why Josh had sent the ones he suspected were sick to her. The tell-tale pock marks on her face and hands were proof that she'd had and survived small pox at some time in her long life. Her steel-gray hair was cropped short and her eyes were such a dark brown they looked almost black.

"I'm Lizzie," I said by way of introduction, just managing to catch myself before I held out my hand to shake hers. "Mr. Hampton, um, that is, Mr. Josh said I should come on back. I'm with Sarie. She should be here soon. We're here to help."

She stepped back, motioning me in. "Law, child, I don't know what you can do if'n we're dealin with what I think we're dealin with but come on in here out of that hot sun."

I stepped inside and waited for my eyes to adjust to the dim light then looked around at the three people sprawled on quilts around the one-room cabin. They stared back, watching me with distrust and, in the case of the youngest one, fear.

"You had the pox?" Viola asked.

"Yes, ma'am, when I was a child."

She studied my face, looked down at my hands. "Don't see no sign of it nowhere. You one of the lucky ones, I reckon."

"Yes, ma'am. My mother knew the signs and called the doctor right away. They were quick and caught it early enough to keep me from scarring too badly."

"Count your blessings, child. I seen too many people like me who is marked up somethin terrible, all over their faces and hands, and if they're like me, probably their feet, too." She eyed me for a moment then grinned, revealing several missing teeth. "Welp, come on in here and see what you think."

Taking my arm, she led me over to the first patient. "This here's Ned. He was the first of us to show any signs. See here." She leaned down and picked up one of his hands. Even in the dimness, I could see the red rash clearly.

I leaned over and reached out to check for fever but he

jerked away from my hand. "Oh, no, missus, you'll get it, too."

I smiled as I knelt in front of him. "No, Ned, I'm like Viola, I've already had it. Once a person's had small pox, there's no danger of ever getting it again. I'm perfectly safe, I assure you. Just relax and let me feel your forehead to see if you have a fever. Do you feel hot?"

He relented, leaning toward me and allowing the back of my hand to rest on his forehead. It was very warm but not burning as I'd expected it to be, even though I knew from my studies the fever was usually relatively mild, rarely going above 101 degrees. Still, with this heat, even a low fever would be horribly uncomfortable.

"You're a little warm. Other than that, how are you feeling, Ned? Any pain in your muscles or joints? Do you have a headache?"

"Yes'm. Feel kinda like a mule kicked me to the dirt and then stomped on me."

I patted his arm in reassurance. "That's a good way to put it. No headache?"

"No'm, but I is awful hot."

I looked up at Viola. "Could you bring Ned a dipper of water, please?"

"Yes'm. I'll get a damp rag, too, to put on his head. Maybe that'll help to cool him a bit."

"Yes, thank you." I turned back to my patient. "Soon as Miss Sarie gets here we'll fix some herbal tea that should bring the fever down and make you a bit more comfortable. I'm sure she'll have something to help with the achy feeling, too. You just lie quiet and let me take a look at the others."

As I worked, my mind kept running through what we could do to help these people. We could try the vaccine but I didn't have any idea where we would get the material we needed. As I examined a small red spot on the next patient's hand, the youngest one, a teenager named Willy, I thought about the progression of the disease, leaving behind a deep scar, or pock.

I turned back to Ned. "How long have you had the rash on your hands, Ned?"

Viola answered for him. "First noticed it this mornin so it must have started sometime durin the night."

"And you, Willy?"

Again, Viola answered. "Mr. Josh said Willy only had a fever and a headache when he brung him to me this mornin. The red spots are new."

I smiled at Willy and Ned. "All right. You probably have another day or two before that blisters. When it does, do your best not to scratch." I laid a hand on Willy's shoulder, giving him a reassuring pat. "I'll bet Miss Sarie has something to help with that, too."

As I stood up and moved on to the last patient, my mind was working furiously. When I'd seen the rash on Willy's hands, I had remembered that at one time, doctors in England and here in the United States had done something called variolation, a sort of arm-to-arm vaccination on small pox patients. If we couldn't find the infectious material from a sick cow or rodent, we could try that. The risk for complications and, yes, possibly even death, was a little higher than with the cow pox vaccine but it could be done. And if it would save lives, it had to be considered.

As a worst-case scenario, I thought, it might work but I still hoped we could find a cow or a rodent with the milder form of pox and use that instead.

I knelt down beside the last patient as Viola told me his name was Noah. He appeared to be in his late thirties, maybe early forties. He smiled winsomely at me as I reached out to check his forehead for fever. He, like the others, felt warm to the touch but not overly so.

"How are you feeling, Noah? Any headache or pain?"

"No'm, I's fine, just hot is all."

I picked up one of his hands to check for the rash when he suddenly scooted away from me, eyes wide with fright and mouth gaping open.

He threw one hand up as if to ward off an attack, pointing behind me with the other and yelling, "No, missus, no! Keep it away from me!"

I looked over my shoulder and saw Sarie standing in the doorway, her face covered with the white handkerchief and white gloves covering her hands. With the bright sun streaming in behind her, giving her body a haloed effect but leaving her face in shadow, she looked like a being from another world and I could only imagine what Noah was thinking.

I reached out to reassure him everything was fine but he pressed as hard as he could against the wall. I smothered my amusement, smiling reassuringly at him. "It's all right, Noah. Shh, now, it's only Miss Sarie. She's here to help. She's not going to hurt you." When he continued to cower against the wall, I patted the back of his hand, hoping to distract him enough to continue my examination.

Sarie came the rest of the way in and knelt down beside Ned. "How are you feeling, Ned?"

The sound of her voice seemed to calm Noah and he allowed me to check his hands for signs of the rash. As his feet were bare, I checked those, too, but like his hands, found them clear.

Sitting back on my haunches, I watched Sarie for a minute. "It looks as if Ned and Willy have progressed to the second stage. Noah doesn't have the rash yet but he is warm. Both the others have the rash on their hands which probably means they were already infected before Mr. Hampton brought them here. It takes one to two weeks after infection before the rash appears." I turned back to Willy. "Did you come from the slave trader, too?"

"No'm, I come here 'bout three years ago from Mr. Walton's place."

"You're a house servant?"

"Yas'm. I helps with the washin and cleanin and such."

"Were you around Ned and Willy anytime after they came, Noah?"

"Yas'm. We sleep in the same cabin."

I looked at Sarie. "He says he doesn't have a headache or any pain so it's possible he may not have contracted it yet but we can't be sure. It's best not to take any chances so we'll keep him here for now and watch for the rash to appear."

"All right."

"Ned and Willy both have fevers, headaches and the achy feeling that accompany the first phase and the rash that comes with the second phase. How do you think we should treat them?"

Sarie shrugged. "Only thing I know to do is treat what's ailing em till we decide what we're goin to do. Probably best to start with a willow bark decoction. Best thing for the fevers and it'll also help with the headaches and ease their pain a bit."

I nodded. Sarie knew so much more than I did when it came to natural treatments but, oh, man, what I wouldn't give for a huge bottle of aspirin right now. And as long as I was making a list of all the things I wanted, I might as well add surgical gloves and masks. "All right. I assume you have willow bark in the satchel. What else do you need?"

"Boiling water and maybe some honey and wild mint to sweeten the taste a bit. Willow bark by itself is awful bitter and hard to get down." She turned to Viola. "Viola, you reckon you could put a large kettle or pot of water over the fire and let it boil?"

"Yes'm, I'll do that." She hurried to the door, shouted for someone named Jonas. Turning back to us, she said, "I'll send Jonas down to the creek right away to get some fresh water. Is there anything else you need?"

Sarie gave her a wan smile. "Prayers are always welcome." She looked at me. "I need to talk to you outside."

I patted Noah's arm and stood. "Lie back and rest. We'll get you ..." I smiled at Ned and Willy to include them, "... all of you, feeling better soon."

When I stepped outside, Sarie was waiting for me beside the big cook pot of cattails. "I reckon there's not much we can do for them at this point except to make em as comfortable as we can and wait for the rash to move to the next phase—is that what you called it?" She didn't wait for my answer. "I'm gonna ask Mr. Josh if he can send Elijah back to our place and tell Maggie and Abbie to start makin up some calendula infusion to help with the rash. I brought some with me but it's not gonna be anywhere near enough, especially if more of the slaves come down with it."

CC Tillery

"Will that help?""

"It's the best thing I know for skin rashes. I ain't got no idea how much it will help but it's at least something."

I nodded, mentally adding a vat of calamine lotion to my wish list. I remembered my mom smothering me in the stuff when I had chicken pox. It didn't help much, but just the bright pink spots on my skin were enough to remind me not to scratch. The thing that helped the most was the oatmeal baths she gave me.

"We could try oatmeal baths. That's what my mama did when I had the chicken pox. The oatmeal soothes the itch and helps to dry the spots out a bit. I'm not sure but that could be the best thing with this."

"Oatmeal baths? You mean like cook up a big batch of porridge and have em get in the pot?"

"No, I mean grind up the oatmeal and put it in the bathwater, swish it around and bathe with that. What my mom did was toss a handful of finely ground oatmeal into a warm bath and then she had me soak in it for fifteen or twenty minutes. I remember it helped with the itch better than anything else."

"Don't see how we can do that. These slaves ain't got a way to take a bath other than go down to the crik."

"We could make an oatmeal salve and smear it on the spots as they show up."

"Like we do for the chicken pox?"

"A bit thicker than that maybe, using ground oatmeal."

"It could work, I reckon. If nothing else, it might make em more comfortable. Like I told you afore, that's about the only thing we can do for em once it moves on to what you called the final stage. How did she grind the oatmeal into a fine powder anyway?"

"In a blender but I don't guess we can find one of those. They haven't been invented yet. But maybe a mortar and pestle would work. It might take a little bit of work but it could be worth it."

"How about a corn mill? Would that do it?"

"What's a corn mill?"

"It's a contraption that we use to grind dried corn down

into corn meal so we can make corn pone and corn bread."

I thought about it a minute. "That might work. Do you have one?"

"No, but I'd say they have one here somewhere. I'll ask Mr. Josh when I ask him about sendin somebody over to talk to Maggie and Abbie about the calendula infusion."

"Speak of the devil," I murmured when I saw Josh coming toward us on the path. I touched Sarie's arm. "I thought of something while I was examining our patients in there. We'll talk after you get finished with Mr. Hampton." I put my hands on my hips and scowled at Josh. "Where are your gloves and handkerchief?"

"I told you I've already been exposed. I'm not in any danger."

"Yes, you are if you haven't already contracted it. At least put a handkerchief over your mouth and nose."

He grinned. "You worried about me, Miss Lizzie?"

I started to deny it, but the truth was, I was worried about him. "Yes, I'm worried about you and everybody else who lives on this plantation. This is not the time to be careless."

He pulled a bandanna out of his back pocket and waved it at me before tying it around his nose and mouth.

I gave him a curt nod. "Thank you. Sarie needs to talk to you. I'm going to go back in and get that willow bark concoction started."

Viola and I stood by the fire staring at the large pot, full to the brim with water just beginning to boil. "How much water does this thing hold, Viola? Miss Sarie said we need a couple of teaspoons of willow bark for two cups of water to make one dose."

"I reckon it holds about four-five gallon or so."

I calculated in my head: four cups to a quart, four quarts to a gallon. "So this should make way more than we need right now. I wonder if it's all right to go ahead and make it and then heat it back up later when we need to give them another dose."

"Better to make it fresh ever time," Sarie said, making me jump and drop the spoon I was holding.

Viola quickly stepped back to avoid the splash of hot water as the spoon fell into the pot.

"Good law, Sarie, you scared the life out of me."

She shared a knowing grin with Viola. "Sorry, Lizzie, next time I'll have the butler announce me. What are you so jumpy about anyway?"

I sniffed. "I'm not jumpy. I was concentrating on the correct measurement of willow bark."

"I reckon the best thing to do is measure the water into another smaller pot and add the right amount of willow bark for the number of doses. We got three patients so you'll need six cups of water and six teaspoons of willow bark. That needs to boil for a good twenty minutes then you can strain it and add the honey. Oh, and throw in a handful of wild mint leaves with the willow bark."

I turned to Viola, who was already holding out a smaller pot. "Do you have a measuring cup?"

Sarie rolled her eyes. "Eyeball it, Lizzie. It don't have to be that exact."

"Excuse me?"

"Oh, for heaven's sake, guess. The dipper there is about a cup so add six dips to the pot Viola has. Then add the willow bark, stir in a handful of mint leaves and hang the pot over the fire. When it comes to a boil, let it alone for twenty minutes and then strain the liquid into the cups afore adding the honey."

"Wouldn't it be easier to mix the honey in while the water's boiling? That way the honey will dissolve."

"No, you have to add the honey last because boilin it takes the sweetness from the honey and it don't heal as good."

I turned to Viola. "Viola, could you bring us the biggest jar of honey you can find? I have a feeling we're going to need a lot of it."

"Yes'm, Miss Lizzie. I reckon I have to go up to the big house to fetch it but I be right back."

After she left, Sarie moved over to stand beside me as I set the smaller pot on the hook over the fire. Speaking in a low voice, she said, "While she's gone, tell me what you thought of."

I used my apron to blot the sweat off my face. "There's another way we can vaccinate the ones who are sick. And really, we should vaccinate everybody here on the plantation, just to be safe. If it works, that is."

"Mr. Josh said they don't have any cows infected with cow pox, so unless we can catch some kind of forest critter that's infected with that other thing you said, we should probably try it."

I nodded. "This is a method they used in England and America up until the end of this century when it was replaced with the cow pox vaccine. It's called variolation and it involves using people who are sick with small pox to vaccinate other people."

"How can that be safe?"

I sighed. "I'm not really sure. I only know that I read about it and it is doable. They even had what they called variolation houses and clinics all around England so people could get the treatment. One man, a doctor, well, actually a family of doctors named Sutton were very successful and had clinics all over the country. They kept their method a secret but at the end of the century one of the doctors published a book that told the secret to their success."

"What was it? Do you remember?"

I nodded. "He used a shallower scratch than most people did. Simple, really, and it worked. But like I said, it's more dangerous than the cow pox vaccine and the type of vaccination I received." I looked into her eyes. "Do you think we should risk it?"

She shrugged. "I reckon I don't see as we have no other choice."

I nodded toward Viola's cabin. "I'm not sure how we should do this but I guess we could make it on a strictly voluntary basis. Explain it to them and let them choose whether or not they want to risk it."

She shook her head. "Mr. Hampton ain't never gonna allow that. He makes the decisions for his slaves."

I muttered a not-too flattering curse.

"What?"

"Never mind. We could do it without telling him. If anybody does, God forbid, die or get small pox anyway, we could tell him, I don't know, that it's the nature of the disease. Surely he can't blame us. If we don't do it, he's guaranteed to lose some of them."

"We could, I reckon. But I think we should tell Mr. Josh and let him decide whether or not we do it." She ripped the handkerchief from her face then peeled the gloves from her hands and stuffed them into her pocket. "Mercy, that feels better."

I grabbed her hand. "Sarie, you need to put those back on right now."

She shook her head. "No, I don't. I'm gonna be your first volunteer. When we get home, you can do Maggie and Abbie, too, if it works." Before I could protest, she went on, "I believe we, *you* can do this and I believe it could work. I'm trusting you, Lizzie."

I hesitated, not sure I wanted their deaths on my conscience if it didn't work. Sarie surprised me by squeezing my hand. "It's only fair if we're gonna do this that we try it out first. That way you can practice how you do it afore you go sticking needles into anybody. I bet Mr. Josh will insist you give it to him, too."

"All right," I finally said, "but only if it works and they agree to it, and because if small pox is as common as you say, it will keep them safe for the rest of their lives."

"All right. I thank you, Lizzie."

I waved that away, uncomfortable at her words of gratitude, which Sarie rarely spoke. "Let's get back to the willow bark. Surely that water has started to boil by now."

I worried about my decision as we completed the willow bark decoction, adding a spoonful of the honey Viola brought back, then dispensing it to Ned, Noah, and Willy.

It worked just as Sarie said it would, cooling their fevers and helping with the pain and headache.

By that time, we had two more patients and were discussing whether we'd need to waylay another cabin in case more showed up. Viola offered her son's and his wife's cabin and we went to check it out while Sarie stayed with the new patients to examine them. I made sure she placed the handkerchief over her face and the gloves on her hands before we left.

The cabin was much the same as Viola's and we were on our way back when Josh and Abbie appeared on the path from the barn. I rushed toward the two, knowing Sarie would be upset to see her sister here, even though she had predicted it. "What are you doing here, Abbie?"

She held up a huge canning jar. "Calendula. Isn't that what you and Sarie requested?"

"We did but you shouldn't be here." I turned to Josh. "Why did you bring her here? It's dangerous."

Josh merely shrugged. "You want to explain, Miss Abbie?"

Abbie's eyes flashed with anger. "Don't yell at him, he didn't *bring* me. I followed him. Well, most of the way." She frowned at me. "Why is it dangerous for me and not for you or Sarie? I know what's goin on, Lizzie, and I can help."

Sarie stepped out of the cabin, pulling the handkerchief down off her face. "Abbie, what in hellfire are you doing here?" She glared at Josh. "Why did you bring her here?"

This time Josh held up his hands, palms out. "You want to tell your sister, Miss Abbie?"

"I come on my own. Fact is, he didn't see me till I was almost here and I told him the only way I was goin back was if he knocked me in the head and carried me back." She sighed. "I was worried about you and I'm not leavin, Sarie, so you might as well let me help. And don't give me none of that 'dangerous' talk. That don't work with me." She gentled her voice. "Sarie, let me help. Please."

"Does Maggie know you're gone?" Sarie asked.

Abbie shook her head.

I turned to Sarie. "Sarie, why don't you take Abbie back home? There's nothing more you can do here today anyway. I'll stay here tonight, if that's all right with Mr. Hampton." I looked at Josh and got a nod of agreement. "I can take care of our patients and anybody else who shows symptoms."

"But what about the ... what did you call it?"

"Variolation. We really can't do anything until the rash

moves to the next stage. That could happen as soon as tomorrow. You can come back in the morning, and if we can, we'll get started with the treatment."

"Can I ask what you're talkin about, Lizzie?" Abbie said, drawing my attention to her.

"Sarie can tell you all about it on the way home." I looked back at Sarie. "Go on now, take Abbie home. I imagine Maggie's worried sick by now. You can tell her and Abbie everything that's happened and what we plan to do."

Sarie eyed me suspiciously. "Are you sure?"

"Yes, of course. It's only a matter of waiting at this point."

"All right, then. I reckon we'll take Buck and go. Mr. Josh can bring you back if needed."

"Good. Get a good night's sleep. I have a feeling we're going to be busy tomorrow."

Sarie took Abbie's hand. "I reckon so. Come on, let's go home, Abbie. Leave the calendula with Lizzie. She and Viola can get a batch goin."

"But what about—"

Sarie cut her off. "We're goin home, Abbie. Lizzie can handle it here." She turned to me. "You need us to bring anything back, Lizzie?"

"Some sharp needles would be nice. Maybe some more calendula flowers if you have any."

She nodded. "I'm sure we do but you might want to check with Viola and see if they have any fresh. Those work, too, only use six spoons to two cups of water instead of three."

"All right. We'll take care of it."

She stared into my eyes for a moment, nodded and whispered, "I'm trustin you on this, Lizzie." Stepping back, she took Abbie's hand. "Come on, Abbie, we've got some things to do afore tomorrow mornin."

Abbie followed her though she kept her eyes on me for as long as she could.

After they had ridden away, I turned to Josh. "I can bed down with Viola, if that's all right with you ... and her, too, of course."

"There's no need for that. I can have Selma prepare a

room for you in the main house."

"Thank you, but I think it would be better if I stay here with my patients in case they need anything through the night. I also need to talk to you. And I could use a walk. Would you wait a few minutes? I need to take the calendula in to Viola and check to see if it's all right that I stay here tonight."

"Of course."

"I'll be right back," I said as I headed into the cabin.

When I came back out, Josh held out his arm and I took it. We walked in silence until I deemed it far enough away from the cabins that I felt I could talk freely. There was no need for the slaves to know what I planned on doing before I got his approval.

I explained it all very carefully to him and it didn't surprise me a bit when he immediately volunteered to be the first to get the variolation, just as Sarie had predicted.

I smiled. "I'm afraid you'll have to get in line. Sarie's already insisted I give it to her first and to her sisters next if it works."

He laughed. "I should have known. Miss Sarie's not afraid of anything and always wants to be the first. She's been like that since we were children."

"You used to play together?"

"Pa insisted we all, my brothers and sisters and myself, attend the local school for the first few years of our education. Said it was just as important for us to learn about our neighbors as it was for us to learn to read and write. I liked it so much, I begged him to let me stay there when he said it was time to go to a finishing school to prepare me for college."

"That's nice. And did he let you stay?"

"Unfortunately, no. He sent me to a school in Raleigh first then on to Duke to complete my education."

I started to ask what he'd majored in but I didn't know if college students had majors then. Maybe they had a set curriculum for every student and didn't focus on one specific area of study like business or medicine the way we did in the future.

"Yes, well, Sarie is determined to have the variolation before I attempt to give it to anyone else." I looked up at him and grinned. "She's like my lab rat."

His eyebrows arched. "Your what?"

Oops. I really needed to be more careful about what I said to him. I waved my hand in the air. "Oh, that's something my father says all the time. He's a doctor and doctors sometimes need to test something before they use it on a patient. Doctors and scientists often test unknown theories on mice or rats. Hence, you, Sarie, Abbie and Maggie are going to be my lab rats."

He laughed. "Lab rats? Not very flattering but I'm willing to be a rat if it helps."

I held up my hand, fingers crossed. "I'm hopeful that it will but I just don't know. What I do know is that they've been using this practice since the early 16th century with some success. I believe it's worth trying."

"Then I believe it, too, Miss Lizzie."

"You can call me just Lizzie, Mr. Hampton. I won't mind."

He nodded. "If you'll call me Josh instead of Mr. Hampton."

As we smiled at one another, I did my best to ignore the increased tempo of my heartbeat as I looked into his beautiful green eyes. Like a deep forest, a woman could get lost in those eyes if she wasn't careful. It alarmed me when I realized I might be falling for him. Or was it just his faith in me that had me fighting for my balance?

CHAPTER TEN

Time Passes Slowly

When Sarie arrived the next morning, she had both Maggie and Abbie with her. She also brought along another jar of dried calendula flowers to make more medicine, a packet of delicate sewing needles Abbie used to do her fine embroidery, a dozen or so handkerchiefs and a couple pair of white gloves she said had belonged to their mother.

We had two more people who had fevers and headaches, one of whom also complained of soreness. Viola and I had spent part of the night setting up pallets and bedding in her son's cabin. Along with making the calendula infusion and willow bark tea, neither one of us had slept very much.

As soon as Sarie saw us, she ordered both of us to lie down and take a nap. There wasn't anything I wanted more than to close my eyes for a few minutes but I needed to talk to her first.

I smiled at Abbie and Maggie. "Why don't you two go on in Viola's cabin and get a pot or two of water boiling? I need to talk to Sarie for a few minutes and then we'll come in and help." I put my hand on Abbie's forearm when she began to move away. "Before you and Maggie go in, put on your gloves and tie the handkerchiefs around your mouth and nose. And keep them there until you come out."

Abbie covered my hand with hers, her eyes filled with concern. "You look awful tired, Lizzie."

"I am tired and I'll have myself a nice lie-down as soon as I fill Sarie in on what happened during the night. She can bring you up to speed ..." The collective frowns on the sisters' faces alerted me to the fact they didn't know what I was saying. I waved a hand in the air and stopped talking for a moment as I searched for another way to say what I wanted to say. "What I mean is she can share everything I tell her while I catch ... take a nap."

Sarie and I helped them don the gloves and tie the handkerchiefs around their faces then watched as they walked inside the cabin. I could hear the smile in Abbie's voice as she greeted Viola.

Taking a deep breath, I turned back to Sarie. "Do you think it was wise to bring them here?"

She snorted. "You try and tell Abbie she couldn't come. I swan, that girl is more stubborn than a constipated mule. And when she told Maggie what we were dealin with over here ..." she raised her hands in the air, palms out "... there weren't nothin I could do to get em to stay at home."

"Sorry, I didn't mean to jump all over you. It just surprised me to see them here but you were smart enough to teach them how to protect themselves." I reached out to touch her but the look on her face stopped me. "Let's just hope it's enough."

"I reckon you can hope all you want. Me, I'm gonna be doin an awful lot of prayin till we get through this." She looked toward the cabin then turned her attention back to me. "Did you remember anything else during the night about the, what was it you called it?" Before I could answer, she said, "Variolation and how to do it?"

I nodded. "I did. It was Dr. Sutton's son who wrote the book telling their secret."

She frowned. "That ain't no help, Lizzie."

"No, it's not, but the fact that he also explained in the book that they were careful to select pus from only the most mildly affected patients should help."

"What do you mean, mildly affected?"

"They only took the pus from patients who had a more mild form of the disease and used that for the variolation on other patients. When I remembered that, I started thinking it's best if we only vaccinate one person, wait for the pock to appear and use them to vaccinate the next. I don't know for sure but I'm hoping and praying the disease will kind of cycle down as it's passed from one patient to the next."

"I ain't sure I understand what you're sayin."

"What if we variolate one person from Ned, wait for that person to break out and then do you. Then when you get the pustule from the second patient, we use your pus on Maggie and Abbie." I waved my hand. "It's hard to explain but I'm thinking the disease will become less severe, and if we use the pus from some of the later victims, maybe it will lower the incidence of problems."

"That makes sense but won't that take too long?"

I winced, knowing she was right. "It'll take a while."

"Well, then, I hate to disagree with you, Lizzie, you bein the expert and all, but I don't want to wait that long. Every day we wait, the chances that one of us gets infected increases."

"Yes, it does but—"

"Did you remember anything else that could help?"

I sighed. "Well, yeah, I remembered that Dr. Sutton said not to bleed anyone before performing the variolation."

"Bleed?"

"A long time ago, doctors used to open a vein in a person's arm and let them bleed almost to death before they gave them the variolation. Actually, doctors used to bleed their patients for almost every sickness. They thought a person's blood was making them sick and figured if they drained out as much as they could, it would make them well. A rather barbaric practice, if you ask me, but one they believed in. It's a miracle anyone survived past the 18th century."

Sarie nodded. "Well, let's hope what we're doin works better than that. Has Ned broken out yet?"

"It usually takes two or more days for the disease to progress to that phase. I'm guessing sometime tonight or tomorrow. You'll be the first to know since I'm pegging you as my first ..." I rubbed my hands together as I laughed wickedly, " ... victim. That is, unless I give the honors to Josh."

She frowned, signaling she didn't find this funny. "You told him?"

"Yes, I did, and like a true Southern gentleman, he gallantly volunteered as soon as I explained what we were going to do."

"Then I reckon he don't have any problem with us vacci—" she stumbled over the word.

"Vaccinating."

"Vaccinatin the slaves."

I smiled smugly. "Nope, not a one. I forgot to ask him what he would tell his father."

"I don't reckon Mr. Hampton would have any objections if it keeps his property from harm."

I wanted to snarl at that but Sarie had heard it already. I was just glad Josh didn't seem to feel the same way when it came to the slaves.

"But if you kill em all ..." She gave me a measured look.

Abbie poked her head out of the cabin door. "Lizzie, I think you and Sarie need to come see this."

"What is it?" I asked.

She stepped out. "I reckon Ned's moved into what Lizzie calls the next stage."

I glanced at Sarie. "Those prayers you have so much faith in would sure be welcome about now."

She didn't answer as she went into the cabin.

Inside, we hurried over to Ned's pallet. When I saw the blister on his face, oozing pus, it suddenly hit me we didn't have a way to vaccinate him. Kneeling down beside him, I vowed mentally that I would do whatever I could to help him get through this horrible disease. I didn't fool myself that he would come through unscathed but I would try everything to see that he lived through it.

He opened his eyes and tried to smile at me but seemed too weak to make the effort. "I got it, don't I, Miss Lizzie?"

With what I hoped was a reassuring smile, I placed a

gentle finger on his cheek just above the pustule. My stomach clenched at the thought that saving his life and the lives of the others rested squarely on my shoulders. Moving my hand to his shoulder, I rubbed it gently. "I'm afraid you do, Ned. Lie back and try to rest. We're going to do everything we can to get you through this."

He closed his eyes again but not before a tear escaped. I watched, tracking it as it rolled slowly and gently back into his hair.

As it had out in front of Viola's cabin yesterday, the prayer simply formed in my mind: "Dear God, please give me the knowledge and the courage to help these people."

I took a deep breath as Sarie knelt beside me, a questioning look on her face. Tilting my head toward the door as a sign for her to follow me out, I reached out and braced a hand on her shoulder as I stood. "We'll be right back," I said to Ned then turned to Abbie and Maggie, whispering, "Whatever you two do, don't touch him, especially his face. Keep the handkerchiefs and gloves on. Sarie and I need to step outside for a moment."

"But—" Abbie started but I shook my head to stop her question.

"Sarie and I will handle this part. Promise me you'll both do as I say. If you want something to do, get busy making another batch of the willow bark tea and give some to everyone. It'll help them feel better. Sarie, would you come with me, please?"

"A-course."

Sarie, thank goodness, was wise enough to hold any questions until we got a few steps outside the door. And even then, she whispered, "What do we do next?"

I turned and looked into her eyes, trying to convey the seriousness of this. "Are you sure you want me to do this on you and your sisters? Josh has volunteered—"

She cut me off. "No, Lizzie, we agreed I would go first. I'm ready, more than ready, but I need you to do somethin."

"What is it?"

"How long does it take to know whether or not it works?"

I shrugged. "It usually takes about a week for the

variolation scab to form and fall off. If it takes, that is, but we need to check it daily to make sure there's no infection or any other adverse effects. If it falls off clean then I guess that means it worked. That's how it works with the vaccination, anyway."

"So we should wait another week before we do my sisters?"

"Yes. Once we know it works, we can vaccinate them."

She nodded. "All right, we'll do me first and then them later." She tugged on her gloves. "Can we get rid of this stuff after we do?"

I shook my head. "Just to be safe, I'd like all of you to continue to wear it until we see if this works. We should know in a week if you can go without it." She frowned. "I know it's hot and uncomfortable but it's for your protection, Sarie."

"All right. And if it does work, then my sisters and I will be protected from small pox for the rest of our lives. Is that right?"

"Yes, you should be."

"Then we'll do it and pray it works. What can I do to help?"

"We'll need a dull knife, something like a butter knife should do, and something to sterilize it with so I can take a scraping from Ned's cheek. Then we'll need to sterilize a sharp needle to make the scratch."

She surprised me when she grasped my hand hard in hers and gave me her first real smile. "But not too deep, right? You won't forget that part, will you?"

I smiled back at her, grateful she was trying to calm the nerves that had my stomach jittering. "No, I promise I won't forget that part. After I've scratched you, I'll spread a small amount of the infected material from Ned onto the scratch. Then all we can do is keep an eye on it and wait to see what happens."

"I thought you said they did it with needles."

"That's a vaccination. We're not doing that, we're doing a variolation which is slightly different.

"All right. And we don't do Maggie and Abbie till we know

it works."

"Yes. I think we should do you today. I can't tell right now how severe Ned's case is and the severity affects the variolation. Could be the next person who comes down with it will have a milder case and that would make it safer for your sisters." I wanted to take her hand but Sarie had made it clear she didn't like to be touched so refrained. "I'm trying to keep everyone safe, Sarie, or as safe as possible."

She nodded. "All right. I reckon we ain't got no choice but to do it your way."

Josh knocked on the door frame as Sarie and I dropped a couple of needles in a pot of rapidly boiling water. Coming inside, he moved over to Ned and knelt down beside him, whispering something I'm sure was meant to reassure.

I watched him out of the corner of my eye as Sarie bent over the pot of boiling water, the steam flushing her cheeks prettily.

"How long do we need to leave em in there?" she asked, drawing my attention back to her.

I felt my cheeks go hot and hoped she would think it was from the fire and not from Josh's appearance. "Oh, at least thirty minutes."

Josh straightened up and walked over to us. "What are you cooking?"

Sarie chuckled and I smiled. "Needle soup. Would you care for a bowl?" I asked.

His forehead furrowed as he peered into the pot. "Needle? As in a sewing needle? What for?"

"Yes, we're, that is, I'm going to use them for the first step of the variolation on Sarie and they need to be sterile."

He drew a small knife out of his pocket. "I believe you requested a dull knife, Miss Lizzie. Is this what you meant?"

I took it from him and examined it. "Is this silver?"

He nodded. "It's from a set my sister has in her hope chest. I would've brought one of my mama's but if she noticed it was missing there'd be hell to pay." He grimaced. "Excuse my language, ladies."

"This should do the job." I slipped it carefully into another pot of water, bubbling frantically just like the other one. "Will your sister miss it?"

"Most likely not. She's too young to be thinking of marriage. At least, I hope she is. Frannie loves her dolls and spends most of her time playing with them. Boys, according to her, aren't worth the time or trouble."

I smiled even as I wondered why his sister would have a set of silverware at such a young age but didn't think it was appropriate to ask. "I'll do my best to return it to you without any damage."

He waved that away, turning to lay a hand on Sarie's arm. I watched her tense at this but, unlike what she had done with me, she didn't rebuke the gesture. "Miss Sarie, I wish you would think about letting me be the first of Miss Lizzie's ..." he looked at me, "... what was it you called it? A lab rat?"

I smiled. "Yes, not very flattering, I know, but that's precisely what she's going to be in this situation."

"What in tarnation's a lab rat?" Sarie asked.

"A term referring to an animal you use for a medical experiment." I looked back at the pot. "Have they been in there for thirty minutes yet?"

Like me, Sarie peered into the furiously boiling water. "I'd say they have. Does the knife have to be in there for that long, too?"

"Yes, but we won't be using it until we've scratched your arm." My stomach turned just thinking about it. Rubbing my hand over it in a soothing motion, I said, "Let's give it another few minutes. While we wait, we can sterilize your arm."

She blanched. "Are you sayin you want me to stick my arm in a pot of boilin water?"

"No, we'll wash it with warm water and some of Viola's lye soap. I wish I had some rub—" I closed my mouth when I remembered Josh was standing beside me. Did they even have isopropyl alcohol in the mid 19th century? I didn't know but I added it to the growing number of things on my list.

Luckily, neither Josh nor Sarie noticed my slip.

Sarie watched as my hand continued to rub my stomach. "You ain't nervous, are you, Lizzie?"

I nodded, licking my lips and trying to work up enough saliva to wet my suddenly dry mouth.

"You have to do this, Lizzie," Josh said. "I brought two more people to Viola's son's cabin, both complaining they don't feel well. This is the only chance we have."

I looked into his eyes as tears pushed behind my lids. I could see the faith in his and it calmed me a bit.

Taking a deep breath, I blew it out slowly and squared my shoulders. "All right. Sarie, you'll need to roll up your sleeve as high as you can. I want your upper arm bare so I can get it as clean as possible before ..." I waved my hand as I lost my courage again. "I'm sorry. I'm not sure I can do this. I don't want to hurt you, Sarie." I looked down at my hands, noticed they were trembling.

"You have to do it, Lizzie, you ain't got no choice."

Grasping my hands together, I took another deep breath and held it for a few seconds before blowing it out slowly between my dry lips. I could only be grateful we'd sent Maggie and Abbie with Viola to her son's cabin. They wouldn't be witness to my humiliation if I couldn't gather enough courage to do the procedure.

Looking into Sarie's eyes, I nodded then dipped several ladles of water into a basin sitting on the table. "You're right, Sarie, of course you're right. I'm sorry." I took several deep breaths. "All right, let's get you cleaned up. Here, sit at the table and try to relax. I'll do my best not to hurt you."

"Law, girl, it's only a small scratch. I've had worse from pickin blackberries or gatherin eggs from the chickens."

I nodded, my mind on what lay ahead. "Josh, would you bring that kettle of hot water over here and add some to the cold in this basin, please? Sarie, I'm going to lay out some clean rags for you to rest your arm on after I get it cleaned."

I washed Sarie's arm, nearly taking off the skin with the rough cloth just so I could be sure it was as clean as possible. I only stopped when Sarie winced. "I'm sorry, did I hurt you?"

"You keep scrubbin at me like that and you won't have to scratch me with one of them needles," she said, but she smiled when she said it.

"You're a brave woman, Miss Sarie," Josh said. "Lizzie, why don't you do me at the same time?" He rolled up his sleeve, revealing a tanned, muscular arm.

I felt the heat redden my cheeks. Settle down, Lizzie, I told myself. It's only a man's arm. You've seen thousands of them before and even touched a few in your time. That didn't help, it only heated my cheeks more. Keeping my eyes on Sarie's arm as I dried it seemed to help so I concentrated on that task.

"All right, I think we're ready." With a pair of Sarie's mother's gloves on, I picked up a needle from the clean rag we'd set them on to cool.

Trying to come up with a way to distract her, I remembered something one of my professors had said in a reproduction class. "Close your eyes and think of England," I said to Sarie as I lightly scraped the needle down her upper arm.

"What in the Sam hill does that mean?" she asked.

I looked up, smiling at her as I blotted the end of the tea towel over the scratch. "It's done."

She glanced down at her arm. "Oh, ain't you the clever one? I didn't feel a thing. Now what do we do?"

"Now we use the knife to take a scraping from Ned and apply it to your arm."

Josh held his own arm under my nose. "And mine," he said.

I looked down and saw the long, shallow scratch on it, oozing blood.

Since I didn't have time to get angry, I only sighed. I stared into his eyes. "Are you sure? This could mean your life, Josh."

"I reckon I'm as sure as Miss Sarie." He smiled reassuringly.

I studied him for a moment, noting his sincerity. "If you're sure, I don't guess I can stop you. Just let me do it."

Smiling crookedly, he took up one of the rags and blotted at the blood. "Looks like I got what I wanted, didn't I?"

"It sure looks like you did. You fool."

He shrugged, still grinning.

I used a slotted spoon to dip the knife out of the boiling water, holding it in the air for a few moments so it could cool. When I took it over to Ned, he opened his eyes and raised his head when he sensed me kneeling down beside him.

I smiled in what I hoped was a reassuring manner. "I'm just going to rub this knife over this blister, Ned. It shouldn't hurt but you let me know if it does."

"Yes'm, Miss Lizzie. Will that help to make me better?"

"No, Ned, I'm sorry, but there's very little we can do once you have the disease except treat the symptoms and get you through it." I took his hand, squeezing gently. "It will help to keep Miss Sarie and Mr. Josh and anybody else from getting it. You'll be a brave hero, Ned, to a lot of people."

"Yes'm, if you say so. Don't feel much like a hero though, laying here and not doing much."

"You're doing a lot. It may not feel like it, but you are and you are most definitely a hero in my eyes."

He sighed as he lay his head back down, turning his cheek toward me to make it easier for me. I wished fervently for the words that would tell him how much I admired his courage but stayed silent, knowing I could never say exactly what I wanted to. And if I could, I would never be able to push the words beyond my heart which was firmly lodged in my dry throat.

Thankfully, Josh said it for me. Kneeling beside us, he leaned down, taking Ned's hand in his. His voice barely a whisper, he looked into Ned's eyes. "Thank you, Ned, for your courage and generosity. No one will ever forget it was you who saved us. I promise, better days are coming for your people. All you have to do is make it through this and you will. God will see to it."

Despite the tears I couldn't stop from falling, I scraped the knife as gently as I could over Ned's cheek as Josh spoke, gathering the infectious pus I hoped would save everyone else from enduring this appalling disease.

Taking a deep breath, I squeezed his shoulder. "All right, Ned, that should do it. I didn't hurt you, did I?"

"No'm, I's fine. Just a little tired is all."

I tried my best to smile at him but my mouth wouldn't

cooperate. "I'll get you some tea that'll help you sleep for a bit. And we'll put some of the calendula infusion on that cheek to soothe it." I swallowed audibly. "Thank you, Ned."

"Yes'm."

I looked helplessly at Josh. As if reading my mind, he reached out and grasped my hand in his. "Thank *you*," was all he said, echoing my words to Ned.

I nodded as I rose to my feet. "Stay with him. I need to get this on Sarie's arm while that scratch is still fresh."

Sarie waited patiently at the table. When our eyes met, I could see she was trying hard to hide her anxiety.

"All right, Sarie, here we go," I said as I picked up her arm and lightly smeared the infected pus on the scratch I'd made earlier. "We need to let it dry before we put a light bandage on it."

I turned to Josh who was standing by my chair. "We need to sterilize another knife. It isn't safe to use the same one."

He grinned at me then plucked the knife from my hand. I gasped as he rubbed in over the scratch he'd made on his arm.

I knew I had to get out of there before I broke down completely. As I stood up, I blurted, "I have to go outside for a few minutes. You two stay right here and watch each other. There shouldn't be any reaction but ... just stay here and watch each other." I covered my mouth as bile rose in my throat.

Josh immediately took my arm. "I'll go with you, Lizzie."

"No, no, stay here, please. I need a few minutes alone," I said fiercely from behind my hand. Close to panicking, I turned for the door. Maybe if I got outside, I could breathe again.

I bolted out, almost running Viola down on the path as she approached the cabin. I think I muttered an automatic courtesy, "Excuse me," but with my hand covering my mouth, she probably didn't hear or understand. Running blindly, I made it to the edge of the creek where I knelt down, buried my face in my hands. I don't know how long I knelt there but it was probably a good ten or fifteen minutes at least. When I could, I cupped my hands in the cold water then splashed it on my heated face several times, hoping to dispel the redness I knew rode my cheeks and bloodied my eyes. After that, I concentrated on taking long, deep inhalations and releasing them slowly, hoping to get my hitching breath under control.

And all the while one thought circled endlessly through my brain, "Did I just kill Sarie and Josh?"

There was no way to know right then, of course, but that gruesome thought stayed with me for the next few days which passed with a slowness that was agonizing. I constantly checked the scratches, breathing a little easier when the sites on each of Josh's and Sarie's arms formed a red, raised bump that didn't show any sign of infection. And easier still when the blisters formed and finally scabbed over. As if on schedule, both of the scabs separated and fell off in twelve days. Only then did I stop thinking about killing my friends.

During those hair-raising days, we tended to Ned, Willie, and ten more slaves who also moved into the second phase of the disease. I refused to use the procedure on anyone else until I knew for sure it had worked. In spite of my arguments and protests, Sarie went ahead and gave it to Maggie and Abbie after Abbie convinced her she had seen they would not succumb to small pox. Later, Abbie admitted to me what she had told me once before, that she could not see what the future held for her or her sisters, or anyone she loved for that matter, and had lied to Sarie. It was all I could do not to rail against her for putting her and Maggie in such danger.

After that, we waited and we prayed. Or at least, I did. With my confidence shattered, I just couldn't bring myself to do anything more until I knew for sure that it had worked.

I also questioned whether or not I really wanted to finish medical school when—if—I was able to get back to the future. If this had thrown me into a tailspin, would I be any good at medicine or would I constantly find myself questioning every treatment, every decision I made on behalf of my patients.

I just didn't know.

Thankfully, Ned survived, though I knew he would carry the pock marks for the rest of his life. Willy, however, and three others who contracted the disease within the first few days of the beginning of the outbreak were not so lucky and succumbed to the dreadful illness a week or so after we knew the variolation had worked on Josh and Sarie.

Willy's death, along with the three others, threatened to send me into another tailspin. I moped for days until Sarie snapped me out of it a short time after the crisis passed. "Four out of almost a hundred," she said with awe. "Think about how much worse it could've been if you hadn't been here and had the courage to try to save em, Lizzie. They's a lot of people that are still alive because of you." She surprised me when she drew me into a tight hug. "You hold on to the ones you saved, girl. Grieve for the others but you hold on to the ones who are still alive. You hear me?"

I hugged her back, mumbling, "Thank you," as I fought tears.

It was then that I realized my experiment could be considered a success. I had, as Sarie pointed out, with the help of my friends, not only saved multiple lives but Sarie had finally, after weeks, begun to accept me. More important than that, I thought, she seemed to finally believe that I had come from the future. And maybe, with her help, I could someday go back.

But Pokni's admonition kept recurring to me and for the first time I began to question if I really wanted to go back to my domineering father, my unfinished education, and a boyfriend I was no longer sure I loved. To give up my close friendship with Abbie and a young man I was quickly coming to care for. You can do so much good here, my inner voice would whisper, but was it enough to keep me in a place so primitive and uncomfortable?

I simply wasn't sure but hoped when the time came, if it ever did, I would make the right decision.

CHAPTER ELEVEN

Chimes of Freedom

Although I considered myself more spiritual than religious and hadn't been brought up under any particular denomination, the sisters were churchgoers when time permitted and as their guest I was required to tag along with them to Brown Mountain Baptist Church, their chosen place of worship. My first visit was a trepidatious one, as in my time, I had heard of churches in the Appalachians where the congregants handled snakes and spoke in tongues. Although I found the congregation a little too enthusiastic at times, raising their hands and hollering Amen or Hallelujah or Praise God throughout the ceremony, most seemed sincere in their faith and somewhat reluctantly accepted me into their midst. During my time on the mountain, I had found the mountaineers an eclectic group, most of whom did not welcome outsiders, looking upon them with suspicion, but my association with the sisters along with my medical knowledge seemed to open doors to me that I am sure would have otherwise been closed.

At times, I spied Constable Jackson mingling with the congregation and suspected his reason for being there had more to do with keeping an eye on Sarie than actually revering God. I watched him surreptitiously as he conversed or prayed, noting his eyes never strayed far from Sarie's face. Did he still love her and was this his misguided way of trying to find a way into her heart? Or hate her for rejecting him and hope one day to ensnare her in some way? I suspected the latter and hoped for Sarie's sake that his eyes would soon wander in another's direction.

Josh was always present with a warm smile and greeting to the other parishioners. Whenever he entered my field of vision, my eyes were drawn to him and I found it hard to concentrate on anything else. I had become intrigued by him, curious about how he had helped Samuel, and spent many a night trying to figure out what he could have done. I searched my mind for all I had learned or read about slavery and finally concluded Josh must have helped Samuel escape, which brought back vague memories of the Underground Railroad. I remembered it had been mostly active in the North but could it have been here on the mountain as well?

At the beginning of each autumn, the church held a picnic for the congregation, a way of celebrating the end of a hot summer and beginning of cool weather heralding a colorful display of dying leaves on the mountain. In preparation for the event, Maggie spent the day prior baking pies and cooking dishes for the picnic, refusing anyone's help. Since she was a gifted cook and I had no ability in this department, nor was I inclined to, I was happy enough to let her have at it without any interference from me. No meat was prepared due to Abbie's sensitivity to animals and their suffering, resulting in the sisters becoming vegetarian, which meant I had become one as well. When Abbie told me the brutal way chickens and hogs and cows were slaughtered, I swore to her I'd never eat meat again and surprisingly found I didn't miss it.

The day of the picnic, we rose early and packed the food Maggie had prepared in two large baskets before setting off for the church. The weather couldn't have been more perfect, with a warm breeze blowing and blue skies dotted with clouds that looked like fluffy puffs of cotton, the sun shining a golden light on the mountain. A hint of autumn was in the air, some trees already giving way to the first traces of reds and golds, the ground smelling loamy and rich. For once I found myself at peace with my predicament and held on to this feeling, knowing it wouldn't last long. The sisters seemed in a happy mood with Sarie even breaking into a smile occasionally and Abbie especially in high spirits which I found infectious. For the first time on the mountain, I found myself completely in the moment, enjoying the day as we walked along, feeling carefree and content, listening to Abbie's clear voice as she sang her favorite hymns.

When we arrived, it seemed most everyone from town and the mountain was in attendance at the picnic. Long, wooden tables set up under a copse of trees groaned under the weight of dish after dish of foods and breads, pastries and pies. I walked along, sniffing with delight at all the different fare presented, thinking, I have to taste this or that, and walked straight into Josh Hampton's muscular chest. I stepped back, flustered, my face reddening at the thought of how handsome this man was and how good his body felt against mine. I reached out to touch him then quickly drew my hand away. "Oh, I am so sorry. I wasn't paying attention at all where I was going."

He grinned, reaching out to steady me as my feet got tangled and I came close to falling. "If I hadn't looked up, I'd have run right into you, Lizzie." He glanced at the table. "Sure looks good, doesn't it?"

"There's so much food, I don't think I'll be able to eat but a small portion, even if I take just one bite of each dish."

He nodded. "We've got some mighty fine cooks on the mountain." He nodded toward Maggie, fussing over one of the tables. "Miss Maggie's one of the best."

I nodded. "You should have smelled the cabin yesterday. I had to force myself to stay outside just to keep from sampling everything she made."

He grinned. "Whoever marries her is sure gonna be a lucky man."

I watched him, curious if he wanted that right for himself. It was hard to tell with Josh. He seemed to treat everyone with the same amount of warmth and respect, even though I knew most of the single women on the mountain craved more than that from him.

He fell into step as I walked along, and we began surveying the tables, each of us commenting on this dish or that one. And when it was time to eat, we easily accompanied each other as we filled our plates and found a place to sit under a large maple tree with leaves just beginning to tint red. I didn't feel awkward with him as I did with so many people in this place and realized as we talked about his life on the plantation how lonely I was and how much I craved friendship and that he might possibly make a very good one. From time to time, young ladies would walk by, sometimes with arms linked, trying to catch Josh's attention, giggling behind their hands. I couldn't help but smile at this, stealing glances at Josh who either didn't notice them or studiously avoided them.

As we ate dessert, I noticed a man I had spied from time to time, who seemed mysterious to me. He didn't interact with anyone unless they approached him first and I had never seen him smile. I had noticed him wandering around town, seeming in a melancholy mood, and was curious about what had happened in his life to make him so miserable. I nudged Josh, nodding in the man's direction. "Who's that man over there, Josh? He always seems so sad to me."

Josh looked in the direction I indicated and I noticed his expression changed. "That's William Waightstill Avery. He's a well-known and respected lawyer around these parts, but something happened to him that I reckon eats away at him to the point he's a changed man from the way he used to be."

I leaned closer, intrigued. "What happened?"

"Oh, let me see. It was back in October of '51, I think, when Mr. Avery traveled to the courthouse in Marion to argue a case against an attorney from Burnsville by the name of Samuel Fleming." He glanced at me. "Keep in mind I wasn't present during any of this and what I'm telling you comes from others who were there and have culled together the story."

"Of course."

"I was told that during the trial, Avery defended his client's position so strongly, saying some not so nice things about Mr. Fleming, that Fleming took offense. That evening after court was over, Avery was walking around Marion when he ran into Mr. Fleming who challenged Avery to repeat the remarks he'd made in court to his face. When Avery refused, Fleming got mad and challenged him to a fistfight. Avery turned and walked away and that made Fleming fly into a rage, I reckon, because he drew a cowhide whip out from under his coat and lashed Avery with it several times. Avery tried to fight back with his fists but he was smaller and unarmed and took quite a beating before Fleming was through with him. Stunned and dazed, Avery wandered back to his hotel, in a stupor."

I remembered the whipping Samuel had endured, the damage the whip had done, and couldn't repress the shiver that swept through my body as Josh continued.

"Dr. John Erwin, Avery's cousin, came by the hotel, treated his wounds and gave Avery a pistol. Well, this confused Avery, who I'm told was a passive person, not prone to violence. He didn't know what to do so he waited until after dark to return to his home in Morganton.

"The next week, he went about his business, attending court in Caldwell County as he had planned, even as rumors flew around about him and Fleming. It's said that Avery's father, brothers and one of his uncles pressed Avery to kill Fleming but he didn't do anything even though word started going around that Avery didn't dare show his face in Morganton. The people of Morganton were indignant on Avery's behalf although he continued to act as if nothing had happened." He glanced at me. "Some thought he was hoping things would calm down and everything would go back to normal. But he must have been seething underneath or maybe just wanted to put an end to it all because of what happened in November, when the Superior Court convened in Morganton.

"The first day, he went about his affairs as normal. Unknown to him, the next day, Fleming rode into town with his young son, leading some horses they were planning to take to Charleston and sell. At one of the hotels in town, Fleming asked the owner if he'd heard if any threats were being made against him." He glanced at me, raising his eyebrows. "Could be he was concerned about what Avery might do in retaliation. I know I would be. Anyway, the owner told him no, so when Fleming left the hotel, I reckon he felt safe because he left behind his saddlebag with his pistol in it. He walked around the town then made it a point to stop by the courthouse where Avery was. After the noonday recess, Fleming sauntered into the courtroom, entered the enclosed bar and stood at the clerk's desk in front of Avery. Many thought he was taunting Avery, and I'd say he probably was. When an Asheville lawyer called out to Avery, he walked across the courtroom and leaned forward over a desk to talk to him for a few minutes. Without warning, he stood up suddenly, drew a pistol from his pocket and fired directly at Fleming. The bullet struck him on his right side and he reached into his left breast pocket and jerked out his watch as if it was a weapon then sank to the floor and died without making a sound. Avery didn't say a word, just threw his pistol at the dead body. He was arrested, of course, and charged the next day, and the case was called for Friday of that same week.

"Avery's lawyers—he had three of them—argued that Fleming brought it on himself, that he had degraded Avery to the degree that he went mad, leaving him with no option but to fight back and get rid of the threat."

"But that didn't work," I interrupted, "did it? I mean lots of people, including a judge and several lawyers, saw Avery shoot and kill Fleming. What is it Be...my friend Ben calls that?" I waved my hands in the air. "I can't think of what it is right now but it means something like it's a foregone conclusion. They had to find him guilty. Right?"

Josh shook his head. "That wasn't the jury's verdict. It only took them ten minutes to declare Avery innocent after which he was released."

"But that can't be justice, not if he killed a man in front of a whole courtroom filled with witnesses."

Josh shook his head "Maybe, maybe not, but you saw

the damage a whipping can do. I doubt Avery suffered like Samuel did but I'm sure it brought about pain, not to mention humiliation, one white man whipping another. But most everybody agreed with the verdict. As soon as it was announced, every person in that courtroom got up and made their way over to Avery and shook his hand."

"Really?"

"Yes, they did. And ever since, Avery's continued to practice law and enjoy the respect of most of the citizens of Morganton. But as you've noticed, it seems he's suffered personally. I understand he's often seen lost in thought as if he doesn't know where he is or what he's supposed to be doing. Some people say he must not be able to sleep 'cause he's often seen out walking the streets at night. Many believe he'll never recover from what he did." He sighed. "I've never killed a man but I'd say it takes its toll, Lizzie."

I looked back at Mr. Avery, who now sat alone, not eating or drinking, simply staring off into space, a look of dejection on his face. "I think they're right, Josh," I said. "Maybe that's punishment enough."

After the meal, both so miserable we felt we'd pop, Josh suggested we go for a walk down to the river to help the food digest. "It's pretty down there and cooler by the water."

Smiling at him, thinking this would be the ideal time to ask him what I wanted, I accepted his hand when he offered to help me to my feet. As we left the picnic, I did not miss the hostile looks cast my way by several young women nor Abbie's knowing smile.

As we walked along, he took my hand and tucked it into his elbow. People passed us by from time to time, smiling their hellos and bidding us good day. Josh glanced at me with a smile. "I never got the chance to tell you how much I, no, my father and I appreciate what you did for our slaves, Lizzie. I reckon you saved a good many souls."

I shook my head. "I don't know about that, Josh, but I'm glad it worked." I frowned at him. "Although somebody ought to knock you upside the head for putting yourself in danger."

He gave me his crooked grin, one I found too charming to resist, and couldn't help smiling back.

"Well, now, could be you saved my life, too, with that variolation, Lizzie. I could have gotten the small pox just as easily as the others."

It frightened me the despair I felt realizing he could have died.

He squeezed my hand as he nodded at a man of regal bearing coming toward us. The man nodded back, smiling. He stopped to shake hands, saying, "Good to see you, Josh. How's your family doing?"

"Everyone's well, James. I'm awful sorry to hear your mother and father are in failing health."

I watched as pain flitted across his eyes. "Well, they're getting on in years, Josh. It's to be expected although it will sure be hard losing them."

Josh nodded in sympathy then seemed to realize I might not know the gentleman. He gestured toward me, saying, "James, I'd like you to meet Lizzie Baker. Lizzie, this is James McDowell." He turned back to Mr. McDowell. "Don't know if you heard or not, but she saved our plantation during an outbreak of small pox."

Mr. McDowell looked at me with interest. "So you're Lizzie Baker. Well, young lady, I'd like to sit down with you and hear about that miracle you worked. The whole mountain's talking about it."

"I'd be happy to, Mr. McDowell."

He shook his head. "Oh, no need for formalities. Call me James, please."

I smiled. "Thank you, James. Please call me Lizzie."

He tilted his head in acknowledgement before returning his gaze to Josh. "I reckon I'm a mite late to the picnic. You reckon there's any food left?" He lifted his brow inquiringly.

Josh rubbed his stomach. "There was when we left but it's so good you best hurry."

Mr. McDowell put his hand to the brim of his hat in a farewell gesture and bid us goodbye.

I turned to Josh. "Is he related to the McDowells of Quaker Meadows?"

"He's the son of the owners Captain Charles McDowell and his wife Anna."

"It's such a beautiful place, Josh. I love going by there."

He nodded as we resumed our walk to the river. "Do you know the history, Lizzie?"

"No but I'm hoping you'll tell me."

"Well, the house was built in 1812 at Quaker Meadows by Charles the year prior to his marriage to his cousin Anna of Pleasant Gardens. Now Quaker Meadows was initially named by its original owner Joseph McDowell after his home in Frederick County, Virginia, and this property played a major part in history. Two of Joseph's sons, Joseph and Charles, both leaders during the Revolutionary War, gathered the Overmountain Men, patriot soldiers from Virginia, Tennessee and North Carolina, for a council under a giant oak tree on Quaker Meadows…" He looked at me. "Have you seen it?"

I nodded. "Abbie pointed it out, said it had a history to it, but never explained. It's a beautiful tree."

"It is that. It came to be known as the Council Oak because that's where they laid plans to defeat the loyalists under British Major Patrick Ferguson at the Battle of Kings Mountain which became the turning point of the war in the South."

"I never would have thought the Revolutionary War would come to Burke County, Josh."

"Well it did and I'm proud to say we played an important part in it."

We walked along in silence for a bit and when we were far enough away that no one was nearby and could hear us, I lowered my voice and leaned close to him. "Is it the Underground Railroad? Is that what Samuel meant when he said you helped him?"

Josh drew back, his brows raised high, alarm flashing across his face. "Where'd you hear that?"

"I didn't. I just put two and two together." Josh looked behind him and I followed his gaze. "No one's near, I made sure before I spoke."

When he didn't respond, I continued. "If that's what it is, I commend you for it, Josh. I think slavery is barbaric, something that eventu…" I closed my mouth, thinking, don't give yourself away! "That I hope will eventually be unlawful. And if you're involved, then you're definitely doing the right thing in my eyes."

We had stopped walking and were facing each other. Josh glanced around before putting his hand on my elbow and nudging me along. "It'd be best for you if you didn't voice these thoughts to others, Lizzie. Slavery is a contentious subject on this mountain and you're liable to make enemies of the wrong people."

"Wrong?"

"Those who respond with violence rather than words. I imagine you've met one or two already."

"As in your overseer."

"He's one of many."

I nodded, thinking of Constable Jackson.

We had reached the bank of the river, shining silver in the sunlight, and stood there, admiring the water as it glided over rocks and raced along to wherever it eventually emptied. I admired how pretty this place was and wondered what it looked like in my time. Were there buildings where now stood only wildflowers and trees and scrub brush and lush grass? Was the river even here or had it or man altered its course?

Josh drew me out of my musing by saying, "Let's sit here and watch the sunset. You're always guaranteed a pretty one from this spot."

We sat close to one another, not touching but very nearly so. I was once more aware of how handsome he was, how masculine he looked, and for a fleeting moment stared at his lips, wondering how they would feel against my own. With a jolt, I realized I loved Ben and shouldn't be having these kinds of thoughts about another man. But my inner voice whispered I would probably never see Ben again and a sadness so profound it hurt to breathe came over me.

Josh, noticing this, said, "Are you all right, Lizzie? Should we go back?"

I forced myself to smile. "I'm fine." To take my mind off Ben, I said, "I was hoping you'd tell me about how the Underground Railroad works, Josh, if you don't mind."

He regarded me for a long moment, as if unsure of my interest.

"I'm asking for me, no one else. I'd like to be involved if I could or would be needed."

He looked across the river, seeming lost in thought. He finally glanced around us then turned to me. "I think it's been in existence since the early 1800s, Lizzie, run by abolitionists all over the South and North. I reckon you know it's not an actual railroad or even underground but a network of people helping to move slaves along to safety."

"I was wondering why it's called that, Josh. Do you know?"

"I'm not sure but rumor has it a slave owner tracking his escaped slave claimed that he disappeared as if he must have gone off on an underground railroad and the name took hold. Whether it's true or not, it's been called that since the early '40s, I guess, and from that have evolved code words we use that are connected to the railway system."

"Such as?"

"Well, I'd be what you'd call a conductor. I move the slaves from our hiding place here on Brown Mountain, called a station or depot, to the next which is over in McDowell County. The stations are run by stationmasters who provide a home or business to harbor the runaways. Stockholders contribute money or goods such as clothing to help the slaves as they go along."

"Where do they go?"

"Most go north, hoping to reach Canada, where they can't be legally retrieved by their owners. Some go south to Florida or Mexico."

I thought of my time, when it was so easy to travel from one place to another by car, train or plane, where anyone could just disappear on a whim. "How do they get there, Josh?"

"On foot mostly. Some ride in wagons that have a false bottom where they can be hidden or hide underneath hay or piled blankets. Others may ride the train with a white man claiming they're his slave. We always warn those on the road to travel by night. Our watchword for those going north is keep your eye on the North Star, which will keep them headed north."

"I've seen what happens when they get caught, but what about you, Josh, what would happen to you if you were caught helping them?"

He shrugged. "I could be charged with constructive treason and at the very least would spend time in jail. With Constable Jackson in charge, I'm sure I'd get worse than that. Not to mention, I'd probably be disowned by my father." He gave me a wan smile. "I wouldn't get off light by any means, Lizzie. But I don't think about that. It bothers me more than I can tell you what those poor souls go through day after day after day."

I nodded, thinking about Samuel's small hut and the primitive conditions he lived under. "Was Samuel the first you helped?"

He shook his head. "I reckon I've helped close to ten or so now. Samuel was the first to be caught."

"By Eustus?"

"No, by a bounty hunter working for Eustus. There are plenty of those around. I figured the Fugitive Slave Act of 1850 would put an end to them but it didn't, only seemed to produce more."

"I can't say I've heard of that. What does it entail?"

"It requires federal marshals to capture escaped slaves which is bad enough but goes further to deny jury trials to anyone imprisoned under the act, making it worse for the ones captured."

"Is that even legal?"

He shrugged. "It's a law so I guess it is."

"Have all those you helped been on the mountain?"

"No, I've helped move seven from other areas, the other three were from plantations in Burke County." He glanced around again. "I have to be careful around here because if too many escape, then that would raise suspicion and you know how Constable Jackson is when he suspects someone."

I thought about Sarie and the scrutiny she endured from that vile man. Without realizing it, I put my hand on his arm.

"Josh, you need to be careful. He's a cruel, mean-hearted man. I'd hate to think what he'd do to you if he caught you."

He smiled at me, patting my hand. "Don't worry about me, Lizzie, I'm very careful."

Realizing how warm his hand was on mine, I quickly withdrew it and glanced away.

As if realizing my discomfort, Josh said, "Look to the sky."

When I did, I gasped with pleasure. The sky over the river had turned a beautiful creamy orange and pink as the sun descended behind the mountain. I sighed. "I should do this more often."

"What's that?"

"Take time to enjoy such beautiful moments."

We watched in silence for several minutes and when I felt a chill in the air, said, "Maybe we should head back before anyone misses us."

He gave me a wicked smile. "They'll just tell each other we're courting, Lizzie, it's a natural thing, you know."

I couldn't help but smile back. "And I'd have most of the single young women of Morganton and Brown Mountain scheming of ways to get me off this mountain and back to Knoxville." As we turned to head back to the picnic, I said, near a whisper. "I want to help. You'll call on me if I can?"

He stared at me while he considered this before finally nodding. "If you can."

CHAPTER TWELVE

Let's Keep It Between Us

As my time on the mountain slowly ticked by, I grew closer to Abbie with every passing day. She became a trusted and valued friend, someone I could talk to freely, the only one of the sisters who truly accepted my story of how I'd come to be there and believed that one day I would make it back to my time. Most times, I wanted that more than I could say and came to rely on her faith when feeling homesick.

I can't say I felt the same for Sarie or Maggie. Even though Sarie seemed more inclined to talk or listen to me after we had worked so closely during the small pox outbreak at the Hampton Plantation, I still found myself unable to grow close to her or even look upon her as a trusted friend. Initially after the outbreak, she seemed more willing to accept I had come through the lights, but as time went on, I could see disbelief creeping in and that alone was enough to make me uncomfortable around her. Sarie was pragmatic after all and something so other-worldly would be hard for her to accept. But more than that, Constable Jackson had planted the seed of doubt in my mind about Sarie and her father, and at times I speculated about his disappearance and if she had had anything to do with it. I couldn't get out of my head the packet she had given to Susie and how it had changed Jim. Of course, I didn't know if it was the tea he drank or Sarie holding the skulls over his head that caused his breakdown. But Sarie and her sisters had their own version of justice and I began to wonder if she had outright killed her father. If she had, was it a matter of self defense or maybe to protect one of her sisters? Or had she somehow tricked him into touching one of the lights and watched as it sucked him in? I couldn't say, of course, but the feeling wouldn't go away.

As for Maggie, I really didn't know what to make of her. Whereas Abbie was the sister of my heart and Sarie a puzzling enigma, Maggie was just there and I could never get a true sense of her. The only time I really spent with her was in the chicken coop every morning gathering eggs from the always broody—at least where I was concerned—hens. I had tried talking to her at first, hoping it would make the detested chore go by more quickly, but Maggie never had very much to say and usually let a nod or frown serve as her answer. If she did deem to open her mouth to speak, it was mostly in one-syllable words, and those often seemed strained or forced. To me, she seemed happiest living in her own world in her own mind. I would see her at times, just standing still and staring off into space for several minutes. Those little mind trips she took usually ended in a dreamy smile and flushed cheeks. It was as if she were daydreaming or perhaps remembering a happier time in her life, one where she could be herself and had everything she ever wanted.

Adding to the puzzle, she went off to walk in the woods by herself almost every single day, usually when Sarie was occupied elsewhere and wouldn't see her leave. She always came back with some sort of plant or root that could be put to good use as medicine or food, which was her reason for going, but it didn't explain why she invariably returned with a wistful smile and a flattering flush on her pretty face.

Since I had shared a couple of walks in those same woods with Josh, I naturally assumed Maggie was doing the same with some man. Given Sarie's views on the male gender, it seemed natural to me that Maggie didn't want her older sister to know that she was attracted to, or possibly even loved, a man.

One night when we were in bed waiting for sleep, I asked Abbie if she knew where her sister went on the mysterious walks but she only mumbled something I didn't catch as she dropped into sleep. Since she claimed to have no sense of what happened with her sisters, I decided to not pursue it with her.

So the whole Maggie romance with a mystery man was all speculation on my part, probably nothing more than a way to get my thoughts off of my own dilemma and focus on something else entirely.

Until one early morning while Maggie and I were alone at the cabin, going about the dreadful daily chore of collecting eggs from the chickens. Sarie and Abbie had left about a half hour before to gather the last of the hyssop leaves and flowers that they used to make their rheumatism salve.

As Maggie and I stepped out of the chicken coop, a horse came barreling around the side of the house carrying a young man yelling at the top of his lungs, "Maggie, Maggie!"

She bobbled the basket of eggs, almost dropping them. I grabbed the handle before all our hard work went crashing to the ground, not to mention, saving us both from the tongue-lashing Sarie was sure to deliver when she came home and found all the eggs broken.

Maggie murmured, "Randall?" drawing my attention back to her. I watched her cheeks flush bright pink and her lips curve into that dreamy smile that always lit her face after one of her little jaunts into the woods.

Fascinated, I narrowed my eyes as she hiked up her skirts and ran toward the young man. He executed a quite dashing leap off the still-moving horse, landed a few feet in front of her and took her by the shoulders when she reached him. I was sure he was going to pull her into his arms but she glanced over her shoulder at me and mumbled something as she shook her head. He cut his eyes to me then looked back at her.

I walked slowly toward them. I didn't want to impose but I wanted to hear their conversation almost as much as I wanted to go into the cool cabin.

"You have to come quick, Maggie," Randall said. "Constance is having pains. It's too early, ain't it? I'm afraid she's gonna lose the baby."

This stopped me in my tracks. Surely Maggie wasn't involved with a married man.

"Calm down, Randall. It's a little early but just by a couple of weeks. I told all y'all that this could happen. Remember?" She smiled. "I'm sure the baby will be all right if it's born now. Just let me get my bag. Lizzie and I will be there soon as we can." She turned to me. "Leave the basket of eggs on the table, Lizzie, then grab my bag and meet me in the barn. I may need your help." She turned back to him. "Where's Martin?"

"He's with Constance, said he wasn't about to leave her with nobody to look after her but Sally. I was over helpin him shoe one of the horses in the barn when Sally started raisin a ruckus in the house. Martin went in to see what was happenin and came tearin back out to tell me to ride for you."

This just kept getting more and more interesting. Who the heck were Martin and Sally, I wondered? How did they fit into the picture?

"I'll get Buck for you, Maggie, and bring him round here," the young man said, his cheeks flushed almost as red as Maggie's. "You go on inside, get your bag and do whatever else you need to do. I'll meet you back here in a bit."

Oh, this was interesting. They both could hardly take their eyes off of each other and were blushing like a couple of teenagers who'd just gotten caught fooling around under the bleachers at the homecoming game.

"Yes, thank you, Randall," Maggie said, almost formally. "I'll leave a message for Sarie and Abbie so they won't worry about me and Lizzie. Oh," as if an afterthought, she added, "this here's my cousin Lizzie from over Knoxville way. Remember I told you about her?"

I wondered what exactly she had told him as Randall glanced at me, nodded and said, "Ma'am."

I nodded back but I doubt he saw me, his eyes were all for Maggie. "I'll be back quick as I can," he said, reaching out to touch her hand.

Maggie's cheeks went a brighter shade of red. I could actually see her try and fail to contain the bright smile as she forced herself to turn away from him and face me. "Come on, Lizzie, let's go in and get my bag. Do you know anything about deliverin babies?"

I smiled as I followed along behind her into the cabin, puzzling over this intriguing scenario. I was grateful Maggie seemed to want my help and even more thankful that I was on the cusp of finding out what her little secret was.

"Well, I can't say I've ever delivered a baby myself but I've seen several film... I've seen it done in one of my ... I mean, I've helped my father a few times."

"Good. Constance is close to her time. She's had a right normal pregnancy but it's her first and I ain't for sure how she'll do, if she's strong enough to get through the delivery." We walked inside and I was so enthralled I barely noticed the welcome coolness of the cabin. "Could be, it's nothin to worry about," she went on as she took her saddlebag from the nail, "but we won't know till we get there and have a look." She dug into the bag, checking the items inside, then brushed a hand over her hair as if to smooth it. "Oh, you reckon you can write a message on the wall for Sarie and Abbie?"

"Sure." I walked over to the fireplace, used the poker to separate a small piece of charcoal. "Now who exactly are Randall and all the others? I don't believe I've ever heard you or your sisters say anything about them. Do they live here on the mountain?"

She answered readily enough but her cheeks stayed flushed and she directed her attention to the contents of her medical bag. "Oh, that's right, you ain't had the chance to meet Martin and Constance Landon since they ain't been goin to church for the last few months. Constance had some problems early on with her pregnancy and I suggested she stay in bed as much as possible. Martin loves her enough to see that she did what I said." She shook her head. "Most men wouldn't," she murmured.

"All right, Constance and Martin are married, I take it.

But what about Sally and Randall? Are they married, too?"

She chuckled. "No, Sally's a dog. She belongs to Constance and is real protective of her. Randall's Martin's brother. He don't go to church so you wouldn't have met him there."

"Oka—all right. Is there anything else I need to know? In order to help you deliver the baby, I mean?" I picked up the cooled charcoal, scribbled a message on the wall then glanced back at Maggie.

She tied the flap closed on her bag, hefted it over her shoulder and turned to look at me. "I don't reckon so. Like I said, it's been a normal pregnancy, other than some cramps and slight bleedin during the fifth month which stopped when she took to her bed." She narrowed her eyes as she thought, then went on, as she headed for the door. "The baby's active, and while Constance has gained a little more weight than normal, it's not overly much. Could be, she's havin twins but we won't know until she delivers."

"Twins? Oh, wow. Is that a problem?"

She opened the door and walked out onto the porch. "Well, depends on the health of the babies, and the mother, too, a-course. Constance ... well, she was spoiled growin up. Her pa saw she never wanted for anything. Surprised me when she married Martin, him not bein as well off as her pa, but she wanted him and she got him. Surprised me even more when she buckled down and worked the farm side by side with him instead of expectin him to do all the work." She smiled at me over her shoulder as she stepped off the porch. "She's strong, a lot stronger than I thought she'd be, and she wants this baby so I don't think we'll have any problem deliverin it, but ..."

"Every birth is different and you just never know what might happen," I finished for her.

She nodded as she walked toward Randall and the waiting Buck. I slowly followed, thinking to give Maggie and Randall a minute to make eyes at each other some more but then hurried after her. I was just too interested to miss any of what promised to be a real eye-opening journey into the world of the one sister I didn't know all that well.

The ride to the Landon farm didn't take long, only about ten minutes or so. Randall set a brisk pace with his pretty little mare and Buck, being male, followed happily along beside her. That gave me some time to focus on the all too obvious love between Maggie and Randall.

I enjoyed myself if only because I knew Sarie would definitely not approve of their affection for each other. Plus, it was one of those beautiful fall mornings on the mountain that made you want to capture it in your mind so you could pull it out later and revel in the memory. The trees and wildflowers were a kaleidoscope of color, the bright blue sky as clear as polished glass. The softness of the air caressed my face, delicate as a mother's loving touch and smooth as silk.

Maggie and Randall talked mostly about the baby. Randall believed it would be a boy but said he'd be happy with either a niece or nephew as long as it made his brother and sister-in-law happy. Maggie wouldn't commit to either sex, though she hinted at the surprise the Landon family might have in store for them. Randall was too busy making cow eyes at her to catch her subtle clues.

Their voices jumped every time the horses' hooves hit the ground and I wondered how they could understand what the other said. It didn't seem to bother them, though, and when they'd exhausted the baby topic, they moved on to the weather and what the upcoming winter might bring. I tuned out at that point as my thoughts turned to wondering whether I'd still be here then. I sincerely hoped I'd be home where I could have heat at the turn of a dial and warm light with the flip of a switch. And hot showers. Oh, how I missed those. Almost as much as I missed my cozy little off-campus apartment with my soft bed and comfortable sofa where I could stretch out and read one of my favorite books from the neat little bookshelf under the window.

I considered whether I could convince Abbie to come through the light with me, if we ever found it. I truly did not want to leave her behind and thought she might love the future and possibly feel at home there. I was just putting together a list of things that would convince her when my attention was drawn back to where I was with the wild barking of a dog.

Randall kicked his horse into a gallop. Maggie dug her heels into Buck's sides with only a trite warning to me, "Hold on!"

I wrapped my arms tighter around her waist, trapping the saddle bag between us. Squeezing my eyes closed, I did my best not to think about how far down the hard ground was or how much it would hurt if I fell off of a galloping horse. Before I had the chance to wonder how many bones I'd break in the fall, Maggie pulled back on the reins, bringing Buck to an abrupt stop.

Instead of waiting for me to get down, she dropped the reins, swung her leg over Buck's neck and slid down to the ground, landing with her skirt bunched up around her thighs. It must not have bothered her because she turned back to me and wrenched the saddle bag out of my hands.

I flopped forward, hugging Buck's neck as I thanked God I had made it safely, though I felt as if my teeth had been jarred out of my head.

Already at the front door of the cabin, Maggie yelled at me over her shoulder, "Get down, Lizzie. I might need your help."

I sat up and swung my leg over Buck's ample backside, sliding to the ground. Taking a moment to catch my breath, I hurriedly straightened the skirt of my dress—man, what I wouldn't give for a pair of jeans—then ran to follow Maggie inside.

The cabin was much like the sisters' cabin, except it only had one room. After entering I had to stop for a minute to let my eyes adjust to the dimness. Once they had, I could see Maggie bending over a bed in the far corner, her voice soothing as she reassured the woman lying there and the man sitting beside her.

Randall remained just inside the door with one hand on the head of a large dog whining mournfully and the other hand wiping the sweat from his forehead.

I turned my attention to our patient, who moaned through her gritted teeth as she clutched her husband's hand. Her eyes stayed locked on his as he whispered something to her.

When she finally relaxed, I breathed a sigh of relief in unison with hers, wondering if I should be boiling water or tearing up sheets or doing something productive. I felt entirely useless in this situation so braced my shoulders and walked over to the bed to stand by Maggie, hoping she would give me something to do.

She placed a hand on the man's shoulder, giving it a pat before she said, "When did the pains start, Martin?"

He kept his eyes on his wife, shaking his head as he answered. "This mornin, early, but I don't know exactly when."

"Constance?" Maggie said.

"They started a couple hours before the sun come up."

"Why didn't you wake me, Connie?" Martin asked.

"You need your rest. You ain't been sleepin too good lately and I wanted …" She trailed off to smile at Martin as he raised her hand to his lips and kissed the knuckles. "I had a feeling it would be today and I wanted you to get a full night's sleep."

"All right," Maggie said. "Martin, I need to check Constance and see where we are. You and Randall go on outside for a few minutes so we can have us some privacy."

Martin raised his wife's hand to his face and kissed the palm before nodding. "I'll be right outside, Connie. Maggie'll call if you need me."

Constance nodded, watching as he walked out the door with Randall. Then she turned her attention to Maggie. "Law, I've never seen him so scared, Maggie. He's always—" She gasped and her lips tightened. "Oh, oh, here comes another one," she said through her gritted teeth.

"Lizzie, get over here and sit behind her so you can brace her back," Maggie said as she ran her hands gently over the patient's swollen abdomen.

When the contraction ended, Maggie raised the skirt of Constance's nightgown, murmuring something about needing to get a look. Her small hands disappeared under the skirt. After a minute, she lowered the nightgown. "Looks fine, Constance. You're doin good." Her eyes darted to me.

"Come on, Lizzie, I need to show you how to make buckeye bark tea." She patted Constance's hand. "You're goin to be all right. I'm just goin to show Lizzie how to make some tea that will help with the pain. If you need me, just yell out and I'll come running."

I knew how to make buckeye bark tea, but there was a warning in Maggie's eyes so I didn't point that out. I only followed her over to the fireplace where there was a kettle hanging over the fire.

Picking up a towel folded neatly on the hearth, she used it to lift the kettle off the hook and set it on the hearth.

I sidled up next to her and whispered, "What's the matter?"

Maggie pulled a jar of buckeye bark out of her saddlebag. "I reckon she's havin twins."

"Is that a bad thing?"

"Not usually, but in this case, unless I'm mistaken, one of the babies is breech."

Breech? I knew what a breech birth was but didn't have a lick of experience with it. My first thought was, of course, caesarean section but without the proper tools and medicine we might just as well go ahead and kill both the mother and her baby outright. I had watched a film about a breech birth sometime during my first year of med school. The only thing I remembered was the doctor turning the baby using external manipulations a few weeks before the due date. The baby had turned back, though, a day or two before the mother went into labor. When the time came, the doctor had tried turning the baby again but to no avail. She'd finally stuck her hand into the woman's womb, grabbed the baby's feet and pulled it out that way. It had not been easy on the mother. The baby did survive, but I can't imagine it had been easy on him, either.

I shuddered as I realized I was about to get the live version of that film. I wanted to paraphrase the character from "Gone with the Wind", I think her name was Prissy, who screeched, "I don't know nothin bout birthin no babies, Miss Scarlett!" Instead, I said a quick prayer that Maggie knew how to handle a breech birth and all I would have to do was follow her instructions.

I watched her calmly spoon buckeye bark into a delicate china teapot sitting beside the fire, taking heart that she didn't seem a bit nervous. "What can you do?" I asked.

"We can deliver the first one but I'm afraid we might lose the second. I ain't never had a breech birth before. Granny delivered one once but the baby was born dead, had the cord wrapped around its neck. You reckon you know anything that might help?"

I took the jar and screwed the lid back on. "I've heard—or read—about a technique used to turn the baby in the womb but I don't remember how it was done."

Picking up the kettle again, she poured hot water over the tea. "I've heard of that, too, but I don't know how to do it neither. If we can figure it out, I think we should try it. It may be the baby's only chance."

"I remember there were two ways it was done. One is external and probably less dangerous for the mother and the baby. You try to maneuver the baby into a better position so it can be born normally, head first. I think that might be the best way but I can't say how painful it will be for the mother … or the baby. The other way involves putting your hand inside the mother's womb …" I couldn't contain the wince "… try to get a firm hold of the baby's feet, or one foot, and pull it out. It sounds more dangerous to me, not to mention, a lot more painful. And I'd think you would run the risk of breaking something, the baby's leg or at least spraining the leg muscle pretty badly. Not to mention peritoneal tearing for the mother. That has to hurt."

Maggie nodded as she placed the lid on top of the pot. "All right." She set the teapot on the table and moved to a bucket of water to wash her hands. "Let that steep for a few minutes then bring it over. I'm gonna try to explain to Constance what's goin on and what we want—no," she shook her head, "what we need to do. She's gonna be awful scared."

"I imagine so but maybe if we act like we know what we're doing it will reassure her."

Maggie nodded. "I reckon that's what we'll do. That tea

should be done in a minute or two. When it is, pour her a cup then bring it over. We'll tell her together."

"Maggie?" I said as she turned.

She stopped and raised an eyebrow at me.

"I just wanted to thank you for letting me help ... or try to help."

"Why wouldn't I? You told Abbie you were trainin to be a doctor and I've seen the good of some of the things you've told us to do." She smiled. "Ain't none of us dead or marked by small pox, are we?" She lowered her voice to a whisper. "I still don't know if you come through the lights like you said, but however you got here, I'm glad you did."

I smiled back, pleased she trusted me. "Thank you. It means a lot to me that you're willing to give me a chance to prove myself."

"That tea should be ready now. As you keep tellin us, don't forget to wash your hands thoroughly."

And with that, she turned and walked over to the bed where Constance watched us anxiously. "What were y'all whisperin about?" she said, in a frantic voice. "Is there somethin wrong with my baby?"

Maggie sat beside Constance, saying, "Lizzie ain't never birthed a baby afore and I was just tellin her what to expect, but there is somethin I need to tell you." She took a deep breath. "Here's what we think is happenin and what we're gonna do about it."

Maggie explained the situation to Constance, and while she was scared, all she said was, "Can Martin come in and sit with me while it's happenin? I'd like him to be here. I'm always stronger when he's with me."

Maggie smiled as she nodded. "A-course, Lizzie will go get him right now."

When I came back in with Martin, Constance was in the middle of a contraction. I watched her, noting her flushed, sweating face, the way her teeth ground together as she tried not to scream, how she writhed on the bed. I glanced at Martin, who looked to be in as much pain as his wife as he shook his head, looking powerless to help her.

When it was over, Maggie smoothed a light blanket over

Constance's knees, telling her how well she had done. She smiled at us and gestured for Martin to join her. "Constance wants you to be with her while we deliver the babies."

His face went pale. "There's more than one?"

Constance reached for his hand, trying hard to smile. "We're gonna have two babies, honey. Maggie says the first one'll be delivered normally but the second one is—what was that word you used, Maggie?"

"Breech."

His face went pale as watered milk, reminding me of one of my favorite songs "A Whiter Shade of Pale" by Procol Harum.

"Martin," Maggie laid her hand on his shoulder, gently guiding him toward the head of the bed. "I think it'd be best if you sit beside Constance and brace her shoulders while she pushes. It'll also help if you hold her hand, giving her something to squeeze when the pains come."

I suddenly realized I knew something else that might help with the pain. I hesitated, thinking I should ask Maggie first, but when Constance gasped again, I blurted it out, "Breathe your way through the pain, Constance. Like this." I demonstrated the breathing used in natural childbirth. Constance followed my technique, panting along with me. I didn't really know how much it helped since I'd never had a baby before, but if nothing else, it might keep her mind focused on something other than the pain.

After she made it through the contraction, she smiled at me. When she spoke, her voice was hoarse. "I thank you, Lizzie, that did help."

"Good. Something else you can try is staring at a focal point while you breathe through the contraction."

"I ain't for sure what you mean," she said.

I looked around the room. Like most of the cabins I'd seen, there weren't a lot of pretty little knick-knacks sitting around but there was a beautiful cradle sitting under one of the windows. Draped over it was a baby quilt with colorful rainbows arched within each quilted square. It would make a fine focal point. "When the next contraction comes, do the breathing and keep your eyes focused on one of the rainbows on that gorgeous quilt draped over the cradle. Don't think about anything else except how warm that's going to keep your precious baby." I looked at Martin. "You can help her, Martin. Just keep supporting her back, breathe with her and encourage her. That sometimes helps the mother to stay focused."

I turned to Maggie and found her smiling at me. I smiled back, hoping that meant I had done the right thing.

The first birth was relatively easy and fast. Well, in my opinion. I didn't do much but remind Constance to breathe, stand by Maggie and pass her clean towels and rags and such, but when she handed the tiny little girl to me and told me to clean her off, all I could think was how much I admired her unruffled manner. Unfortunately, that was the last moment of peace any of us would have for a while.

After I handed the baby back to Maggie, she checked her then diapered her before re-swaddling her in a clean blanket. She handed her to Martin, saying, "Don't forget to help Constance breathe when the next one comes." Then she took me by the arm and pulled me over to the table. "I'm gonna try to turn the baby from the outside first. If that don't work, we'll have to ..." she shook her head. "Let me see your hands."

Puzzled, I held out my hands. She frowned. "Mine are smaller so I guess it'll be me who goes in. If I can't do it, we'll have to try to deliver the baby feet first or bottom first if that's the way it's in the womb."

I took her hand, holding it until she looked at me. "You can do this, Maggie, I know you can."

She sighed. "I'm glad somebody knows I can 'cause I ain't so sure."

I squeezed her hand. "You can and I bet if Abbie were here she'd be telling you the same thing. She'd know."

Maggie nodded as she took a deep breath. As I watched her struggle to gain the confidence and courage she would need, inspiration struck. "All right, here's what we're going to do, Maggie. You're going to try turning the baby and while you do, tell me everything you're doing. Just think of me as your slightly dim student and walk me through the whole process. Can you do that?"

"I think so." She chewed on her bottom lip for a second. "But if I say it out loud, won't that scare Constance?"

I hadn't thought about that. "Yes, it might. But you can say it silently in your brain. Make believe you're telling Abbie or Sarie about the birth. Would that work?"

"I think so."

"All right then, let's get this baby born. Remember, I'll be cheering you on the whole time. You can do it, Maggie, I know you can."

She took another deep breath then nodded. "Thank you, Lizzie."

I smiled. "No problem."

Maggie went to the washtub, washed her hands then walked over to the bed where Constance breathed her way through another contraction. This one seemed longer, possibly more painful, and I did not miss how terribly pale and drained she looked. I was sure she was more than ready for this whole thing to be over. I know I was.

Maggie's eyes darted from me to the baby, still in her father's arms. I immediately understood, took the infant and placed her in the cradle, taking a moment to stroke her silky cheek.

"All right, Constance," Maggie said, "let's try to get your other baby out. Martin, you take Constance's hand and don't let go." She placed her hands on either side of Constance's swollen stomach. Concentrating on turning the baby, she remained quiet as she tried to manipulate the baby's position. Constance cringed and gasped, and after several minutes, screamed so loud I fought the urge to cover my ears.

Maggie immediately removed her hands. She swiped the back of her forearm over the sweat dotting her forehead.

Constance bit her lip. "I'm sorry, Maggie, I couldn't help it. It hurt awful bad."

Maggie sighed then looked at me. "What do you think?"

"Let me try and if I can't do it, then we'll ..."

"All right." She moved aside and I took her place. I ran my hands over Constance's stomach, trying to get an idea of just how the baby was positioned so I could tell which would be the best way to proceed. It only took Constance a couple of minutes to scream this time. I removed my hands right away and stepped back. "I'm afraid we're going to have to try the other way," I said to Maggie then lifted the hem of Constance's nightgown. I probed the opening of the birth canal and ran into an obstruction not even an inch deep. Maneuvering my finger to feel the outline I looked up at Maggie and smiled.

"I can feel a foot right inside there."

She nodded as she put her hand over mine, pushing it aside so she could feel. Then she took a deep breath, slowly and gently moving her fingers into the canal. "I have the foot," she said. "Should I pull or try to get the other one?"

"I think you should try for the other one. Who knows, we might get lucky."

Drawing in a calming breath, Maggie eased her hand farther inside. Her eyes narrowed for a moment then she smiled. "I've got it. Constance, I need you to tell me when the next contraction starts so I'll be ready."

Constance grimaced. "Right now," she gasped.

Maggie didn't say a word but her eyes narrowed in intense concentration as she slowly pulled the two feet out of the womb. She rested when the contraction diminished but was ready when the next one came.

Constance let go a little scream when her baby came out in a whoosh of fluid and wails, as if protesting this rough treatment.

Maggie smiled, passing the baby to me as she picked up a sharp knife to cut the umbilical cord. When she'd finished with that, she turned her attention to the afterbirth.

After I cleaned the baby and swaddled him in a blanket, I handed him to his mother who had tears of happiness in her eyes, just as the father did. Maggie went to the crib to retrieve his sister then lay her in her mother's arms next to her brother.

Randall burst in as the babies' cries throttled up to full-blown screams. He went directly to Maggie, pulled her into his arms and gave her a smacking kiss on the lips.

It was a wonderful moment, full of love and laughter, and all I could think was I'd sell my right arm for one of Pokni's hand-rolled cigarettes and a bottle of wine to sip while I smoked it. Or maybe champagne would be more apt since I'd just helped bring two lives into this world and that was truly something to celebrate.

We left sometime later, after Maggie made sure both babies were in good health and nursing well. Maggie kept Buck to a walk as we made our way back to the cabin. She didn't speak, seeming lost in her own thoughts, as she hummed softly to herself. But there was something I wanted to ask her and I figured alone in the woods on the back of a horse where she couldn't walk away might be the perfect place.

I took a deep breath, then said, "Maggie what kind of an arrangement did Constable Jackson have with your pa about Sarie?"

She stiffened, not saying anything for a long moment. Finally, "Who told you that?"

"Constable Jackson. He waylaid me one day coming back from Pokni's. Told me he found it suspicious your pa disappeared right after they had made some sort of agreement about Sarie. Said he intended to find out what happened to him and once he did he'd hold Sarie to that agreement."

I watched as her shoulders seemed to slump with defeat. "Sarie don't know I know this but I heard Pa and Constable Jackson talking." She glanced over her shoulder at me. "This was right afore Pa disappeared. Pa owed a debt to Jackson." She shrugged. "Don't know what for, I didn't hear that part, but Jackson told him in payment he'd take Sarie as his wife and release Pa from the debt. Constable Jackson's had his eye on Sarie for years now. I reckon he loves her, though he don't act it, but it's like he can't take his eyes off her and can't just leave her be. Pa was more'n happy to agree to it but Sarie wouldn't hear of it. She don't want nothin to do with men, I reckon 'cause of the way Pa treated us since we were young'uns. Sarie got the worst of it 'cause she'd always take the blame for somethin to save

Abbie and me from his fists or belt. She don't know men can be kind and gentle, thinks they're all brutal and mean like Pa and Constable Jackson. So she told Pa she wouldn't marry the constable and they had an ugly row. I was glad Abbie had been called away somewheres, don't remember where now, so she didn't see it or hear what they said to one another. Pa finally told Sarie she'd marry the constable, didn't have no say-so one way or t'other about it, and left to go buy some moonshine. Sarie followed him out the door and we ain't seen him since."

"Do you think she did something to him, Maggie, to make him disappear?"

She shook her head. "Don't know and don't rightly care. All I know is our life's been easier since he left. Don't have to put up with his drunken ways or tiptoe around one another like we used to, worried he'd get mad and decide we needed a beatin." She shook her head. "He liked to killed Abbie one day. She was passed out for two days, couldn't talk when she come to."

"I know. Abbie told me but she doesn't hold that against him."

"Our Abbie is sweet and innocent, she ain't cut out for this cruel world. But Sarie and me, we hold it against him for her." She sighed. "I pray she did do somethin to him, Lizzie, so that he don't never come back. If he did, I might just kill him myself, and that's all I'm gonna say on the matter."

"Of course. I understand." As we rode the rest of the way home in silence, I wondered what I would do if faced with the same situation. Raised by an abusive man then given to another one as payment of a debt. Would I agree? No, I thought. I'd refuse, no matter what it took.

In the barn, after we had both dismounted from Buck, Maggie grabbed my hand before I left to go to the cabin. "It'd mean a lot to me, Lizzie, if you didn't tell Sarie about Randall and me. She don't trust men, don't want nothin to do with em, and I ain't sure how she'd feel about me and him." She looked away then back to me. "I ain't ready to tell her yet. Can you understand that?"

I nodded, smiling at her. "Love's a beautiful thing,

Maggie, and I'm happy for you. But don't worry, I won't tell Sarie. That's up to you."

"I will tell her," she said, nodding with determination. "But at the right time."

"Of course." I gave her a brief hug then left, hoping things worked out for her and Randall.

CHAPTER THIRTEEN

Let Me Die in My Footsteps

Time slowly passed by, each day helping the sisters with chores or tending to the sick or injured, each night sneaking out with Abbie to roam the mountainside in search of the lights. Abbie said they were seen more often in late summer and early autumn and as the days progressed, sliding from summer to fall with winter looming on the horizon, I began to despair. The times I found myself alone in the cabin, I would retrieve my hidden items from the cedar chest, holding my watch close and thinking of my father, who had raised me since my mother's death and whose overprotectiveness had driven me to distraction and rebellion. His love for me had pushed me away but, oh, if only I could go back and tell him I understood why he treated me the way he did. If only I had listened to him and not gone with Ben, I'd be back at home, in my time, living a comfortable life. Most of the time, I hated this time, the crude way of living, unsanitary conditions, inconveniences that would never be attained if I lived the rest of my life here. Sarie treated me at times as if I were an unwelcome visitor and I feared she would one day tell me I had to leave. But where would I go? I knew no one other than the sisters and those I met in Morganton and on the mountain, and these were only superficial relationships at best. Except for Abbie. And perhaps Josh.

I saw Josh from time to time and he was always friendly and warm but never mentioned the Underground Railroad or anything of substance. I had begun to think he had decided he didn't need my help when one evening, while out searching for the lights with Abbie, Josh appeared from out of nowhere, out of breath and in a panic.

"I've been looking all over the mountain for you," he said, when he reached us, his eyes on me.

"What is it? What's wrong?" I glanced over his shoulder, fearful I'd see the constable trailing after him, ready to arrest him for treason or me for murder.

"I have ..." he glanced at Abbie and hesitated. "One of the slaves has been hurt. I need your help."

I knew in an instant he meant a runaway.

"Is he bleeding bad?" Abbie asked. "You need a blood stopper?"

He shook his head. "He fell and injured his leg. He can't hardly walk, he's in so much pain. I'm sure the bone's broke. It looks like it's poking through the skin."

"Oh, Lordy," Abbie said. "We best go get Sarie."

"No," Josh said in a loud voice.

She frowned at him and started to speak but I put my hand on her forearm, stopping her. "That's all right, Abbie," I said in a soothing voice. "I can handle it. I'll go with Josh."

"I best come with you."

"No, that's all right, we won't need you," Josh said, taking my arm.

"If the bone's pokin through the skin, you're gonna have to cut off that leg," Abbie said, following us with determination. "You'll need the Blood Stopper for that and Sarie for lopping it off."

"Oh, I doubt we'll have to remove the leg," I said.

"That's what Sarie always does, says infection's sure to set in and kill em, so it's best just to bypass that and take the leg."

"Maybe so, but I think I'll try to save it first."

"Do what you want but you'll end up choppin it off," she said, continuing to trail after us.

Josh and I looked at each other. "It's all right, you can

trust her," I whispered.

"What in tarnation are you two whisperin at one another about?" she said with irritation as she caught up to us.

"It's just that we may need to ask you to keep this a secret," I said.

She studied us for a long moment then shrugged. "Well, I reckon you better than anybody on this mountain knows that I keep secrets right well, Lizzie."

Josh gave me a puzzled look but didn't pursue her statement and I was thankful for that.

I nodded. "All right then, you can come with us."

He led us to an abandoned farm near the bottom of the mountain. Abbie looked around as we crossed an open field of long grass and wildflowers. "Ain't this old man Scarbrough's place?"

Josh nodded. "Ours now. Pa bought it right after Mr. Scarbrough passed a couple of months back. Says he intends to farm it but hasn't gotten around to it yet."

Abbie snorted. "Your pa'd own the whole mountain if he could just to brag about it."

Josh laughed. "Not a truer statement could be made."

He opened the large barn door and we went inside. I glanced up and could see stars sparkling in the evening sky through gaps in the planks overhead, could feel the cool wind blowing through those on the sides. I breathed deeply, liking the lingering odor of apples and horses and dried horse manure. Josh crossed over to the ladder leading to the loft and began to climb. Abbie and I looked at each other. With a shrug, I followed. When I reached the top, I moved aside for Abbie to step onto the wooden planks beside me.

I followed Josh to the far wall, the light so dim I could barely see in front of me. He fumbled in the dark and eventually found a kerosene lantern. After he turned up the flame, he held it over a black man lying on his side on the floor, holding his leg. Sweat covered his body and he grit his teeth as if to hold back a moan.

"What's his name?" I asked Josh.

"Zebediah. You don't need to know anything else."

I nodded as I dropped to my knees beside him and

placed my hand over his. "I'm here to help, Zebediah. Let me look at your leg."

When he removed his hands, Abbie gasped. "Lordy mercy, you can't save that leg, it ain't worth the bother. We need to go get Sarie so she can take if off."

"You can't cut off my leg," the man said between clinched teeth. "I need it to travel."

"Shh, let's not worry about that just yet." I motioned for Josh to hold the lantern closer so I could study the injury. Sure enough, the bone protruded from the skin but it looked like a clean enough break. The problem lay with maneuvering it back into place. "I think I can do this," I said, my mind whirling with images of broken bones during med school and what needed to be done. I looked up at Josh. "This is going to be quite painful. Do we need to keep him quiet?"

"Best if we could," he said. "There might be hunters nearby."

I raised my eyebrows, meaning bounty hunters?

He nodded.

Abbie, not seeing this, said, "Ain't no hunters down this way, Mr. Josh, they'd be up on the mountain if they was a-huntin."

"Just in case," Josh said. "Someone may come traveling through on their way up the mountain."

"We left our medical bags at home. Well, it wouldn't do any good anyway. I don't have anything in there to knock him out," I said, more to myself than them.

"Knock him out?" Abbie said.

"Yes, make him unconscious so he won't feel the pain. It's going to be quite intense."

Abbie thought for a moment, then began to search. She eventually came back to us, raised a thick stick of wood and hit the man on the side of the head. His eyes rolled back in his head and he collapsed on his back.

"That do it for you?" she said.

I bit my lip to keep from laughing, horrified I found this funny. After ascertaining he still breathed and probably wouldn't suffer anything more than a bad headache, I smiled at her. "I can always count on you, sweet friend." I smiled wider at her proud blush.

I turned back to Zebediah. "Okay, um, all right, let's get to it then. Josh, do you have any kind of whiskey we can use to sanitize the wound?"

He withdrew a flask from a saddlebag lying next to the man. I poured the liquor over the wound, flushing out debris and blood, glancing at Zebediah from time to time to make sure he remained unconscious. "We're going to need rags to blot the blood then to bind the wound." I looked at Abbie and Josh. "Any idea where we can get them?"

Josh searched through the saddlebag and pulled out a white linen shirt. "This do you all right?"

"Is it clean?"

He raised it to his nose and sniffed. "Smells clean."

"It should work then." I tore off a swatch and wiped the leg around the bone as gently as I could. Zebediah began to tense and I stopped, watching him. When he stilled, I turned my attention to Josh and Abbie. "I'm going to need both of you to hold his leg straight while I try to maneuver the bone back inside and lined up with the tibia."

"The what?" Abbie said.

"Lower leg bone."

When Zebediah groaned, we all watched him but he remained tranquil.

After I directed Josh and Abbie to kneel on either side of him, I straddled Zebediah's leg at the ankle, considering how I should manipulate the bone. After a few moments, I sat back on my heels, wiping my brow with the back of my forearm. "Where's that flask?"

Josh picked it up and handed it to me.

I took a swallow, almost gagging, thinking this must be what turpentine tastes like. I began to choke and my eyes watered considerably.

Abbie frowned at me. "I didn't know you was a drinker," she said accusingly.

"I'm not. Just need a little push is all," I wheezed, wiping my eyes as the whiskey warmed its way into my stomach. I glanced up, caught Josh grinning at this and gave him a quick smile. I nodded at each of them. "Let's do it. Abbie, Josh, hold his leg as still as you can while I see if I can maneuver that bone back inside. If he starts to wake up, Abbie, you know what to do."

She nodded as she pulled the thick stick toward her.

They both put their hands on each side of his leg, determined looks on their faces. I grabbed his lower leg and began the process of trying to get the bone to slip back inside the skin and into position with the tibia. It took quite a while but finally it disappeared back inside his leg and looked to be in place. I ran my hand over the bone, checking to see if it had aligned properly. "Wish I had some rods or pins," I mumbled.

"What for?" Abbie asked.

"In my..." I hesitated, stopping myself before I said "time". "In my studies, we learned how to insert metal rods or pins, screws and plates to hold the bone in place. We certainly can't do that here. I'm hoping if we bind it securely enough and keep him off the leg for a few weeks, it will heal on its own. Otherwise, we may have to call in Sarie. I'm not about to cut off a limb in this day and a..." Shoot! I thought, I have got to learn to think before I speak. I darted a glance at Josh, noticed his furrowed brow. I needed to distract him. "We'll need to stitch the skin. Josh, is there anything in that saddlebag we can use?"

. He pulled it closer to him and rummaged through. "I found a needle and thread, you think you can use it?" He held it up. The thread looked to be silk, which would be better for skin than cotton.

"It will have to." I doused the wound with the liquor, stopping when Zebediah began to stir. Abbie picked up the stick, watching him. When he settled back down, I sanitized the needle and thread and began the process of closing the wound while Josh tore the shirt into strips and Abbie searched for two straight sticks. Afterwards, I placed a stick on each side of the leg and wrapped it as tightly as I dared, hoping I didn't cut off his circulation. Finished, I stood up and stretched my back, joined by Abbie and Josh.

"Can you check on him daily?" I asked Josh.

"I'll try but there may be days I can't get away."

"Why don't we do it this way? I'll come check on him tomorrow, you come the next day and we'll alternate days."

"Might be best to come at night," Josh said, "in case anyone's watching."

"What's so special about this feller you got to keep him here and be so secretive?" Abbie said.

I blinked, having completely forgotten about her. I didn't know what to say so turned to Josh for an explanation.

"He's a runaway."

Abbie's eyebrows went up. She considered it for a long moment before speaking. "Well, I reckon we ought to be extra careful. You know how Constable Jackson is about runaways. If he knows this feller's on the run, he'll be all over this mountain lookin for him."

"I know."

"What about food and water?" I asked Josh.

"I've got enough food and water stored in the corner over yonder to last him a few days. We'll have to bring more as the days go by, especially if you want him off the leg for a few weeks."

"If he wants to keep it, he'll have to stay off it. We could make crutches for him but that's going to hamper him when he travels."

Josh shook his head. "He needs to travel fast when he goes. We'll have to wait." He rubbed his hand over his hair, making it stand on end. He looked cute that way and I suppressed a smile, feeling that tug of attraction for him. "Look, y'all go on back home. I'll stay with him tonight and leave for home before dawn." He touched my hand with his. "You'll come check on him tomorrow night?"

I nodded.

"*We'll* come check on him," Abbie said.

I clutched her hand. "Abbie, you can't get involved in this. It's too dangerous."

"Well, I reckon I'm involved right now, ain't I? And I ain't gonna leave you to do this all by yourself, not with Constable Jackson already suspicious of you."

"You're sure? You don't have to, you know."

"I reckon you'll be safer if I'm around, won't look so suspicious if he catches you out at night if I'm with you."

I kissed her on the cheek. "You're an angel."

"Don't know as I'd say that," she said, as if embarrassed. She glanced at Zebediah. "I reckon he'll be out most of the night. We'll bring him somethin tomorrow night for the pain. You best leave that flask by him to get him through till we come."

"I will," Josh said.

"We'll also bring medicine for fever and infection," I said, "although it'd be better if we did that tonight."

"I'll walk y'all home and you can give me whatever you think he'll need," Josh said.

"We best get on back home else Sarie and Maggie are liable to come lookin for us," Abbie said.

We climbed down the ladder and walked outside into the cool night air. I breathed deeply, feeling a bit chilly as sweat dried on my body. I longed to climb into a tub filled with hot, soapy water but those days were gone, I thought miserably. I'd be lucky to get a whore's bath before I went to bed. I wondered if I'd ever stand under a warm shower, washing my hair with scented shampoo, my body with gently foaming soap.

We walked home in silence, careful not to speak in case anyone was nearby. The cabin was dark when we arrived and I waited with Josh outside while Abbie went inside to fetch herbs from her medical bag.

He stepped close to me and grasped my hand. I looked at him. "What you did," he said, "how you helped Zebediah, how you helped our slaves with the small pox, you're an amazing woman, Lizzie. I don't reckon I've ever met a woman like you." The door opened and he released my hand. I looked down at it, still tingling from his touch.

Abbie returned with a poultice made from witch hazel to put on the wound in case of infection, along with a jar of catnip tea to help calm Zebediah and one of feverfew if he developed a fever.

"I thank you," Josh said after she explained to him how to use the herbs. Before leaving, he reached out and touched my arm.

I smiled at him. "I'll see you soon."

As he walked away, Abbie leaned close and whispered, "That feller's sweet on you."

I was distracted, my eyes following Josh, thinking how wide his shoulders were, so wasn't sure I heard her right. I cocked my head at her. "I'm sorry, Abbie, I wasn't listening. What did you say?"

She gave me a knowing look. "I said that feller's sweet on you."

I frowned.

"He is," she insisted. When I didn't respond, she said, "Well?"

"Well, what?"

"Are you sweet on him?"

I rolled my eyes. "It's getting late. Let's go to bed, Abbie."

"I reckon I got my answer," she teased, leading the way into the cabin.

My dreams that night alternated between Ben and Josh, each so different from one another mentally and physically. I had been in love with Ben when I came to this time but knew there was a great chance I would never return to him. Of course, being in love with Ben, I was attracted to him but didn't recall the pull toward him that I felt when I was with Josh nor the great anticipation at the thought of seeing him, the tingle that ran through my body at his touch. I wished Abbie had not asked the question because I knew the answer although I had tried desperately to keep from thinking it. I *was* sweet on him.

CHAPTER FOURTEEN

Heading for the Light

The next night, Abbie and I returned to the barn loft. Along with our saddlebags, we carried a lantern with us so we could see our way to Zebediah without stumbling around trying to find the one Josh left. Zebediah lay shivering under a blanket, his eyes closed. He didn't stir at our presence, and when I knelt beside him, I smelled a strong odor of liquor.

"Why, he's passed out drunk," Abbie said with derision.

I felt his forehead with the back of my hand. "He's burning up, Abbie."

His eyes flew open and he flinched away from my touch.

"It's all right," I said. "We're here to help."

He looked from me to Abbie, and when he spoke, his words were slurred. "You was here last night."

"That's right."

"You saved my leg."

"I hope so."

He struggled to sit up but seemed too weak so shortly gave up and lay back down. "Mr. Josh stayed with me most of the night. He left some tea for me and I been tryin to drink it but it's hard to stay awake."

I nodded. "You just rest, Zebediah. We'll see what we can do for you. Is your leg hurting?"

"It's painin me something awful. I reckon that's why I been sleepin so much, I been drinkin that moonshine to help with the pain."

I glanced at the flask lying beside him. I picked it up and shook it. Empty. There was also an empty jar nearby. "You had more than just the flask?"

"Yes'm, they was some in the jar there but it's all gone now, I reckon."

I glanced at Abbie, who shook her head with disgust. Because of her father, she couldn't tolerate anyone who drank alcohol. I gave Zebediah some of the tea Abbie had provided to help calm him. After he drank the cup and lay back down, I pulled the blanket off, motioning for Abbie to bring the lantern closer. His leg appeared to be red and swollen, puffing out around the bandages.

"Looks to be infected," Abbie said.

I nodded. "I was afraid this would happen. Let's get these bandages off, put some of that poultice on it you gave Josh last night."

She knelt beside me and we set to work, Zebediah moaning as we maneuvered his leg. With the bandages off, the leg looked worse than I had imagined it would. Infection had definitely set in and I prayed this wouldn't lead to gangrene.

Abbie leaned close and sniffed.

"What are you doing?"

"Checkin for gangrene. Has a real sweet odor to it but I can't smell it so I don't reckon it's set in yet. A-course, that don't mean it won't. That's why Sarie says to go ahead and lop the limb off so you don't have to face that on down the road."

"We didn't bring any moonshine, did we?"

"What in tarnation do you want that for? He's drunk as a skunk already."

"To wash our hands. I don't want to touch his leg until we're sanitized."

"I reckon you're out of luck."

"Do you have any chamomile ointment in your saddlebag?"

"I reckon I do. You gonna put it on his leg?"

"Later, if the witch hazel doesn't work. But first we're going to put the chamomile on our hands. It has an antiseptic quality."

"Anti what?"

"It will help kill bacteria or germs on our hands. We'll save the witch hazel for his leg."

After we rubbed the ointment into our hands, I tenderly touched the puffy area over the broken bone, making sure the fracture was still aligned properly. As I worked, I told Abbie to give Zebediah a cup of the feverfew tea for the fever. I found the witch hazel ointment Abbie had given Josh and lightly rubbed it over the inflamed skin and around the stitches which were still in place. Then pulled fresh bandages out of my saddlebag and with Abbie's help wound them around his leg and the wooden sticks Abbie held in place to keep the leg straight. Afterward, I sat back, wiping sweat from my forehead. I glanced at Zebediah, who lay still, his eyes slit, watching us. Perspiration glistened on his body and I knew we had hurt him while tending to him but he hadn't uttered a word of complaint.

"I hope this helps, Zeb. If Josh comes by, tell him I'll be by sometime tomorrow. I don't know if I want to wait a full 24 hours before checking your leg again. We're leaving you a jar of the catnip tea and one of the feverfew to drink." I wracked my brain, trying to recall any information about these two herbs, afraid I might be overdosing him. But I had not studied herbal medicine so had no idea what the side effects were or how much to give him. I looked at Abbie. "How often should he drink those?"

She shrugged. "I reckon every couple of hours might be all right. If not, we'll know when we see him."

I nodded. It was the best we could do. As we gathered our things together, I said a silent prayer his leg would heal and gangrene would not set in. I had no idea what we would tell Sarie if we needed her to cut it off. I knew she would blame me for placing Abbie in danger by exposing her to a runaway slave, and I couldn't blame her.

Zebediah was near sleep when we left. I shook his

shoulder to get his attention. "Make sure you try to drink these teas every couple of hours, Zeb. It will help with the pain and the infection."

"Yes'm," he said, closing his eyes.

Abbie snorted. "Don't know as he'll remember what you told him, drunk as he is," she said with disdain as we climbed down the ladder.

Once outside, Abbie doused the flame in the lantern and we made our way through the field, guided by the silvery light provided by the full moon. We hadn't gone far into the forest when a looming, dark form stepped from the woods into our path, right in front of us. The trees around us blocked out the light from the moon and I couldn't make out what stood before us. Abbie and I both gasped, clutching at one another, until we realized who the culprit was.

Constable Jackson studied us for a moment, cocking his head. "It's a bit late to be out gatherin herbs, don't you reckon?" he said.

I started to respond but Abbie placed her hand on my forearm and squeezed. "Ain't no law says we can't go anywhere on this mountain we've a mind to, be it day or night," she said as she stepped around him.

He moved back, blocking our way. "Well, now, Abbie, that just might be true but I've been standin out here watchin y'all, askin myself what the two of you are doin trespassing on Mr. Hampton's place."

I could feel Abbie go rigid beside me.

"Nothing wrong with walking through his field, is there?" I said.

He shook his head. "But there is if you trespass in his barn. That's where you been, ain't it?"

"We been out searching for evening primrose," Abbie said with annoyance. "They're easier to spot at night because that's when they bloom, even you should know that. We ain't got no interest in Mr. Hampton's barn unless he's still got old man Scarbrough's tobacco crop stored in there. We could use us some tobacco." She turned to me. "You reckon we ought to go check?"

"Ain't yours to use," Jackson said.

"Well, it's old man Scarbrough's, not Mr. Hampton's, way I see it. If he didn't take it with him, it's anybody's that wants it."

"That ain't how the law works, Abbie," Jackson said with impatience. He studied us for a moment. "I reckon y'all ought to get on back home. It's late."

"We ain't found the primrose yet," Abbie said. "We'll go home then."

So we spent the next hour searching the mountain for evening primrose, in case Constable Jackson continued to watch us, then returned home. As we walked along, I said, "You think he'll go check the barn since he thinks we were there, Abbie?"

She shook her head. "He didn't think that, he was just trying to trick us, make us tell him where we were."

"But he might have seen the light when we were in the loft."

"If he did, he would have come in the barn. He didn't see us till we were close to him."

"If he checks the barn, he'll find Zebediah."

She glanced at me. "He won't. He's already on his way back to town."

"How do you know that?"

"I just know things, Lizzie. If that slave was in trouble, I'd know it so don't go worrying about it until I tell you to."

The next morning, after gathering eggs with Maggie and helping fix breakfast, I groomed the horse, which to me was more pleasure than work. Buck was a pleasant soul with a gentle nature and I would find myself confiding in him as I brushed his coat and worked tangles out of his mane and tail. At times, he'd turn and stare at me with his large, dark eyes and I sensed understanding there. Abbie told me horses were especially sensitive to human's feelings and I felt this horse sensed my loneliness and feeling of isolation and was very forgiving of my tendency to kiss him and hug his neck, whisper my worries into his large ears. I, quite frankly, looked upon him as a friend.

After grooming the horse, I found Abbie harvesting the

last of the summer produce from the garden. As I plucked a squash off a vine, I whispered, "I'm going to go check on Zebediah."

She glanced at me. "I reckon Mr. Josh'll be doing that."

"I'm worried about that leg, Abbie. It needs to be tended to more than once a day."

She wiped sweat off her brow, leaving a smudge of dirt. "If you go, you're liable to get caught out by Constable Jackson."

"We got caught last night, in case you forgot."

She straightened up.

"I can say I'm gathering herbs in that big meadow outside the barn. It worked last night. Besides, he can't tell us where we can and can't go. And I can always claim Josh gave me permission to be on the property."

She considered that for a moment. "All right. I'll get my herb basket and we'll go on down."

"No, you should stay here and finish what you're doing. I'm caught up on my chores, I have the time. When I get back, I'll check our herbs to see what we need so we can go gathering this afternoon." Before she could protest, I picked up my herb basket in which I had stuffed my medical bag and went on my way.

I didn't meet Constable Jackson on my way to the barn. When I arrived, I stayed in the meadow a good while, waiting for him to show himself, working my way around the side of the barn and to the back, looking for another entrance. Unable to find one, I peeped around the side, checking the meadow and what I could see of the forest on the far side. When I didn't spy anyone about, I walked around to the front and slipped inside the door. I figured if the sheriff caught me, I'd tell him Josh gave me permission to be there and I was checking for tobacco for Abbie.

Zebediah was lucid when I arrived and immediately began complaining about the pain in his leg. He still had a fever but his skin didn't feel as hot as the night before. As I placed the back of my hand against his forehead, I thought it would make things easier if I had a way to gauge how high his temperature was. I remembered from my studies that a

German physicist by the name of Daniel Gabriel Fahrenheit had invented the alcohol thermometer in 1709 followed by the first modern mercury thermometer in 1714, going on to one with the standard temperature scale, called the Fahrenheit Scale, in 1724. Well over a hundred years back. But I had yet to see a thermometer on the mountain of any sort. When I asked Abbie if she had one, she gave me a look like she didn't know what I was talking about.

I gave Zebediah more of the tea then checked his leg, grimacing at how puffy and red it remained. I had just begun to remove the bandages when we heard the door creak open downstairs. I put my finger to my lips in a shushing motion and crept over to the top of the ladder to look down. Josh stood below, one foot on the first rung. "Come on up," I whispered.

He glanced up and smiled at me, and I admit to a feeling of giddiness at seeing him. When he got to the top, he nodded at me then turned his attention to Zebediah. "How is he?"

"Abbie and I came last night and rebandaged the leg. He was feverish and it looked to be infected."

Josh turned to me, his forehead furrowed. "How bad?"

"Not gangrenous yet but it looked bad. I was just taking the bandage off when I heard you."

He nodded. "I'll help you."

Once the bandage was removed, I had Josh light the lantern so I could see better in the dim loft. As he held it over Zebediah's leg, I studied it for signs of gangrene or red lines running up his leg, which would mean a blood infection. I leaned close and sniffed then sat back on my heels. "I think it looks a little better than it did," I told Zebediah who sighed with relief. "We'll continue with the ointment and teas. Hopefully each day it will get better and we can get you on your feet soon."

"I shore will be glad for that," Zebediah said. "I thank you and Mr. Josh for what you're doin for me, but I don't feel safe here, Miss Lizzie."

I began rubbing ointment onto the leg, trying to ignore his grunts of pain. "I know, Zeb. We'll get you back on the road as soon as we can, I promise you that."

After Josh helped me rebandage the leg and we made sure Zebediah had enough food for the next day, Josh and I took our leave. Once outside, as we walked through the meadow, I told him about the encounter between Constable Jackson and Abbie and me the night before. "So," I said, "if he asks you, you've given us permission to come onto this property to gather herbs and into the barn to check for tobacco, right?"

He grinned at me. "Of course, Lizzie. I'll support you no matter what you say."

I smiled my thanks at him. "Might be a good idea to come during the day, too, so that the light from the kerosene lantern won't be as noticeable as it would be at night. We were lucky he didn't see the light."

"That's a good idea, Lizzie. I reckon that'd be best." Josh reached out and took my hand. I hesitated at first but then decided there wasn't much harm in that. But once we were inside the forest, trees looming over us, blocking out most of the light, he pulled me off the trail and kissed me. I stiffened at first and he began to pull back but then my body responded to him and I put my arms around him and kissed back. Afterward, we pulled apart, looking into each other's eyes.

He cupped my cheek with his hand. "I knew it'd be special," was all he said before leading me back onto the path and home.

Special, I thought. What a perfect word for that kiss.

As the weeks went by, I found myself going to the barn daily. Sometimes Abbie accompanied me, but if she had other chores or patients to attend to, I went by myself, always on the lookout for Constable Jackson. I told myself I was worried for Zebediah, but after the fever and infection had passed, I could have gone every other day or every few days. The real reason, of course, was one I would not admit to myself. Always, when I opened the barn door, I would listen for Josh's voice and look for his face peering over the loft at me. Those times when he was not there, I tried to convince myself what I felt wasn't disappointment. As time wore on, it became harder and harder to do.

When Zebediah and I were alone, I tried to draw him out about his past history. I was intrigued as to how he came to be in North Carolina and who he was running from. He seemed reluctant at first but finally told me his mother and father came from differing tribes in Africa. They entered the country at Charleston and were sold in a slave market to William Walton, Jr., then sent to his plantation at the mouth of the John's River where they were trained by other slaves to speak English and to farm using American methods. "I'm American, born and bred, though that don't get me nothin other than being slave to a white man," he said with some bitterness. I could only nod in commiseration. As a child, he had been sold to a man in South Carolina who owned a large cotton plantation, where he worked the fields from sunup to sundown six days a week. He showed me scars on his back from whippings he received if he didn't meet the quota each slave was required to pick each day. "I reckon I got the arthritis in my hands," he said, showing me his fingers, which were bent and gnarled, "from pickin cotton all day. I couldn't pick like I used to so I figgered it was time I left. I couldn't take them whippins no more."

I held his hands in mine, marveling at how he could do anything with the fingers so swollen and twisted. "I'll bring you some salve made out of velvet dock next time I come. It should help."

"I thank yee, Miss Lizzie."

I began to massage his hands, hoping to give him some relief. "There's no need to call me Miss, Zebediah. Lizzie will do."

He didn't respond. When I looked at him, he was frowning as if I'd offended him.

"That is, if you want."

"But it ain't proper, Miss Lizzie. You a white woman, I ain't nothing but a slave."

"You're a person, aren't you? One of God's creatures, Zebediah, as am I. The only difference is the color of our skin and that you're a man and I'm a woman."

"I ain't never heard nobody talk like you," he said with wonder.

I smiled at him. "Well, hopefully when you reach Canada, you'll hear a lot more of it."

He seemed to ponder this a moment then a smile lit his face.

"We'll do everything we can to see you get your freedom, Zebediah," I promised. "No one should live the kind of life you've had to."

The smile faded as he nodded. I don't know if he didn't believe me or perhaps didn't want to allow the thought of it when he was in so much danger of being caught.

And so the weeks went by, stealing away for daily visits to check on Zebediah, seeing Josh from time to time. Neither of us mentioned that kiss or even came close enough to touch but it was there, between us, and I wondered if he considered it a mistake, and why I didn't.

But we stole glances at each other which apparently were evident to Abbie, who said with great irritation during one visit, "It's a wonder this whole dadgum barn don't just go up in flames."

I turned to her. "What are you talking about, Abbie?"

"The heat between the two of you." She motioned to me, then Josh. "Whoo-whee, it's hotter than hellfire when y'all look at one another like that. And it makes me wonder, what in tarnation are you waitin for?"

I glanced away, embarrassed, and made sure when Abbie was with me not to look at Josh directly. Something which I found harder than I thought. I liked to watch him, see a grin slide across his lips, study his broad form, handsome face, so had to limit myself to sideways glances and surreptitious looks when he and Abbie weren't aware.

Finally, a month and a half after I first met Zebediah, when I climbed the loft, I found Josh helping Zebediah walk around on his injured leg. His gait was stiff and I could tell from his occasional grimace it wasn't very comfortable but hoped with time and movement he would be able to travel a distance.

"You'll probably always have a limp," I told Zebediah as I

Josh.

Josh nodded. "I'll bring it tonight when we leave."

For the first time since the kiss, I touched him, reaching out and grasping his forearm. "Josh, no."

"It's his choice, Lizzie. I've seen what they go through. I reckon I'd be of the same mindset if I was in his shoes." He turned his attention to Zebediah. "We'll meet back here an hour after full dark."

"I'm coming, too," I repeated.

When he looked at me, I said, "I can be a distraction if they start following you. Constable Jackson knows the sisters and I gather herbs at night, he won't question me."

Josh thought about it for a long moment. "All right, but if things get dangerous, you can't stay with us, Lizzie. I won't have him connect you to this."

"All right."

I was antsy the rest of the afternoon, worried about what would happen that night, hoping we could help Zebediah escape to freedom. Once it was completely dark, I stole out of bed, quickly got dressed, and tiptoed to the top of the ladder leading downstairs.

"Where you goin, Lizzie?" Abbie asked, raising up on an elbow.

I turned back to her, whispering, "I have to use the privy, I'll be right back."

She sat up. "Don't see the need to get dressed just to go pee. Besides, we got a chamber pot right here."

I didn't know what to say to this.

She sighed. "We ain't never lied to one another, Lizzie. Now ain't the time to start. You been fretful all afternoon about somethin or other and I been waitin for you to tell me what's goin on."

I came back to the bed. "Josh and I are going to help Zebediah get off the mountain tonight. I'm on my way to meet them."

She threw back the covers. "Well, I reckon I'm goin, too."

I put my hand on her arm to stop her. "It's too dangerous, Abbie. We could get caught."

"I'll know if we're in danger and that's the very reason

you need me."

I couldn't argue with that so simply shrugged.

She quickly dressed and followed me out of the house. Near the path that would take us down the mountain, she stopped. "I forgot somethin, Lizzie. I'll be right back."

She took a step or two then turned back. "You can either wait or go on. I'll catch up with you."

"I'll wait."

She returned, tucking a packet into her apron pocket.

"What's that?"

"Somethin that might just help us if we get caught."

I gave her a look but she chose not to explain as we hurried down the mountain. Josh hadn't said what time they were leaving and I was worried he'd go without me, thinking to save me from danger.

We found Josh and Zebediah standing outside the barn, discussing the route they would take. Josh scowled when he saw Abbie.

"She insisted on coming, Josh. She has the sight, she'll be useful because she'll know if we're in danger."

He studied Abbie a moment. "I'd heard that, Abbie, but didn't know if it was true."

"Well, it is, and I'm a-thinkin we need to leave now. They'll be on the mountain tonight lookin for him but they ain't started yet."

Josh handed Zebediah a paper on which he had drawn a map. "Safest way is to cross the mountain. If we get caught or separated, use this map, it'll take you to the station in McDowell County. If you lose the map or get lost, keep the North Star right in front of you and follow it. Travel at night, like we talked about, stay in the woods, and you'll eventually get to where you need to go." He patted the satchel Zebediah had over his shoulder. "You got enough food to see you for a bit but you may have to fish or hunt to get you through if we get separated."

Zebediah nodded as he took the map, folded it, and placed it inside his shirt. "I thank you, Mr. Josh. I reckon we best get on now afore it's too late."

Josh motioned for us to be quiet and we all stood

listening for sounds of anyone nearby. He finally gestured for us to follow him and we all set out single file, through the tall meadow grass and onto the mountain.

We had been traveling an hour through dense woods and brush and I had just begun to worry if Zebediah was going to be able to make it on his injured leg when Abbie suddenly stopped. We all followed suit, looking at her.

"They're comin," she said.

We listened but I didn't hear anything other than the wind rustling the leaves of the trees. "Will they see us?" I whispered.

"Don't know that, just know they're comin. They got a dog on our trail." She reached into her apron, pulled out the packet and gave it to Zebediah. "This is pepper, sprinkle it behind you as you go. The dog will start sneezin, mayhap lose your scent." She pushed him. "Go now. We'll cover for you."

I quickly hugged Zebediah. "Good luck. If you can find a way to let us know you got to safety, please do so."

"I will, Miss Lizzie," he said, hugging me then turning and running as well as he could on his injured leg.

Josh started to follow but Abbie held him back. "No," was all she said and that one word crushed me, for I feared she sensed Zebediah would be caught. "We need to split up," Abbie continued. "Mr. Josh, you go on up the mountain, Lizzie and me will go to the west. We can send em off on another trail if we meet up with them."

We heard a dog braying behind us and all panicked and began running, Abbie holding my hand. We hadn't gone far when I saw a bright light to the right of us moving through the trees. I stopped, staring at it, thinking it looked awful familiar, startling when I realized this just might be the same one I came through. I heard shouts behind us but ignored them, watching the light.

"Lizzie, we got to go," Abbie said, pulling my arm, urging me to continue running.

I remained where I was, studying the light which continued to come toward us, noting the bright orange circle with the dark center. "Oh, God."

"What?" Abbie said. She followed my gaze, then noticed the light. She turned back to me, her face grave. "Is that it, Lizzie? Is that the one?"

I stared at her, unable to answer, my mind in turmoil. Should I chance it, step through and see where I ended up?

"Go to it," she hissed.

I was frozen to the ground, questioning if this was indeed the right one.

I heard Josh shouting at me to run, the dog braying in the background, a man yelling at us to stop, felt the energy from that light as it moved closer. I could only stare at it, mesmerized by that bright, pulsing dark center. The wind seemed to pick up and I could feel the light pulling me as if magnetized. My hair whipped around my head and the fine down on my arms stood straight up.

"Go," Abbie hollered, pushing me toward it. I wanted to tell her no need to push, all I had to do was reach for the center and the light would pull me in, but found myself unable to speak the words.

"Lizzie, don't go near it, it's dangerous," Josh yelled, his voice closer. That seemed to break the light's hold on me. I turned and saw Josh running toward us, a panicked look on his face.

I turned back to Abbie. "Come with me."

Tears sprung to her eyes. "Oh, Lizzie, I wish I could but I'm needed here."

"You'll love it there, Abbie. It's so much easier. I'll be with you, you'll be happy."

"Oh, darlin, I reckon I'm happy enough here." She glanced at Josh then said, "Go to your Ben, Lizzie, unless there's a reason for you to stay here."

"Lizzie," Josh said, his voice closer now. I looked back to see him drawing near, holding out his hand. "Don't go near it, Lizzie," he said, reaching for me, "step back, take my hand."

I looked at Josh, I looked at the light, which was now in front of me, hovering, as if waiting for me to make up my mind, waiting for me to reach out my hand and touch it. Ben or Josh, my mind whispered. Which is it? No, it has to be more than that, I answered. My dad waited on the other side, my privileged, comfortable life versus a brutal, primitive one here. But there was Abbie, my dearest friend, and I had done some good here … All this running through my mind in a fraction of a second.

"Stop right there, don't take another step," Constable Jackson roared behind me, near enough that I knew he would reach me in another second or two.

I smiled at Abbie, tears running down my face. "I love you, Abbie," I said as I reached out my hand.

4/10/19

Acknowledgements

We would like to thank the following people for their generous help with the historical aspects of this book:

Ed Phillips, Director of Tourism at the Burke County Tourism Development Authority

Laurie Johnson of the North Carolina History Room at the Old Burke County Courthouse

Dottie Ervin of the North Carolina Room at the Burke County Library

Thank you all for taking the time to answer our many questions and for guiding us in the right directions when we visited your lovely town.

A lot of research went into the writing of this book. We consulted multiple websites, books and booklets, and though we'd like to list them all here, there are just too many. So we'll settle for the ones we used the most:

Brown Mountain Lights, Morganton, NC; A Viewing Guide by Joshua P Warren

Murder in the Courthouse, Adapted by Cheryl Oxford from "The Averys: The Saga of a Burke County Family by Edward W. Phifer

Burke County Courthouses and Related Matters by Sam J. Ervin. Jr.

Burke: The History of a North Carolina County, 1777-1920 with a Glimpse Beyond by Edward William Phifer, Jr.

A huge thank you goes to our husbands, Mike and Steve, who handle the grunt work at the many festivals we attend throughout the year and also put up with the sometimes crazy world of living with a writer-wife. We love you guys!

And finally, to our awesome readers, who have always, always, encouraged and supported us. If it weren't for all of y'all, our *Appalachian Journey* series would have stopped at the first book and the *Brown Mountain Lights* series would never have seen the light of day. We love you all and hope you enjoy the new direction we're taking with this series!

Books in CC Tillery's award-winning, best-selling, internationally published *Appalachian Journey* series:

Whistling Woman, Book 1

Moonfixer, Book 2

Beloved Woman, Book 3

Wise Woman, Book 4

Brown Mountain Lights Series:

Through the Brown Mountain Lights, Book 1

About the Authors

CC Tillery is the pseudonym for two sisters, both authors who came together to write the story of their great-aunt Bessie in the *Appalachian Journey* series. Tillery is their maiden name and the C's stand for their first initials.

One C is Cyndi Tillery Hodges, a multi-published romance author who writes under the pseudonym Caitlyn Hunter.

The other C is Christy Tillery French, a multi-published, award-winning author whose books cross several genres.

To find out more about their work or for more information on their joint writings, please visit their website at cctillery.com.

Made in the USA
Columbia, SC
01 May 2018